PRAISE FOR AIMIE K. RUNYAN

Girls on the Line

"*Girls on the Line* brings to vivid life the unknown story of American women who served on the front lines of World War I as telephone operators, working under shellfire and exhaustion to keep frontline officers connected during battle. Philadelphia socialite Ruby battles family disapproval to volunteer at the front, finding camaraderie and sisterhood among her fellow operators, who risk their lives as much as any soldier and fight to be accepted as soldiers in their own right. Runyan illuminates these little-known women of the past in a moving tale of female solidarity and courage."

—Kate Quinn, *New York Times* bestselling author of *The Alice Network*

"A worthy war narrative with a strong, likable female lead and a solid supporting cast."

—*Kirkus Reviews*

"Runyan's book represents the best of historical fiction . . . [*Girls on the Line*] is about the power of female friendship and feminism, as these women fight for equal rights and recognition. The pages crackle with history, the story of the unsung heroines of WWI, comradery, and finding the courage to be your true self."

—Historical Novel Society, Editors' Choice

"An intriguing and original novel inspired by the female telephone operators of WWI, *Girls on the Line* will delight fans of historical fiction. Now is the time for stories about strong, courageous women, and through her heroine, Ruby Wagner, Aimie K. Runyan crafts an absorbing tribute to a group of extraordinary women who played a vital role in the war."

—Hazel Gaynor, *New York Times* bestselling author

"Once again Aimie K. Runyan shines a much-deserved spotlight on unsung female heroes in history. Set during the First World War, *Girls on the Line* follows the arduous journey of an army telephone operator forced to navigate a world of codes and spies and the complexities of love. Brimming with strong women who are easy to root for, this story of loyalty and sacrifice makes for an inspiring, heartfelt read."

—Kristina McMorris, *New York Times* bestselling author of
The Edge of Lost

Daughters of the Night Sky

"Fans of historical fiction or tales of women defying the odds will be immediately drawn in to Runyan's crisp, effortless prose."

—*New York Journal of Books*

"Without a doubt, *Daughters of the Night Sky* is one of the best books I've read this year. Captivating, emotional, insightful, and heart-wrenching, it is a story I will truly never forget. Knowing how accurate the historical details are makes this beautifully written novel even more exceptional. The characters leap off the page and will stay with you long after the final page is read."

—Soraya M. Lane, #1 bestselling author of *Wives of War*

"Fans of *The Nightingale* will be transfixed by this thrillingly original portrait of wartime valor."

—Jennifer Robson, author of *Somewhere in France* and *Goodnight from London*

"*Daughters of the Night Sky* was everything I love about historical fiction. Runyan crafts the perfect balance between plot, characters, and setting, all while educating the reader in an unknown part of women's history. At once compelling, tragic, and uplifting, this is one that I will not soon forget."

—Camille Di Maio, author of *The Memory of Us* and *Before the Rain Falls*

"Aimie K. Runyan breathes life into the gripping tale of the Night Witches—Russian female combat pilots in World War II. A page-turner!"

—James D. Shipman, author of *A Bitter Rain* and *It Is Well*

"Aimie K. Runyan has combined my three favorite literary topics: historical fiction, World War II, and courageous and strong women. She is an incredible historical fiction writer."

—Cathy Lamb, author of *No Place I'd Rather Be*

"A lively and stirring tale of the brave vanguard of female pilots fighting for Russia and, as often, for respect from their male counterparts. As enthralled as I was by this dive into social and military history, it was the humanity of *Daughters of the Night Sky* that won me over: comrades, lovers, and families swept up and torn apart by war. Runyan delivers a well-paced and heartfelt story that fans of World War II novels should not miss."

—Sonja Yoerg, author of *All the Best People*

"*Daughters of the Night Sky* is a compelling World War II story of bravery, determination, and love set within the Forty-Sixth Taman Guards—Russia's all-female pilot regiment. Author Aimie K. Runyan brings four unique women vividly to life: Katya, a superb navigator; Taisiya, her pilot and best friend; Oksana, who risks all for love of her country; and Sofia, the major who leads the women to triumph. Highly recommended."

—M.K. Tod, author of *Time and Regret*

"*Daughters of the Night Sky* is a heart-pounding, epic tale about an incredibly brave squadron of Russian WWII female fighter pilots. Through the eyes of Katya, Aimie K. Runyan takes us through their harrowing adventures and the roller-coaster ride of love and loss in war. Runyan weaves an unputdownable story of bravery, perseverance, and sacrifice. This is a stunner of a novel that I found truly inspiring and well worth the read."

—Kerry Lonsdale, *Wall Street Journal* and Amazon Charts bestselling author of *Everything We Keep*

"A breathtaking novel inspired by a little-known moment in WWII history. Even though I finished *Daughters of the Night Sky* days ago, the scenes are still playing in my head. Katya is an outstanding heroine: a strong woman determined to follow her passion, but also driven by duty and love. And her fellow Night Witches are glorious characters. I miss them and the vivid scenes set within the planes, at the front, and in war-torn Eastern Europe. This is a story I won't soon forget."

—Barbara Claypole White, bestselling author of *The Perfect Son*

Promised to the Crown

"Runyan debuts with what may be the ultimate marriage of convenience/mail-order bride novel of the season. This lively adventure presents readers with a fascinating glimpse into life in 17th century New France (Canada) through the lives of three disparate women. The hardships and wonders of a new world come to vibrant life through Runyan's vivid prose and well-crafted characterizations, which are both realistic and romantic."

—RT Book Reviews (4 stars)

"An engaging, engrossing debut. Runyan's gift transports you to the distant, frozen landscape of seventeenth-century Canada, but Rose, Elisabeth, and Nicole feel as real as if they live next door. A romantic, compelling adventure."

—Greer Macallister, *USA Today* bestselling author of
The Magician's Lie

"A captivating tale of three courageous women: Rose, Elisabeth, and Nicole, bonded by adversity, friendship, and love. In author Aimie Runyan's skillful hands, their stories are woven together as seamlessly as were their fascinating lives. *Promised to the Crown* is an unforgettable saga of strength and sisterhood, one that will stay with you long after the final page."

—Anne Girard, author of *Madame Picasso* and *Platinum Doll*

"*Promised to the Crown* is a sterling debut with carefully crafted settings, rich details, and sparkling prose. Runyan skillfully weaves her protagonists' stories, transporting the reader to the lovely and dangerous world of colonial Canada, while also painting each character's story in heartfelt, compelling detail. A welcome and unique addition to the genre."

—Susan Spann, author of the Shinobi Mystery Series

"In her original and well-written debut, *Promised to the Crown*, Aimie Runyan evokes the story of three young women who venture from France to Canada in the seventeenth century to marry and start a new life. It is a heart-wrenching and timeless tale of friendship, love, and hope that skillfully blends history and romance to educate, entertain, and inspire."

—Pam Jenoff, internationally bestselling author of
The Last Summer at Chelsea Beach

"This gripping debut brings to life the saga of three courageous women from disparate backgrounds starting over in New France. Aimie Runyan deftly guides us through the hardships and rewards of life on the early Canadian frontier. *Promised to the Crown* is an absorbing adventure with heart."

—Jennifer Laam, author of *The Secret Daughter of the Tsar*

Duty to the Crown

"Runyan follows *Promised to the Crown* with another atmospheric, carefully researched story of four young women building lives in the wilderness. Readers will be completely engaged by the well-developed characters' triumphs and tragedies. The colorful, detailed historical backdrop adds to this feminist tale of courage and survival. Readers are left inspired, believing in the power of love, friendship, and determination."

—RT Book Reviews (4 stars)

ACROSS THE WINDING RIVER

ALSO BY AIMIE K. RUNYAN

Girls on the Line
Daughters of the Night Sky
Duty to the Crown
Promised to the Crown

ACROSS THE WINDING RIVER

AIMIE K. RUNYAN

LAKE UNION
PUBLISHING

Published by Lake Union Publishing, Seattle

www.apub.com

Amazon, the Amazon logo, and Lake Union Publishing are trademarks of Amazon.com, Inc., or its affiliates.

ISBN-13: 9781542004756
ISBN-10: 1542004756

Cover design by Faceout Studio, Lindy Martin

Printed in the United States of America

To my dear friend Carol for sharing Max with me.
I hope my version of Max honors the memory of the real
hero.

CHAPTER ONE

RED DOOR / BLUE DOOR

BETH

April 24, 2007
Encinitas, California

My father raised me under a canopy of plumeria. There were the magenta ones with orange hearts that smelled of ginger. Delicate yellows with white tips that smelled of lemon. The deep reds that bore the unmistakable scent of grape Kool-Aid. Those had been my favorite as a kid. Dad fell in love with the towering trees with their riotous clusters of flowers on his travels to Hawaii in the '50s and spent a good portion of his leisure time cultivating more than a dozen varietals on our almost-an-acre lot in Encinitas.

He created a tropical paradise so lush that we were never in want of shade on ruthless summer days. I was sure the new owners, whose primary fascination with the property had been the dense grove of tropical flowers, were taking good care of them. But no one would *love* them as Dad had. When I finally convinced Dad that his stenosis was bad enough that Mom couldn't care for him at home, his sole stipulation was that he be allowed to bring a cutting of his Singapore plumeria to keep in his room. It laced his new bedroom with the scent of jasmine and memories of his happiest times with my mother.

I'd found him a small private-care home. I couldn't bear the thought of putting him in some sterile institution with dozens of elderly people who all clamored for a few precious moments of the staff's time. The home had only five residents, and the staff was as attentive as I could have ever hoped for. In truth, the cottage-like care home with its welcoming red door wasn't unlike the house he'd loved for so long. It made it a little more bearable, somehow.

He left behind the white ranch house with the teal-blue door nine months ago, and though Mom had been set to join him once she'd sold the house and gotten everything in order, the cancer hit so hard and fast, she never had the chance. One second she was in the kitchen making babka, the next, she needed the round-the-clock care of a nursing home. The disease claimed her in three months. My only solace was that Dad never really saw any of it.

I walked through that red door, not needing to knock, with a cutting from an Aztec Gold plumeria balanced on my hip.

"Hey, girl," Kimberly, the head caregiver, greeted me as she changed a dressing on Mr. Griffith's bad ankle. I flashed her a smile. "Mr. Blumenthal's in his room. Been expecting you for the past hour."

She chuckled as I rolled my eyes dramatically. According to Dad, it took exactly thirty-five minutes to get from my office at UC San Diego to his care home in Encinitas. And he was right . . . if you left campus at ten thirty at night. At five p.m.? Count on an extra hour as you become part of the world's slowest-slithering boa constrictor trying to wend its way north on I-5. A boa constrictor that spews gallons upon gallons of noxious fumes into the air and is equipped with several thousand car horns and is overly fond of using them. I could have stayed at work another hour or two and spent the time more profitably, but Dad would be too tired to enjoy the visit if I showed up that late.

"It's about time, baby girl!" Dad said with a smile as he opened the door to the fifteen-by-fifteen-foot room that was now the nucleus of his universe. "I was beginning to think you'd been held up at gunpoint."

"Traffic was murder, so your analogy isn't completely off," I said, kissing his cheek.

"What have you got there?" he said, inspecting the foliage of the cutting with the tip of a finger. The lush green leaves met with his approval.

"Gwen sent this for you," I said, placing the cutting—already blooming—on the window shelf I'd fashioned for his small collection of plumerias and orchids. "Thanks to your advice, her trees are doing magnificently. She was worried for months about the one this cutting came from, but it pulled through. She thought you'd enjoy looking after this guy."

"It's a beaut," Dad said, gripping his walker so he could lower himself to take in a proper sniff. "Smells good too."

"My Prius smells like a crate of fresh peaches," I agreed.

"Tell that sweet Gwen girl that I'm honored to give it a home," he said. Gwen was a friend and colleague in the poli-sci department at UCSD who had more or less adopted my father as her own over the past ten years. No one else would dare call the tenured professor of feminist political theory "that sweet Gwen girl" and expect to live to talk about it.

"She'll be glad to hear it," I said. Dad had rarely offered cuttings from his own plumerias, except to his dearest of friends and family who'd shown a true affinity for horticulture. Those who'd stooped to calling them by their common name—frangipani—one too many times would never have been gifted a cutting. To give someone a piece of a thing you've spent years of your life nurturing is no small offering. You have to know you're passing it off into the right hands. It's not being snooty; it's taking your responsibilities to heart.

"How are you feeling, Dad?" I asked as he fretted over the new plant's placement on the window shelf.

"Ready to march in the Rose Parade," he said, winking. "So long as they keep the parade running at a half mile per hour with plenty of time for breaks."

"Very funny." I opened his fridge, where Dad made sure there was always a case of my favorite seltzer, while he took his place at the little table he kept next to his kitchenette. It was just a bare-bones setup like you'd find in a business-style hotel, but he enjoyed the independence of making himself some eggs or coffee when the mood struck. The sink held a considerable pile of dishes, though, so I turned on the faucet to scrub them.

"Don't fret about those, Bethie. I'll get to them when you leave. Come visit."

"I can visit and wash," I said. "But it doesn't look like you've been eating in the dining room much. Everything OK?"

"I just don't feel like chatting these days. Except with you."

"You know you can't live on canned soup and microwave popcorn. It isn't healthy for you. You're a doctor, you know better."

"Don't you dare try to guilt me, Bethany Miriam Cohen. You're in over your pay grade. I was a dentist. And I can give you my professional opinion that none of that is particularly detrimental to my teeth."

"Very funny, Dad. You won't say so when they all fall out due to malnutrition."

"You sure you haven't stashed a brood of kids at that apartment of yours? Your lecture doesn't seem like the work of an amateur."

"Low blow," I said, averting my eyes a moment.

Dad shook his head. "Sorry, kiddo. I didn't think."

"Just let it go. It's fine."

"Let me make it up to you," he said. "Dry your hands and let me take you to the finest restaurant my budget will cover."

"The dining room ten feet from your door?"

"The very one," he said, holding on to his walker with one hand and offering me his arm with the other, exaggerating for gallant effect. I kissed his cheek before placing the hand of his proffered arm back on the grip of his walker. His spine was stooped so badly from the years he spent leaning over a dentist chair that he needed both hands to navigate the hallway, no matter how much he might have wanted to walk without aid.

I stayed close by his side, not fully trusting the walker, as he shuffled toward the gleaming oak table, whose battle scars were buried beneath the layers of furniture wax that Kimberly applied twice a week without fail. The diligent polishing made the food taste slightly of oil soap on occasion, but Kimberly insisted on maintaining the formality in dining that the residents had all been accustomed to in their earlier years. Though Dad didn't exactly change into a dinner jacket and shined oxfords, he never left the room without a cursory glance in the mirror to ensure his hair was in place and he looked presentable. There were always cloth napkins and bright, heavy ceramic plates in a merry jumble of colors that made the table look as though the residents were celebrating some second-tier holiday. Not Lenox china and Baccarat crystal, but they showed respect for the meal.

The meal ritual attracted me to this place when I'd begun the hunt for a facility. Even when Dad took me to Disneyland when I was a kid, we sat down to full meals at restaurants three times a day. No gobbling down stale hot dogs and fluffy pretzels from carts for us. "I had enough three-minute meals that consisted of cramming down cold food from tin cans to last a lifetime, kiddo." He rarely mentioned his time in the service, but when he did, it was usually to complain about the food.

"The lasagna looks good tonight, Dad," I said, encouraging him as Kimberly placed the plate in front of him. The mozzarella was perfectly melted, with just the barest hint of browning. The garlic bread looked buttery but not too soggy. He glanced at the food with guarded optimism as the rest of the residents took their usual spots around the table. There was Mr. Griffith, the one nursing a bad gash on his ankle, who was just a couple of years younger than Dad. He always tried to pull anyone who would listen into a conversation about golf. There were Mr. and Mrs. Meyer, a lovely couple who still doted on each other after almost three-quarters of a century of marriage. They had a steady stream of visitors—friends, children, grandchildren, even great-grandchildren. Tonight was a rare occurrence in that they didn't have a guest or three staying for dinner.

I was his only child, a surprise born almost twenty years into his marriage to my mother. I was childless and now single, so I was the only one who visited him with any regularity. At least here, the family of the other residents would include Dad in their visits when I couldn't be there. I knew it wasn't the same as being in a proper home, but it was the closest thing to one I could give him. It seemed like poor repayment for all he'd done for me in my life, but at least he was surrounded by love, and not the cold metallic beeping of machines that tormented Mom in her last days. Sometimes better had to be enough.

CHAPTER TWO

LETTERS FROM ASHES

MAX

June 25, 1942
Los Angeles, California

My pulse quickened at the sound of the low plane overhead. I looked up to see if I could identify the markings, but I wasn't expert enough to decipher anything at such a distance. Mr. Ivey's lips formed a thin line as he handed me change for the newspaper. His eyes turned skyward, rather than acknowledging me. His thoughts were the same as mine: *Ours or theirs?* Everyone along the West Coast shared that thought for a few seconds every time a plane flew over, and had done so since December. The attack on Pearl Harbor was horrific, and none of us thought the Japanese would stop there. There was nothing between them and Los Angeles, Sacramento, or Seattle except a whole lot of ocean.

The newsstand keeper lowered his eyes once more, convinced the plane's intent was likely innocent. "Paul's got his notice. He'll be going over."

Paul Ivey had been a classmate of mine in high school and had always been a nice enough guy. We'd lost touch when I'd gone on to college and dental school, but I'd heard he'd made a cracking trade of cabinetmaking. "Well, we can hope it'll all be over before he sees action."

Mr. Ivey stiffened a bit. "That would be a shame. He's eager to do his share. He enlisted, you know. He didn't wait for the draft like some boys."

The accusation loomed over my head like a pitch-black storm cloud. *You're young, you're strong, you're able . . . where is your uniform?* I couldn't blame him. Those who had children fighting overseas resented anyone who could serve and chose not to. Every new soldier was a chance to end the war sooner and get their boys home safe.

"Pass my best on to Paul, Mr. Ivey. Tell him to save some Nazis for the rest of us."

Mr. Ivey nodded, satisfied. I made no promises to enlist, but I implied my intent. He didn't know what my parents had left behind to build a life here and why they were so adamant that I not willingly run off to a foreign country to risk my life. They'd seen their native Latvia in ruins after the Great War, and it sounded like their beloved homeland was well on its way to living through that fate again. They'd made it clear they didn't want me involved in the war if I had the choice. I was a grown man, free to make my own decisions, but I could not treat their wishes lightly after all the sacrifices they had made on my behalf.

My parents' families had been friends for generations, and so it was no surprise when my mom and dad married as teenagers. Together, they scrimped and saved, skipping meals and working every odd job they could find to pay for their passage to the States. They arrived in 1916, and continued west until they ran out of country, stopping only when they found a place where their accents and religion didn't cause doors to slam in their faces. I came along the following year. Ma especially loved the community; she threw herself into every social or charitable event that could use a pair of hands. Dad's tailoring business flourished in the neighborhood that welcomed them, and we had a good life here. They couldn't fathom my leaving it for the sake of finding trouble.

It was because I didn't want trouble to find its way here that I wanted to join Paul and the others in the fight. I couldn't stand to think of this little version of paradise my parents and their friends had built being destroyed at the hands of madmen.

My parents' house was three blocks south, and I began the walk, resolving with each step not to quarrel with them on the topic again. I'd made my case with them a dozen times. People looked down on me for not enlisting and waiting for the draft to call me up. Not enlisting could hurt my dental practice before it even got off the ground. I didn't bother with the more philosophical reasons for joining up. Stopping Hitler's expansion was just too nebulous an ideal to get my parents on board. Even the rumors of the atrocities against the Jewish people in Germany and the lands the Nazis invaded weren't enough to light their fervor. *"These stories can't be half as bad as we hear, Max. The people wouldn't stand for their friends and neighbors being treated so poorly."* I would try to argue, but Ma would claim a headache or Dad would order me to change the subject.

They wanted me to finish dental school before enlisting, and even then, they weren't keen on me joining up before the draft board forced my hand. They reminded me of the sacrifices they'd made to put me through college and dental school, how they still gave me room and board to make it all possible, and that would shut down any arguments. I tried to see things from their perspective, but with each passing day, each new grim headline, it became harder. I glanced at the front page of the *Los Angeles Times* as I walked. British advances in Egypt. More damage by the Axis and their damned tanks. Nothing to give a person hope that the end of the war might be in sight.

I entered the little Spanish-style house in the Fairfax district of LA that my dad had bought when I was six years old. It was roughly the size of a shoebox, with two small bedrooms, one bathroom, a kitchen, a dining nook, and a living room that Ma optimistically called a parlor. It wasn't much compared to the riches of Hollywood that were practically at our doorstep, but Dad bought it brand-new, and by the sweat of his brow. He'd hemmed thousands of pairs of trousers just to afford the down payment. The way Ma and Dad tended the postage-stamp lawn, touched up the paint each spring, and hosed the dust off the shutters every week without fail, you'd have thought they were the head caretakers of the White House. I told Ma there weren't wooden floors in the whole of Los Angeles that were better polished than the 967 square feet of their house. The only thing that shone brighter than they did was her smile when I paid her the compliment.

I wasn't greeted by the usual scents of baking bread or simmering lamb stew, but by the soft sounds of my mother weeping. Dad sat next to her on the sofa, his arm wrapped around her. He was home from his shop hours early, which had never happened in my memory. He'd closed it once for a week when he fell dangerously ill with the flu, and then another week when I was born, but not since then. He prided himself on keeping the shop open from eight to five, Sunday through Friday, without fail. He did close an hour early on Fridays in winter when the sunset fell before five o'clock, so he wouldn't miss the Sabbath, but only during the four or five weeks it was truly necessary. The only other exceptions were for High Holidays. More often than not, he opened early and stayed late to help busy clients who couldn't schedule a fitting during his shop hours.

"What's wrong? Is Ma sick?" I asked Dad, not bothering with a greeting. I thought better of the question, knowing she wouldn't spend tears on her own account. "Are *you* sick?"

"Have a seat, *bubbeleh*," Dad said, calling me the endearment from my youth no one had used since I was in grade school. "We've had some bad news."

I sat in the armchair Dad usually lorded over, and Ma passed me a wrinkled letter with shaking hands. The first sheet was reasonably crisp and written in English by a woman's hand. The second was written in Yiddish by a man and looked like it had been run over by German panzers a few times before making its way to us.

> *To Mr. and Mrs. Blumenthal,*
> *I had the pleasure of meeting your cousin Hillel Blumenthal when I was serving as a nurse for the Red Cross in Riga. The extent of the atrocities committed against the Jewish people in Latvia cannot be described in words. I saw him six months ago in the Riga Ghetto, and while he was dangerously underfed, he was as well as can be expected. He begged me to send this letter to you, but I did not dare try until I returned home to Sweden. I am sorry to send you such grim news, but I hope knowing the truth can somehow give you some solace. I keep Hillel in my prayers each night, and your family as well.*
> *Yours faithfully,*
> *Freja Larsson*

I turned to the second sheet, and while I was reasonably conversant in Yiddish, I'd had little practice in reading it. My father saw how I struggled with the language and harried penmanship and paraphrased the letter himself.

"Hillel says there was a mass execution of Jews when the Germans invaded last year. Your grandparents, aunts, uncles, cousins were all rounded up. Hillel was spared because of his schooling in Moscow, he thinks. He's been relocated to a ghetto in Riga and thinks it's just a matter of time before the Germans decide they can do without him too. The German army kicked out the Red Cross, so they have no plans to make peace."

I passed the letter back to Ma, whose sobs had grown louder as she heard the news spoken from my father's lips. She had been worried about the absence of letters in the past couple of years, but the mail had never been reliable, even before the Soviets invaded in 1939. We'd heard the Germans had invaded last year, but I got the feeling my parents thought they couldn't be any worse than the Russians. Worry was worry, and it didn't matter which army held the bayonets.

I'd never met any of my family in Latvia, but my parents spoke of them so often, they didn't feel like strangers. I hadn't told my parents, but I'd planned on taking them on a trip back to the old country, once my practice was established, so they could introduce me to my extended family. They'd sacrificed those relationships for my sake before I was even conceived, and it seemed one small way to thank them for the opportunities they had given me. But now, there was nothing to go back to.

I placed the letter on the table Dad used for his evening drink when we sat together listening to the news or radio shows. I crossed the room, knelt before my parents, and took them in my arms. For the first time in my life, I saw my father dissolve into tears, and I couldn't restrain my own.

"I wish I could make this better for you," I said. "Roosevelt will make that bastard Hitler pay for all of this."

"I wish my mother could have met you," Dad said. "You look so much like your grandfather, may he rest in peace, that she'd think she was looking back in time. I wish you'd known what it was like to have big family dinners for the Sabbath. To have a house full of cousins for Passover."

"And so I did. The Katzes, the Greens, the Hirschels . . . they may not have been blood relatives, but it's family all the same. You've given me an amazing life."

"And you still want to fight, don't you, *bubbeleh*?" my mother finally managed to ask, mastering her voice for a few moments.

"I do," I admitted. "Now more than ever."

"Then go," Ma said, cupping my face in her hands. "Go over and make those *mamzerim* pay for what they've done."

CHAPTER THREE

CRUMBLING BOXES

BETH

April 26, 2007
Encinitas, California

I stood in front of Dad's door and paused before knocking, hoping I could dislodge the wayward breath wedged sideways in my chest. For all the times I lamented him not being in the living room and visiting with the other residents, this was one time I was glad he'd retreated to his room. It gave me a few more seconds to collect myself. The breath finally escaped, painfully, and I rapped my knuckles on the door in my familiar pattern—hard, soft, hard, soft.

"Back again, Bethie?" Dad said, opening the door to his room, the perfume of the plumerias and orchids hitting my nose like a tidal wave.

"What can I say? Rush-hour traffic is my guilty pleasure," I said, bending slightly to give him a kiss on the cheek as he stooped over his walker.

"Nothing like the smell of fresh exhaust to invigorate the spirit," Dad agreed solemnly. "Come on in and take a seat."

I noticed the new clipping looked more verdant than it had a couple of days before. Even at ninety he had the gift of making things grow under his care. I grabbed my seltzer and took my spot at his little table. Just across from him, like at the dinner table when I was little. Back then, I chose to sit across from him rather than next to him, to make chatting easier. I couldn't remember a time that he and I were ever at a loss for words with each other. His room wasn't overly large, but he still had four chairs, though it was rare that the third was occupied, and the fourth never would be. I just didn't think Dad could bear not leaving room for her, no matter where she was.

"Spill it, kid. What's wrong?"

"I'm fine," I said. "Perfectly fine."

"So, if you're fine, why aren't you out enjoying the weather or doing something with your friends?"

I was about to rub my temples and bury my face in my hands for a few seconds as I usually did before broaching an unpleasant topic, but I refrained. No need to get Dad's heart racing.

"I got a call from Dr. Kendrick, Dad. Your numbers aren't looking good, despite the new meds." His blood pressure, which hadn't been a problem until his late eighties and which had been well regulated with medicine until now, wasn't responding to the meds. His liver panel wasn't looking good either, though they hadn't gotten a good bead on that trend since his last checkup. Every single test they'd run was dramatically worse than those they'd run just six months before.

"What does he expect? I'm ninety years old. Does he really expect anything to get better at my age?"

"He doesn't expect things to go downhill this fast," I said. "For your age, you were in remarkable health at your last visit."

"He shouldn't waste his worry on an old man like me," he said.

"He's a geriatric GP, Dad. It's his job to worry about old people. And it's my job to worry about *you*."

Dad sat in silence for a few moments. "What else did he say?"

I looked down at my hands, which gripped my can of seltzer like a life preserver. "Six months, maybe less if your numbers don't improve."

"I'd die at ninety years old," Dad mused. "That seems like a good age to me. Your mother was eighty-three. It felt unfinished, somehow."

"You just don't like odd numbers," I said, laughing despite myself.

"True enough. Eighty-four would have sat better with me. Though if I were a more selfish man, I'd have asked her to do me the courtesy of outliving me. I'd always expected that, but now that I know what it's like, I wouldn't wish it on her."

I could make no response to this. Dr. Kendrick had asked what had changed for Dad in the last six months, and while I made some glib comments about diet and lifestyle, losing Mom had to be at the center of it, and the doctor agreed. *Blood pressure and jaundice I can treat, Dr. Cohen. A broken heart is out of my realm of expertise, I'm afraid.*

"The doctor did have some ideas for treatment," I offered. "Some new meds and therapies for your stenosis."

"Bethie . . ."

"I know, Dad, but I had to put it out there."

"I know."

"So, what now? Do we start putting all your affairs in order?"

"Most of that was taken care of years ago by your mother. My plot is next to hers. Plans are already in place with the mortuary. You know where all the paperwork is and what to do."

"Not just that, Dad. I know what to do for you *after*. Is there anything you want to take care of *before*?"

"I've lived a long life, Bethie. Got to travel and see my daughter establish a career to make any parent jealous. And even though it didn't take, I got to walk you down the aisle. I can't ask for anything else."

"Sure you can, Dad. You've got some time. Use it."

Dad thought for a few moments. "I've been thinking of the war more often than I should. Would you mind bringing me my photos and tchotchkes from storage? It might be a good thing to put them in some semblance of order. When I came home, I threw it all in a box and never looked at it again. Nearly pitched it out more than once, but your mother never let me. A few pieces might be fit for a museum, you never know."

I'd half expected him to ask for a last trip to Hawaii, the place he was always happiest. He'd probably not do well on the long plane ride, though, and I'd hate for his last trip to be a hardship.

"You got it, Dad. I'll bring them by on Saturday."

"I don't want you spending the next six months of your life here, Bethie. You're still young. You need to be out enjoying yourself."

"I do, Dad. I promise. But I want to do this for you."

I'd missed that opportunity with Mom. I'd been in the throes of my divorce from Greg. I handled the funeral and everything with all the poise I could muster, but in the period when she'd been sick, I'd not visited her with any reliability. There had been plenty of reasons for not trekking to the hospital. Some valid, others less so. The reality was that I just couldn't cope with all that went along with losing Mom *and* my marriage. I had excuse after excuse until it was too late to say a proper goodbye. She was so sick, she might not have known who I was in those last few days, but it would have been some closure. I wouldn't make the same mistake with Dad.

I kissed Dad goodbye after our visit and then pulled back on the highway. I didn't head south just yet, but east to Mom and Dad's storage unit that I'd clear out once Dad was gone. It felt like bad luck to do so beforehand, so I shelled out the hundred dollars every month to keep their things safe. I pulled up and found the padlock key on my ring. The jumble of furniture, china, and silverware would be a nightmare to go through when the time came. Mom had been a proper balabosta, able to throw together elegant dinner parties within hours. I'd missed out on that gene from her, and my new apartment was small. As much as I loved Mom's elegant sideboard and crystal stemware, I had no space for them, nor would they get the use they deserved.

I'd claim Dad's book collection and Mom's vanity. She and I may have had our differences, but our happiest times had been spent on the bench of that vanity as she taught me the feminine arts. Makeup, hair, and proper attire for every occasion. Growing up I was somewhere between the girly girls and the tomboys when it came to such things, but the older I got, the more utility I saw in learning how to present myself. Mom was always understated and impeccable. She might not have worn Chanel suits or carried Fendi handbags, but you'd never have been able to tell from the way she carried herself. I hoped I'd inherited something of that from her.

I waded through the sofas and tables to the back of the unit where the boxes were stacked. The most battered among them was simply labeled *Max*, and it had been off limits to me my entire life. True to Dad's word, it genuinely looked as though he hadn't touched it since 1945. The movers had been wise to place it on top, as it wouldn't have been able to bear the weight of any other boxes. I pulled it down, getting showered in a layer of dust in the process. Without bothering to open the lid, I placed the flimsy box in my trunk.

Forty minutes later, I pulled into my apartment complex, greeted by the cheerful sounds of children playing in the community pool. Their parents waded in the shallows, clearly eager to wear out the kids before bed. The restless days of spring had set in, making the energetic young families antsy for the freedom of summer.

I lugged the box of Dad's memorabilia up the stairs, the cardboard practically crumbling in my arms. I didn't dare rely on the handles cut into the sides. I set it on my bare kitchen table seconds before one side completely gave way. I knew Dad would have preferred to organize everything himself, but there was no getting the crate and its contents to him as they had been. I scrounged up a few sturdy plastic bins and separated the papers and photos into one and all the bulkier items into another.

A German Luger was at the top of the box, and my heart skittered as I placed it securely in the bin. I had next to no knowledge of firearms and didn't want to risk disaster to see if it was loaded. There were a number of medals, postcards, a couple of watches, and other little trinkets I'd have to ask him about. A delicate carved wooden model of a quaint timbered house had miraculously survived, but wouldn't fare well with much handling. I protected the little structure, roughly the size of a small birdhouse, in a generous length of bubble wrap left over from my move. A Kodak Ektra in pristine condition was tossed in with the photos, and I smiled. As soon as Dad had the chance to look things over, I'd put Greg's name on it with a sticky tag. There wasn't any need to ask if he was interested; my ex-husband was a photography nut and would be glad to have this remembrance of his former father-in-law. The photos seemed as though they'd been developed and left in their envelopes without having ever been looked at, so I suspected they were in as impeccable condition as the camera that took them.

I didn't want to go through the photos without Dad, but I peeked inside one of the envelopes to see if acid in its paper had damaged the contents. I would hate to lug a box of ruined photos to the home and have him be disappointed when we opened them. I was pleased to see the figures in the photo on the top of the stack were still as sharp and crisp as one could have expected from the technology of the day, and hoped the rest had fared as well. Though Dad had never expressed much of an interest in photography when I was a kid, apart from making sure my childhood and his flowers were well documented, he clearly had talent beyond what I had ever seen.

Most of the snaps were of men in uniform, smiling at Dad, who preserved a moment of mirth in their youthful faces in the midst of a horrific war. The one picture that caught my attention was of a beautiful blond woman, petite with fine features that the camera adored. A man stood next to her, his arm draped around her casually. He looked down at her and she up at him in adoration. Her figure betrayed that she was visibly pregnant, despite the loose dress she wore. I had no idea who the woman was in the photo, but the man was my father.

CHAPTER FOUR

HOMECOMING

JOHANNA

June 1937
Outside Berchtesgaden, Germany

Faster, faster, faster. I willed the gleaming Mercedes Roadster forward, though it wove its way up the mountain roads with the speed and grace of a panther under Harald's skilled hand. I preferred to be behind the wheel. And that was a distant second to being behind the throttle. I gripped the brown leather handle on the door with my gloved hand, glad he couldn't see the white of my knuckles.

"Relax, *Liebling*. The farm isn't going anywhere. We'll be there soon." My new husband reached over and patted my knee. I looked over at the chiseled, even features of his face.

Husband still didn't seem real. We met at university five years ago, when I was entering my third year of studies in engineering and mathematics at the University of Munich and he was a young lecturer in history. He gave a talk about the Roman Empire, and though he spoke about the politics and social structure of people who had been dead for nearly two thousand years, and though I didn't have any real interest in the subject, I sat engrossed for the entire two-hour lecture. I would never have the passion for history that Harald did, nor would he have my obsession with the mechanics of flight, but in those two hours, I grew to respect his ability to fascinate a classroom. Our paths kept crossing over the years, and acquaintance grew into something more tender.

I loosened my grip on the door handle. "I know, *Knuddelbär*. I can't help it. Just drive as fast as you can," I urged.

"I'm not going to attract the attention of the police. Not with their short tempers these days," Harald said; his eyes were fixed on the road, but he turned to wink at me. "I'm afraid they won't find me as charming as you do."

"Fools," I said, leaning over to kiss him as he navigated the narrow streets that joined the network of farms on the hills outside of Berchtesgaden.

"Too kind a word for that lot." His face grew gray for a few seconds. "'Thugs' is more apt."

"Quiet now," I said. "If you were to slip and say such a thing with the wrong ears listening . . . I don't want to learn firsthand how accurate your description is."

"You're right," Harald said, reaching for my hand. I slid closer to him on the bench seat. He'd grown vocal in his dislike for the regime, angered for my sake and that of his family. His family were of the old guard—I was now a countess by marriage. Hitler had no love for the aristocrats that he held responsible for Germany's defeat in the Great War. The blood in my veins, on the other hand, was an even more sinister threat, according to this new regime.

We never spoke of the supposed stain on my pedigree, but I was getting more and more questions at work. My father's father had been Jewish by birth, though raised Catholic. We were able to keep his heritage a secret by claiming the records had been lost in a fire, but I knew the day was coming soon where I would have to apply for honorary Aryan status to continue my work. The mention of the forms caused

Harald to grind his teeth, but without them, my work at the German aerospace center, Deutsche Versuchsanstalt für Luftfahrt, or DVL as we called it, would come to an end. Despite the plea from the government for married women to stay home and have children, I couldn't abandon my work. Designing the best planes in the world—the fastest, the safest, the most agile—was the reason I was put on this earth.

I looked over at Harald, his expression serious but relaxed as he navigated the winding roads. He had visited the farm only a few times before and had spent far too little time with my family. We'd hoped for a proper church wedding where Papa could have walked me down the aisle. Mama would have cried decorously into her embroidered handkerchief. Little Metta would have looked at my white gown and flowers with affectionate envy, while Oskar would have smirked at the whole affair like the imp he was. But Papa died shortly after we announced our engagement, so celebration would have been vulgar. This was our first trip back since the funeral, and our first as man and wife. I expected our stay would be of some duration, as Mama had begged us to come home as soon as we could manage, to help her with some of the details of Papa's estate. We left as soon as Harald's term was over, and I hoped we'd be able to stay at least a few weeks of the long summer.

We pulled up to the farmhouse, its balcony spilling over with a riot of purple and yellow spring blossoms. I sprinted to the door even before Harald could get the car completely stopped.

"Mama!" I called.

Mama emerged from the kitchen, a dishrag still in her hands. She dropped it on the floor and dashed to my outstretched arms. "Oh, my little Jojo! Let me look at you!" She spun me around to look at my form in the new blue woolen suit Harald had bought me as a wedding gift. "Not my little Jojo anymore, are you? My Johanna has become a woman. How did this happen so quickly?"

"As it always does, Mama, while we are living our lives." I clutched her to my chest, soaking in all the hugs I'd missed since our last visit.

Harald came to the door, a suitcase in each hand. I rushed to his side to relieve him of mine.

"Sorry, *Knuddelbär*," I said, feeling my cheeks grow warm.

"Say nothing of it, you're excited to be home. As any good woman should be."

"I always knew I liked you, young man," Mama said, cocking her head expectantly in my direction, then raised her hand to shake his. "Welcome, Harald. Or welcome home, I should say. It's not a honeymoon suite in Paris, but I hope you will be happy here."

"I'm certain I will be, Frau Hoffmann. You have one of the finest estates in the Alps. I couldn't help but be happy here."

"You're family now. You must call me Ilse. Or Mama if you're so inclined." Most of the children within a two-mile radius called her so. Her pfeffernuesse had that effect on people. Even as a grown woman, I still had dreams of Mama's spice cookies, especially if I'd had too little for supper.

"I'm honored—'Mama,'" he said, trying the word out on his tongue.

Though he was more than thirty centimeters taller than she, Mama took him in her arms and kissed both his cheeks. "I'm so glad my Johanna has found such a nice young man. She has always been so serious in her studies; I wasn't sure that marriage would ever be for her. It may be greedy to ask for so much, but I wanted both a career and a happy home life for my girl."

"I think such greed is the prerogative of a good mother," Harald said. *Good answer, young scholar. Mama might not be a professor, but you're already teacher's pet.*

Mama showed us to the largest bedroom aside from her own. It had been reserved for guests in my youth, but now it was to be ours. My childhood room wasn't exactly appropriate for a married couple, and this would afford us quite a bit more privacy. As we settled in, we heard the stomping of shoes and the cheerful shouting of hungry voices clamoring for an after-school snack.

Oskar and Metta had grown incredibly in the months since Papa's funeral. I'd left a sturdy boy and a little wisp of a girl in Mama's care, and now a young man and woman stood in their places when Harald and I entered the kitchen. Metta was no longer a waif, but a blooming beauty. Oskar still looked every bit the rascal, however, which gave me comfort. "*Meine Gude*, what have you been feeding these children, Mama?" I asked, pulling them both close. As they exchanged greetings with Harald, I admired how beautiful they'd both become. He was tall and muscular and she was petite and lean, but both had wheat-blond hair and vibrant blue eyes the color of a tropical sky. They both favored Mama in looks, and had been mistaken for twins more than once, while I was darker and stouter like Papa, much to my dismay.

"I think they sleep in fertilizer while I'm not looking," Mama said with a wink. "Thank heaven they wash well."

"It is so good to have you home, Johanna," Metta said. "It hasn't been the same without you."

"And it won't be the same ever again," Oskar said, a shadow passing over his face.

"I know," I said softly. Papa's death had taken us all by surprise, but Oskar had always doted on him so much that it had to affect him even more than the rest of us.

"Don't worry," he said, regaining his composure. "I've taken care of Mama and Metta just fine. Since Papa can't be man of the house, I think he'd be proud of the job I've done in his place." He cast an uncertain look in Harald's direction. He clearly thought Harald had come to usurp his place as head of the household. Let Oskar fume at the intrusion. He might think he was ready to lead the family, but I'd not rob him of the last moments of his childhood.

"I'm sure he would be," I said, patting his shoulder.

"What do you think of my uniform?" He spun on the ball of his foot, and I noticed now that the short pants, knee socks, shirt, and tie he wore were not the usual school attire from a few years back. The clothes looked commonplace enough until I noticed the patch on his sleeve and the engraved belt buckle of the Hitler Youth. "I joined last year before they made it mandatory, and they're already talking of making me section leader."

"You look very dashing," I said, though I had trouble forming the words. I noticed Metta wore the navy-blue skirt and necktie with a starched white shirt that was the uniform of the Bund Deutscher Mädel—the League of German Girls.

"Metta wasn't as eager to join, but I think she's come around," Oskar explained. "It's great fun, isn't it?"

"I enjoy the hiking," Metta admitted. "And the girls are nice."

Metta had always been the shy type, and probably enjoyed the novelty of having a pack of girlfriends around her. Both youth organizations had been growing like algae on a stagnant pond for the past several years. If Hitler could boast any success, it was the stranglehold his youth organizations had over German adolescents.

I looked at Mama, who smiled at her younger children. I saw a slight furrow between her eyes, but she turned back to the kitchen to prepare them some sandwiches and cold milk as she'd done for me after school hundreds of times.

"Let me help you, Mama," I said.

Harald nodded to me, his lips set in a firm line. His expression softened as he asked Oskar and Metta about their studies and interests. I shut the kitchen door behind me and gathered the cheese and butter from the icebox while Mama sliced bread and stoked the fire in the stove.

"They've grown so much since you last came to visit, haven't they?" Mama asked.

"It was wrong of me to stay away so long," I admitted.

"You've been busy with your work and your young man. I never expected to keep you close to the nest, my darling girl. I'm just happy you've come home." Mama leaned over and kissed my cheek. "Don't act as though you need to pay penance for growing up."

"Oskar seems to be enthusiastic about his new venture," I said, looking up from the cutting board to gauge her reaction. I lowered my voice to the faintest whisper I could manage. "But are you sure it's . . . wise?"

"It made your father nervous, I'll admit," Mama said, unable to contain her sigh. "But there's nothing else for him to do. It's mandatory now, so the boys who don't join are bullied terribly. A child can't do so much as join a football league if they're not part of the Hitler Youth these days. And lately, it's given him something to think about other than his grief. It's given him some direction, and it's better than him falling into bad habits."

I shook my head. "I hope you're right, Mama. It may be giving him direction, but I worry about where that direction may take him."

"Even so, Johanna, what could I do?" Mama whispered in turn. "If I pull him out, he'll tell his section leader or whatever he's called, and I'll end up on a watch list. Or worse. Hopefully he'll outgrow this phase and find something more useful to do. In the meantime, there's nothing wrong with him going out into the fresh air and getting exercise."

"We live in the mountains, Mama. There's no shortage of fresh air." But I made no further argument. Despite my misgivings about the organization, to breathe a hint of my disapproval to Oskar or Metta could have dire consequences. Mama was right about the watch lists. I looked heavenward and wished, not for the first time, that Papa were still here to advise us all.

"Have you never told them, Mama?"

Her hands shook for a moment as she flipped the sandwiches, then she stepped back from the stove. "Why would I burden them with this?

What does it matter who their grandfather was? He died before they were born. They're safer not knowing."

"What if the truth comes out?" I asked. "I've had to dance around it often enough at work. They don't want non-Aryans working in technology. They'd be better off knowing so they can be prepared."

"If questions come, I'd rather their lies be those of ignorance instead of fear. It's more believable that way."

"I don't think these Nazis will much care which sort of lie it is if they uncover the truth."

"Then we must pray they never find out. Trust me, my dear. They're children. They shouldn't be burdened with such things."

Mama and I took the afternoon snack into the parlor. Oskar's chest puffed with pride as he told Harald of his accomplishments with his local cell and showed off the gleaming silver pocketknife he'd earned for his efforts. There wasn't much childlike in his demeanor as he addressed Harald, and from the look on my husband's face, I knew he felt as I did: that there was nothing childlike about the threat Oskar and the other youths poisoned by Hitler's ideology posed to all of us.

I'd hoped my family would be spared the fervor for this man, but it seemed his reach extended into the deepest corners of my childhood home. I'd been able to take solace in my work for so long, I'd given myself permission to ignore the politics I served. With each revelation of the Nazi methods, I was less and less able to quiet my uneasy conscience. Creating deadlier planes to protect Germany was one thing. Creating them to serve Hitler was another.

⌇

The quartet was in tune, the champagne was chilled to perfection, and the crystal it was served in sparkled more brightly than the sequins on the evening gowns that swished over the dance floor. The event was flawless. Not even the dowager countess could find fault, not that she attended these things anymore. Because of our work, we didn't live on the family's estate, which suited Harald's mother perfectly. She was free to live in the home where she'd once arrived as a bride, and run the house without my interference, but was happy to cede the bother of entertaining to Harald and me on the weekends we could be spared. On these weekends, I traded in my navy-blue pantsuit for an evening gown and played the part of Countess Johanna. It certainly felt like playacting in an age where counts and dukes seemed as relevant as the horse and cart. But all the same, the part had to be played. That night I wore a dress of claret-red crepe and even indulged in wearing ruby earrings and a matching bracelet from the family vault. At least if I had to play a part, I had the chance to look it.

Only a few years before, the men would have been in tailcoats with white ties, but those had given way to the uniforms of the Wehrmacht and the SS. Harald was one of the few men still wearing civilian formal wear, and he looked like a gem among pebbles, but so he always did to me. I watched as he worked the room effortlessly, having been schooled in the art of parlor chat since he could speak.

"How quaint to see you in your element," a voice said from behind me.

Louisa Mueller, a darling of the Luftwaffe and even Hitler himself, wore a pretty little spring-green frock, light as meringue and the perfect shade to bring out the green flecks in her blue eyes. The effect would have been charming if she hadn't paired the ensemble with the expression of a little boy sitting through an overlong sermon at church in a stiffly starched shirt.

"How nice to see you, Louisa," I said, offering her a hand and ignoring her slight. To her, I was the countess playacting as a pilot instead of the other way around. She shook my hand more firmly than was fashionable, but that was a failing of mine as well.

"How can you dress like this all the time? I feel ridiculous." Her declaration was unnecessary, as her opinion of her finery was all but written across her forehead. Attending such a soiree had to be excruciating for her, but she was savvy enough to know that hers was as much a political career as anything else.

"I don't," I replied. She'd seen me in trousers more often than skirts, but to ask her, you'd think I showed up to the office in taffeta ball gowns.

"You know what I mean. If I had to dress like this every weekend, I'd run mad."

"It's nice to have a break from the flight suit sometimes," I said, though I didn't fully mean it. In that respect, she and I were alike. Given my choice, I'd spend all my time behind the throttle, taking planes to their limits, or else at the drafting table creating plans to make the planes as efficient as they could be.

I was like most pilots, enamored of the sheer power of flight and the freedom that came with a pair of wings. But I was even more fascinated by the systems within the aircraft. How they all functioned together to defy gravity and take us to the heavens. It wasn't just flight that called to me, but the magic that made it possible. It had been Papa who had enrolled me in a glider course on a lark when I was in my late teens. He had no idea the monster he was going to create, but I always sensed he was proud of it.

"I heard you set another record," I said, knowing that stroking her formidable ego would make the encounter pass more pleasantly.

"Another altitude record," she said, waving her hand airily, though pride laced her smile.

"You deserve to feel proud," I said. And I meant it. The more she accomplished, the more funding and public support we got.

"The Führer was pleased," she admitted, standing a little taller. "He's grateful for the good publicity for the Reich."

"Of course," I said, forcing the corners of my mouth upward. She had the Führer's ear, and her opinions could easily become policy.

"I see your husband has not joined the party," she said, glancing at where he stood chatting with some very old friends of his family. She made no attempt to hide a disapproving glare at his lack of uniform.

I worried my face would betray my unease. "Oh, you know academics. They usually aren't all that keen on getting into politics."

"I don't really know anything about academics. My family worked for a living."

"Of course," I said, resuming my plastic smile.

Just then, Harald crossed the room to us, as though he'd heard my subliminal screams to rescue me from her clutches.

"How lovely to see you, Miss Mueller. I do hope you'll forgive me, but I have to claim my wife for a few moments."

Louisa said nothing, but offered him a nod and turned to scan the crowd for a familiar face.

"Thank you," I whispered to Harald.

"I know when someone needs rescuing," he said with a wink.

"She's positively insufferable," I said. "She's perfectly content to be a poster girl for the new regime."

"Shhh," he said. "Too many ears."

"I know," I said. "It's still nauseating."

"It's just politics, *Liebling*. Ignore it all and focus on your work. What you're doing is bigger than some regime that's doomed to fail."

"It's been holding on for quite some time now," I reminded him in hushed tones. "And it doesn't seem to be losing any ground."

"That's always the way before a movement like this fails. The country will come to its senses soon enough."

"I hope you're right, *Knuddelbär*," I said, kissing his cheek and wishing I could dismiss the churning in my gut that told me he had more faith in change than was truly warranted.

CHAPTER FIVE

A PICTURE WORTH A THOUSAND QUESTIONS

BETH

April 27, 2007
San Diego, California

Though it sat at home on my kitchen table, the box with Dad's war memorabilia whispered to me seductively as I gave a two-hour lecture comparing the political systems of the Scandinavian countries, graded a pile of term paper outlines, and attended compulsory Friday drinks with the department chair and the other professors racing for tenure. I walked through my door ready to collapse on the couch and lose myself in Food Network, but I found myself fighting the urge to load up the box in the car and trek back to Encinitas through rush hour and ask Dad about the blond woman with the bright eyes. I hung my purse in the entryway, kicked off my shoes, and removed the lid to the plastic bin that now housed the fading photographs. I admired the picture of Dad with the young woman. He was tall and his spine was straight back then. His eyes twinkled, and he wore a kind smile that the war had turned wary but hadn't erased entirely.

The woman's blond curls and the softness of her expression were a stark contrast to Mom's silky dark tresses and sharp features. They were both beautiful women but resembled each other the way a rose resembles a lily. As I looked at the black-and-white image, I found I didn't harbor any resentment toward Dad if he hadn't been a saint during wartime—he wouldn't have been the first soldier to seek shelter from the hardships of war in the arms of a woman. Dad didn't meet Mom until after the war, so I couldn't fault him for infidelity.

Still, the possibility of this woman's significance to my father sat heavy in my stomach. I'd never considered that he'd had a life before Mom, and I felt childish at my lack of imagination on the subject. He'd adored Mom so much, it was easy to believe he'd just spent the first years of his life waiting for her to come along. Had Dad loved this strange blond woman too? Was the baby his? Did I have an older brother or sister out there somewhere? Nieces and nephews? Maybe even a stepmother of sorts? It would be a family, if they were interested in having me be part of it. But that all seemed impossible. If I knew one thing about my father, it was that he would never have abandoned his child if he'd had any choice in the matter.

But the photo could mean nothing. She might have been a French housewife, wanting a photo with a dashing American liberator that she could show her child one day. *You see that man there? He, and millions like him, is the reason we are still alive and have a country of our own.* The expression on Dad's face might not be adoration, but a charming smile for a pretty woman after too many months without the sight of one.

Or it might not.

I considered the lure of the couch, but decided the exuberant celebrity chefs didn't hold their usual appeal. I went to the kitchen, still foreign and not particularly well organized. I'd left behind the palatial granite-and-stainless-steel Tuscan revival kitchen that Greg and I had crafted from the ruins of a lime-green midcentury nightmare. He'd inherited the house from his grandparents and had made it his mission to update it into something fit for a magazine cover. The project had been a long haul, but we didn't bicker over details like a lot of couples did. The cabinets were darker than I would have preferred, and I know the professional-grade stove I chose didn't fit the aesthetic as well as Greg might have liked, but the overall effect was warm and inviting. There were few things I regretted about leaving my marriage behind, but the kitchen we'd designed together was one.

I pulled out the notebook my mother had given me as a wedding gift with all her recipes copied down in her perfect, efficient script. She had loathed computers and would never have taken the time to type them all out, but each and every recipe in the book was clear enough to read as though they'd come from the printer's. Each recipe had been tested for generations and was positively bulletproof if you weren't completely helpless in the kitchen. There was a bit of her on each page, and looking through the pages was like being transported back to the kitchen of my parents' home where she'd used every ounce of her patience to teach me her craft. I flipped it open to her recipe for the challah bread she made for every Sabbath and holiday meal. I didn't celebrate the Sabbath like Mom and Dad had done, and there wasn't a holiday on the horizon, but the kneading and mixing were therapeutic. And there was nothing like challah for French toast, which was a sort of holiday of its own.

I put the humble ball of dough in a bowl, covered it in plastic wrap, and left it to rise on top of the gently warming oven, as my state-of-the-art warming drawer had been left behind. I heard the ring of my cell from my purse as I was washing the wayward bits of dough from my hands. I dashed to the hall and rifled for my phone with still-wet fingers.

Greg.

I hesitated a moment, considering letting the call go to voice mail, but my finger pressed the green answer button out of reflex.

"Just checking in," he said by way of greeting.

"You don't have to, you know," I said, hoping there wasn't too much of an edge to my voice. I could hear my mother in my ear: *He's being kind, Beth. You might have given up on your marriage, but love doesn't bloom overnight, and you can't stamp it out overnight either.* I stopped the voice before she started in on how I'd made a mistake letting a good man, a good provider like Greg, slip away. She'd managed to get in a few of those digs while she was still alive, and I didn't need to manufacture any more.

"I want to," Greg insisted. "Are you out?" There was a pang in his voice, and I knew he was praying the answer was no. To him, the marriage wouldn't truly be over until I'd found someone else. I'd considered going out on a few dates just to give him the signal, but even dates to help him move on were as appealing as a tax audit.

"No," I admitted, wishing I were a better liar. "Raging Friday night at home baking challah."

"Going back to your roots, then?" he observed. "You only bake when you're upset. What's going on?"

I held in a sigh. I baked plenty when I was in good spirits as well, but it was invariably a source of comfort when I wasn't. I considered telling him about the photo, but he'd launch into a million scenarios about its subjects, all of which would be meant to disprove whatever theories I had. Though there was nothing in the photo that proved Dad had a real connection to the woman, there wasn't anything proving he didn't—but Greg would insist it was nothing. Everything was always nothing until it was something. And even then, it was never as important as I made it out to be.

Until I spoke with Dad, there was no sense in opening speculation with Greg.

"Dad's test numbers aren't great," I said, admitting the real heart of my discontent. I took a seat on the couch, propping my feet on the coffee table. Dad wasn't there to chide me, and Greg wasn't there to shake his head. "He wants to stop all his meds and treatments."

"That's his choice, I suppose," Greg said. "I'm sorry to hear it, though."

"I'm sorry too," I said. "I'm not ready to lose him."

"All the treatments are just a stall anyway," Greg pointed out. "He's in his nineties. It's only a matter of time."

"You can say that about an infant and it's still true, Greg. It's just a matter of a bit *more* time."

"You know what I mean, Beth. Don't make things difficult for your dad."

Of course, I knew what he meant: *You can't do anything about the situation, so there's no need to talk about it.*

"I'm afraid 'difficult' is one of my defining characteristics," I said, pinching the bridge of my nose and letting out a ragged breath. "I thought you knew that by now."

Greg cleared his throat, not offering a real response. "I *am* sorry. You've been through a lot in the last year. If you let me take you to Mancino's, I'll let you cry on my shoulder."

"That's a bad idea and you know it."

"After all the years we were together, we can't share a meal as friends?"

I knew that friendship was the last thing he wanted from me, but I swallowed my response.

"So, how is the tenure application coming along?" Greg finally asked.

"Fine," I said.

"I've heard nothing but good things from your chair," he said. As the co-chair of the economics department, he was looped in on a lot of the university politics I tried so desperately to avoid, often to my own professional detriment. My excuse was that I preferred the theory of politics over the application in academia. "I've got high hopes for you."

"Thank you," I said, happy he didn't quiz me on the finer points of my application. He knew his stuff, no mistake, but he often assumed that no one else was as competent.

We ended our call with his now customary reminder to use the dead bolt. Not too long after, the challah was ready to braid. I took my dough cutter and split the dough into three even pieces, not bothering with Mom's preferred six-strand method as it wouldn't be presented at table. It was neat enough, and even Mom wouldn't have found fault with it. I covered it and let it sit again for a couple of hours before baking.

As the smell of the challah filled the apartment, the musty smell of the dozens of prior residents faded away. I took in a deep breath, and my mother was there in the wholesome sweetness of the baking bread.

I'd come to terms with Mom being gone. We'd gotten along well, but her death wasn't the same loss that Dad's would be. I felt guilt at the thought. As much as parents should love all their children the same, children ought to return the favor to their parents. Still, I felt her absence more keenly now than I had at her funeral. I was sure that Dad's decision to let nature take its course was the impetus. When he was gone, I wouldn't have another family member left alive, and that realization chilled me like a winter breeze off the ocean. I had to do better for Dad in his final days than I'd done for Mom. Be more present. My friends would all tell me I'd done my best, but I'd know the truth and be forced to live with it.

CHAPTER SIX

INSIDE THE DEATH FACTORY

MAX

September 20, 1944
Hürtgen Forest, Germany

The roar of the German guns was so constant, the rare silence was deafening. I spotted my next patient: a fallen soldier who had slid to the bottom of a hill. He was covered from enemy fire for the moment, and I stood a decent chance of getting him out.

I ran to his side and fell to my knees by his head, tossing my kit beside me for ease of access. *A pulse.* If there was none, I had to move on. I pressed my fingers to his neck and felt the faint thump-thump, thump-thump, more significant than the screams and shellfire that swirled around my ears. In our kits, they gave us cotton to keep in our ears to muffle the sound, but I saved it for the short stretches of sleep I was able to steal in the barracks. I needed all my senses to treat the wounded—sometimes a nuance in the voice of a fallen soldier spoke volumes about the extent of his injury. And I wouldn't dishonor the families of these men by missing their sons' last words. Hearing them was a task that had fallen to me more times than I cared to count in the year and a half since I'd been deployed to France.

The soldier—a boy of maybe twenty—was breathing, but it was shallow. He was a private by the last name of Davis, according to the dog tags that had come untucked from his uniform when he fell. He'd taken a bullet to his right shoulder and was bleeding so much he was already the color of ash. The bullet had gone clear through, though, so he might make it. Shrapnel from bullets was hard to remove, if a man was lucky enough to get operated on in time in the first place, and it opened him up to infections from within and without. I sprinkled the wound with crystalline sulfanilamide, an antibiotic powder, and applied pressure to both sides with a bandage. I pressed as hard as I dared and prayed that there weren't stray bone fragments to cause him problems later.

"E-everything looks h-hazy," the soldier stuttered. "And I'm cold."

"Come now, it's autumn in Germany, soldier. You're lying in a mud pit. It *is* cold. And the artillery fire has made everything hazy from here to Paris. Nothing to fret about," I reasoned, keeping the timbre of my voice upbeat. I knew the cold he felt and the haze he saw weren't just due to our conditions, but if I could get him to think so, he might avoid shock.

I described the injury and my treatment on a medical tag, affixed it to his clothes, and scanned the field for litter bearers. I was able to get the attention of a pair who were free of a charge and saw the young private loaded up and carried off back to the casualty collection point. For a moment I watched them retreat, unable to breathe. The rear litter bearer stumbled, and I saw a red splotch grow across his back from the bullet of a German sniper. On occasion, the white fields with red crosses on the medics' helmets served as a target rather than a moral deterrent.

I ran out into the open to assess the three of them. The rear litter bearer was dead—the hole in the back of his chest was the size of a dime, but the crater in the front was that of a softball. He'd died before he knew what happened, and he was all the luckier for it. The other litter bearer was lying over Davis, doing what he could to protect him from fire.

"Let's move!" I yelled to the surviving medic, removing the rear litter handles from his partner's hands, not wasting time to attach the litter straps that would make the task of transporting him easier. I could see the rise and fall in Davis's chest, but it was becoming shallower with each breath. The fall had done him no good, and if my instincts were right, he needed sutures as soon as we could get clear of enemy fire.

It was a solid half mile or more to the collection point. Any closer, and they'd be within range of the German guns. Those closest to the Germans had more than a mile to run with a wounded man to get to safety.

The air was bitter, and I had mud up to my knees. Sweat poured from me, and I fought to get air in my lungs. *If I survive this damned war, I'm going to run three miles a day until my legs give out from under me.*

There were at least two dozen patients for every medic, and Davis's bandages were completely sodden.

"This man needs a surgeon," I called.

The head of our medical detachment, a Major Willis, looked up at me. "Congratulations, Blumenthal. You're promoted. If you can stitch up gums after extracting a tooth, you can stitch up a gunshot wound. I need you here." I felt my cheeks grow cool. If he was keeping me here, it was because he knew we wouldn't be able to treat most of the wounded men on the battlefield in time. He looked to the lieutenant who had carried Davis in with me. "You there, take Keller over there and that litter and get back on that field."

The lieutenant saluted, and the two soldiers disappeared into the haze with their litter.

I pulled the tissue forceps, scissors, suture silk, and surgical needles from my kit, along with a healthy dose of morphine and some iodine. I dosed Davis with the morphine, hoping his heart wasn't too weak to handle the medicine. I cleaned the exit wound again with the iodine, stitched him up from the front, then repeated the process on the back after gently flipping him to his stomach. The bleeding was minimal, and his breathing grew steadier. Now it was up to the ambulance crew. If they could get him transported to a proper field hospital and he didn't catch his death lying in the freezing mud, he'd live to fight another battle.

The next five patients I saw weren't so lucky. The only thing I could do was offer them morphine and make their passing as painless as I could. I wished I could stay with them as they passed, but I had only the time for a few kind words before moving on to the next man. The longer I lingered, the more patients there would be for whom there was no help to offer beyond platitudes.

Night fell, but there was no respite. We worked in the dark as best we could without benefit of the flashlights or candles that would make us perfect targets for the snipers. My hands shook with fatigue, but I forged on until Major Willis ordered me to head back to the field hospital with the next transport behind the lines. I looked out the rear window of the olive-drab truck at the men left behind, the feeling of helplessness seeping into my marrow at the thought of all those who couldn't be saved that night.

~

If there was a single lesson I'd learned in dental school, it was the dire importance of sanitation. Cleanliness wasn't next to godliness when it came to medicine—it was laced in its very scripture. But mere yards from German artillery fire, the bright lights and polished tiles of the hospitals back home seemed as far away as the craters on the dark side of the moon.

I helped the ambulance crew unload the wounded, but instead of eager doctors, patient nurses, and warm beds, they were welcomed by harried doctors onto dirty cots under a tent that was next to useless in protecting them from the elements. One thing, among many, that training never prepared me for was how the men, lying in rows under the same olive-drab blankets, all started to look the same. I vowed that when I returned home—*if* I returned home—I'd know my patients. I'd know their families. I'd know if they were powerful lawyers, humble plumbers, housewives, or students.

Here, they were all soldiers. The doctors developed the unfortunate habit of thinking of the men by their ailments—the right-foot amputation in bed four, the burn victim in bed twenty-three—and I couldn't blame them. The detachment helped them get through the day with their wits intact, and we needed the doctors in good form as much as we needed the bullets in our guns. All the same, I couldn't bear to think of the men as nothing more than the sum of their injuries.

I'd been working for sixteen hours, and the commanding officer of our detachment, Colonel Pankhurst—an eminent physician from Chicago—gave me leave to find some dinner and grab a few hours of shut-eye, but I was more likely to win the war single-handedly with a simple bayonet than to quiet my mind enough for sleep. Davis had been settled on a cot in the middle of the tent, which was the best possible place. Warmer than anywhere else, and in the constant path of the doctors and nurses if he needed help. He looked as pale as hospital linens but hadn't yet fallen asleep.

"You look fit as a fiddle, Davis. Why don't you free up this bed for some poor guy who really needs it?" I said, stooping next to him and tapping on his uninjured shoulder. He was incredibly weak from the loss of blood, but still managed something resembling a chuckle.

"That's right," he said, straining to speak. "Just get me back my rifle and I'll get back out there in the morning."

"That's the spirit," I said. "Don't let a paltry shoulder wound get you down."

"The litter bearer—he didn't make it, did he?" His voice grew even weaker.

"No," I answered, unable to think of a good reason to keep the truth from him.

"It's all my fault," he said. "He should have left me there."

"Enough of that," I said. "And that's an order. That litter bearer was doing his job. If you want to blame anyone, point the finger at the Germans. They're the ones who shot him. And shot you, for that matter. I don't know you all that well, Private, but I assume that getting your shoulder obliterated by a German sniper wasn't on your list of plans for the day, was it?"

"No, Captain, it wasn't."

"Good, because if it was, we'd have to get the company head-shrinker in here to help with that too, and trust me, he's busy. We're trying to sneak him over the border to see if he can't talk some sense into Hitler. I haven't taken much in the way of psychology classes, but my hunch is mother issues. It usually is when you're dealing with megalomaniacal dictators."

"Do you have a lot of experience with megalomaniacal dictators, Captain?"

"You've got me there, Davis."

"I didn't get your name, by the way. You saved my life today. Twice."

"Max Blumenthal," I answered. "And I was just doing my job, kid. Where you from?"

"Boston, sir."

"So, I guess that makes you a Red Sox fan?" I asked.

"You bet, Captain. My dad sends me the scores with every letter. He forgot once and wrote twice to apologize. Who's your team?"

"No major league teams as far west as LA, so I'm a Yankees man."

"We all have our faults, Captain," Davis said, his expression so solemn, I felt a laugh escape from my chest, loud enough to earn an impatient "shhh!" from a nearby nurse. "How did a West Coast man end up over here? I thought they were sending you all to the Pacific."

"I wanted to come over here. This is my fight, not the one in the Pacific," I said, thinking of my extended family in Riga. "I hadn't been drafted yet, so I scraped together the train fare to Maryland and enlisted there. They were happy enough to take another medic."

"I expect they were," he said. "I'm glad you came this way."

"Get some rest, Davis. I'll come check on you when I can. You did good today."

Davis, lids heavy, just nodded, but there was something easier in his expression as he drifted off to much-needed sleep.

"You have a way with the men, Captain," Colonel Pankhurst commented as I stepped away from Davis's cot. "It's nice to see them smile a bit. God knows there isn't much to smile about while you're bleeding out next to dying men in a leaky tent. It'd mean a lot to them if you made a habit of this sort of thing."

"I'd be happy to, Colonel. If you think it'll help."

"I do, son. Keeping their spirits up is as important as antibiotics half the time. I'll see about getting you a few extra hours of R and R a week for it. But dinner and shut-eye first, Captain, or I'll have another patient on my hands."

"Yes, sir," I said, nodding my agreement.

I exited the tent, the blanket of night still over us. The gunfire in the distance had slowed, but it never stopped entirely. Though lights were strictly forbidden, the moon was full. Paired with the orange glow from the artillery fire to the east, it was almost as easy to find my way as it would have been at dawn. The mess hall loomed large, and while the fare varied from miserable to nauseating, it was warm and filling if you didn't think too hard about it. The memory of my mother's chicken soup and brisket was dancing in my head like so many sugarplums, but a flash of yellow from my right stole my attention. I saw a slight figure at the edge of the woods, leaves and twigs crunching underfoot as he tried to escape into the cover of the trees and the gloom of night.

"Freeze!" I called, not for the first time lamenting that medics generally traveled unarmed, else forfeit the protection of our medics' helmets and armbands, such as it was.

The figure did freeze, his hands in the air, his breathing rapid and shallow. By the size of him, he had to be a boy of no more than sixteen.

"What are you doing there?" I demanded. He wasn't in uniform but wore ragged woolen trousers and a coat whose very fibers looked to be held together with dirt and sheer determination not to collapse into dust. His yellow hair, which had given him away, came down to his shoulders, and was pulled back with a leather cord. An unusual fashion for boys nowadays, but war made for odd habits.

"I mean no harm," a voice said in a thick German accent.

"Turn around," I ordered.

Slowly, the boy turned toward me, but I was greeted by the face of a young woman. Her eyes were wide and filled with fear, like a rabbit caught in a snare.

"What are you doing so close to the front?" I asked, thinking, *And on the wrong side.*

"I took some bandages and antiseptic," she admitted. "There is a wounded man I must tend to."

"And that wounded man is likely responsible for wounding some of my own. Give it back and I won't hand you over to the military police. This time."

"He hasn't hurt anyone on your side. I swear it," she said. "He's been against Hitler and his thugs from the beginning."

"Which is exactly what I would say if I were a German who wanted to avoid being handed over to the American military police," I countered.

"Blumenthal, I need a hand in here before you head to the mess," the disembodied voice of Colonel Pankhurst called from the tent.

I grabbed her bicep and her eyes went wide. I *had* to drag her over to him and report her presence. How she'd gotten through the forest and so far behind enemy lines, I didn't know, but she'd stolen army property. She could be dangerous, planting explosives behind the lines, sabotaging our troops from the rear. She could be a spy reporting sensitive information to the German commanders.

Or she might be exactly as she seemed.

"Please," she whispered. She was shaking beneath my grip as though I meant to tear her to shreds with my own teeth. No tears welled in her blue eyes, but there was no mistaking her fear.

I pulled her a step closer, leaned down to her ear, and whispered, "Run."

CHAPTER SEVEN

THE MECHANICS OF WAR

JOHANNA

October 1939
Berlin, Germany

Harald packed his bags as I sat on the edge of our bed in the room we shared. The little cottage on the shore of Lake Wannsee was our haven of peace, despite being so near the humming hornet's nest of Berlin that lay just to the east. It was a shoebox compared to what Harald's mother expected for her son, but every centimeter of it was perfect in my view. It was thirty minutes by bicycle to the air base at Gatow for me, and thirty minutes by car to the University of Berlin for him. The sunset over the lake, the trees, and the birdsong were balm for Harald's excitable nerves. They allowed me to sleep as though I were in our mountain chalet.

We'd hoped fervently that his post at the university would exempt him from military service, but as in many things since the new regime came into power, we were mistaken. I should have been folding the clothes for him, placing them in his bag, and tucking in a hidden memento for him to find when he reached his post—a picture of me, a lock of my hair, or some such romantic nonsense—but there I sat, my knees pressed to my chest so hard, I wouldn't be surprised to find bruises on my breastbone in the morning. I would not dissolve as I sent Harald off to war; he deserved better. But to keep that from happening, I could concentrate on nothing more complicated than holding my body in one piece. The taking in and expulsion of air was Herculean.

"I'll be fine, *Häschen*. I'm a professor, not a soldier, and I've no ambitions of being a hero. I'll find my way into some clerical work. They'll know I'm of better use at a typewriter than at the front."

"And what if they just want to be rid of the von Oberndorff name altogether?" I asked. "I can think of no easier way to dispose of a man than to send him to war." Harald's family had been outspoken about their concerns regarding the party, but too powerful to silence.

"Even if that's so, my love, there is nothing I can do to stop it. If I refuse, I risk the firing squad. At least heading to Poland, I stand some chance."

"I can't bear it. I can't stand the thought of you fighting for that evil man."

"I'm not. I fight for Germany as it once was. What it could be again if we regain our senses."

I said nothing but swallowed a diatribe that would have lasted into the small hours of the morning.

"*Liebchen*, if you want to hasten my return, keep at your research. Give Germany so formidable an air force that no one will dare take us on. We can convince our countrymen of their folly and elect a sane leader in due course. In the meantime, just keep quiet and hope no one digs too far back in your family's past. I couldn't bear to serve knowing you were under arrest or shunted off to a ghetto somewhere."

I wanted to debate with my academic. To ask him how we might dispose of a despot when he'd banned all opposing parties. How we could turn the hearts and minds of men when Hitler had given the common man the two things he'd been craving since the war—jobs and a scapegoat. But those weren't fitting words for a parting. And I knew full well my Harald didn't believe what he said. He knew Germany and its people were sick and the only cures we could conceive of were catastrophic.

It was time for Harald to leave, and I summoned all that I had to stand. To hold him in my arms and give him a proper goodbye.

"Don't fret," he said, answering my silence. "I'll be home as soon as it can be arranged. Be strong and look after your mother. She'll need your support more than ever with Oskar being called into service."

I nodded. We'd taken the trip from Berlin to Berchtesgaden monthly since we'd moved to the capital. Though it left us exhausted, Harald shifted his classes and I my work schedule to allow for a five-day weekend the first week of every month so we could spend three days together with Mama and Metta. Oskar had become a rare fixture in the house the higher he climbed in the echelon of Hitler Youth, and now the army. Mama had sent me the picture she'd taken shortly after he enlisted. He was the exact image of our grandfather on Mama's side—tall, muscular, and serious. Handsome enough to have gained quite a reputation with the bright-eyed, eager girls of the Bund Deutscher Mädel, or BDM.

The time had come for Harald to leave, but I clung to him a few moments longer. I pulled his mouth down to mine and kissed him hungrily. There was no way to know when I'd taste his lips again. Those delicious lips that tasted of currant jam after breakfast and cognac tinged with cigar smoke after dinner. He pressed his forehead against mine, his hands on either side of my head. I tried to memorize everything . . . the sound of his breathing, the scent of vetiver soap, the warmth of his skin pressed against mine.

"I'll be strong," I forced myself to say when I knew he couldn't delay his departure any longer. I summoned enough substance in my voice that if the words had come from another, I might have believed them.

Then he was gone.

I'd been given an extra day's leave, before my monthly trip to Berchtesgaden, to bid Harald farewell. No kindness was spared to the wife of a departing soldier, but I knew if I stayed at home I would let myself soak in my despair over his absence like in a bath gone cold. After ten minutes of brooding, I changed from the frilly housedress that Harald loved on me into my practical gray pantsuit, took my bicycle from the front porch, and rode to the air base.

"I thought you were out today," Louisa Mueller said by way of greeting as I entered the lab.

"And a pleasure it is to see you too, *Flugkapitän* Mueller, I trust you're well," I said as I strode around to the table space I used for drafting sketches of my designs. Improving the braking system for the Junkers Ju 87 aircraft was my mission, and it bothered Louisa that my engineering degree gave me different privileges than she had. She was a talented pilot but had allowed herself to become a show pony for the Third Reich. She flew to set records and to garner attention for the superiority of German aviation. I was the one entrusted with making our aircraft more maneuverable, safer, and in many cases, deadlier.

"Just a surprise is all, *Gräfin* von Oberndorff." She spoke my title like an insult, but it was the one she insisted on despite my preference for *"Flugkapitän"* over *"Gräfin"* while at work. And unlike Louisa, I insisted on neither. Though she was a civilian, she had commissioned the female equivalent of a flight captain's uniform and was never seen in anything else on base. If anyone dared to omit her title, she was quick to bare her fangs. "I simply thought you were off on holiday again."

I controlled my urge to roll my eyes at the insult she didn't even bother to veil. I sometimes wondered if she had any sort of life outside of aviation but didn't care to get close enough to her to find out. If she saw a monthly visit to my widowed mother as a dereliction of duty, she wasn't the sort I could ever consider a friend.

To be fair, part of me understood her stance. There was no equivocation on the party's position of the role of women in the new Reich.

We were to be wives and mothers. Caretakers of the home and moral guides for our children. Not test pilots or engineers. She and I were handpicked exceptions to the rule, and if we didn't insist on a certain level of rigor, we would never be respected.

Just then, Peter, a special protégé I'd taken on to train as a mechanic, entered the office. He was a tall lad, and smarter than the rest of the mechanics put together. He'd been rejected from the program at least six times, though, because he was born with a twisted leg that forced him to walk with an extreme limp. He was the sort to be too proud for a cane, so I never dared suggest it.

"Ma'am, I just completed the adjustments to the steering you requested. Everything seems to be in working order."

"Thank you, Peter," I said, turning my back on Louisa. "Is she ready for me to take up?"

"Yes, ma'am. I can put in the flight request now."

"Good," I said by way of dismissal. He turned and limped back out toward the hangar.

"Is that boy really capable of the work?" Louisa wondered aloud. "He's barely able to stand upright."

"His back and hands are fine. And even more important, his brain. He's one of the best we have."

"Curious," she said, without further comment. Typical. The Reich seemed to think that the handicapped were all somehow deficient. Peter wasn't the only one who had been turned away from a job he was more than qualified for. But it seemed that was the way things were these days.

I put away the plans I'd thought to work on, squared my shoulders, and walked to the airfield without another glance back at Louisa.

The Junkers was waiting for me, gleaming in the autumn sun. The air was crisp, the sky seemed to glitter in anticipation of my ascent. I donned my helmet, climbed into the cockpit, and made a quick check of all the systems. All was in perfect working order under Peter's careful eye. He was as meticulous a mechanic as one could dream of working with, and I made a silent prayer every night that the Reich would not find reason to remove him from his post.

With the flip of a few switches, the engines awakened with a roar, then settled into the efficient hum of their labors. I was given the signal for takeoff and coursed down the runway. Each time the wheels lifted off the earth and the plane rose into the heavens, my stomach clenched and my heart stopped for a few seconds of sheer marvel. Soon, I would put the plane through her paces, testing the steering system as well as the others I planned to improve, but I took just a moment to revel in the miracle of flight.

Up here, there was no war—yet. There were no politics. The scurryings of man were inconsequential from above the mountaintops. At the throttle of an aircraft, I found a solace more precious than any treasure.

Shortly after I married Harald, my mother-in-law, bless her, asked me when I planned to stop flying. She was anxious for grandchildren and for Harald to step fully into his role as Count von Oberndorff, which he had little interest in doing. My answer remained steadfast: *"I'll be able to leave my wings behind when flying ceases to be miraculous."*

―――

Dearest Mama and Metta,

I trust this letter finds you well and that you are finding ways to be useful to the Reich. Of course, I cannot tell you many details about where I am or what I am doing, but I can assure you that I am in good health and spirits. I am liked by my fellow soldiers and have earned the respect of my superiors. A man can ask for little more. There is nothing more satisfying than hard work for the benefit of a truly glorious cause. I was pleased to learn that Harald will be joining up, though of course I wish his service had been voluntary instead of conscripted. Then again, he is a man of books, and not all men are built to take up arms. I hope he will be stationed nearby so that I might have the chance to know him better. Tell Johanna that I am proud of her work at DVL and that I am sure it is a credit to the whole family and to the Führer. I look forward to seeing you all when our work is complete.

    Heil Hitler,

    Oskar

"He seems well," Mama offered after a few moments of silence. Metta and I sat on either side of her at the kitchen table, a plate of pfeffernuesse and a jug of milk untouched in the center.

"Climbing the ranks from the sound of it too," I added. "Or soon will be."

"It was nice he mentioned Harald," Metta said, reaching for one of the cookies, but thinking better of it. The BDM had been strict about their guidelines for optimum health. The members were subject to regular inspections like they were enlisting in the army themselves.

Metta, always the peacemaker, wanted to believe that Oskar's mention of Harald was an affirmation of brotherly love. I saw it for what it was—a barbed insult to his manhood. The Hitler Youth all believed that true men were warriors. That they should be clamoring to join the fight and uphold the honor of the fatherland. A bookish man like Harald was anathema to them. He wasn't different in their eyes, he was lesser. But I dared not defend Harald or denigrate Oskar in Metta's hearing. I hoped that the BDM hadn't claimed her heart as thoroughly as the Hitler Youth had claimed Oskar's, and that she was still very much the gentle creature I'd known growing up, but I was scared to trust her.

It was everywhere—mothers being reported by their own children for "unpatriotic acts" or behaving in a manner that might be considered "anti-German." Muttering a kind word about a Jewish person or a mild critique of the Führer would send even doting children to the nearest youth leader. They grew more fervent with each passing year, their rallies more impassioned, their songs bathed indelibly in bloodlust.

"Yes," Mama said at length. "I do hope the two of them will have the chance to become better acquainted. It's a shame for brothers not to know each other. Even brothers by marriage."

"I agree," Metta said. "It would be good for both of them, I think."

"So, have you given any more thought to your university plans?" I asked, changing the topic. "You know you could stay at the cottage with me and take the bus into town. You've always been good with words; I thought the idea of your studying German or journalism was a grand one."

"I couldn't go so far and leave Mama alone," Metta said. "I'd be miserable the whole time, thinking about it."

"Children are meant to leave their parents behind, darling girl," Mama objected. "I'd love to have two well-educated girls in the family. I'd be able to boast all over Berchtesgaden about my two smart girls."

"And Mama can come stay with us whenever she's lonely. For good, if she likes. It would be snug, but we could manage."

"The BDM doesn't believe that a university course is useful for a woman. And that which is not useful is wasteful. That which is wasteful is an affront to the Führer himself."

"Yes . . . quite," Mama said, her voice faltering despite her efforts.

"I would think a good mastery of the German language would be a noble gift to use in service to the country," I countered. "Surely there could be nothing more patriotic than to be able to use our mother tongue with grace. Even the BDM must agree with that."

"They might," Metta said, looking down at the grooves on our heavy oaken table and tracing the patterns in the grain with her index finger.

"There's something else, isn't there?" I pressed.

Metta looked up at me, her deep-blue eyes assessing my face.

"I've had an offer of marriage." She spoke the words like a child confessing a great wrongdoing.

"Why have you said nothing?" Mama asked, pulling Metta to her and kissing her cheeks. "Who is he? You've not mentioned a beau before now."

"His name is Ansel Ziegler. He's an *Obersturmbannführer* in the SS."

I felt my stomach clench. That Metta had attracted the attention of a young man in the party was no surprise. She didn't show Oskar's enthusiasm for the cause, but she was lifted in their estimation because of his fervor. But to attract the attention of a lieutenant colonel was another matter. If she accepted him, she would be tied to the party, inextricably. From what little I knew of the upper echelons of the party, I doubted a refusal was something he would take with good grace.

"If he's an *Obersturmbannführer*, he can't be a very young man, can he?" Mama asked.

"I haven't asked him, but I would guess he is in his forties," Metta replied, still not meeting our gazes.

I took a steadying breath before speaking so that the fear and distress wouldn't creep into my voice and set her on guard. "You don't seem particularly excited. Perhaps he's not quite the match for you?"

I looked over to Mama, who had kept her expression impassive but had gone white as cream. We could not voice one word against this man, likely more than twice Metta's age, who wanted to steal her from us. I made haphazard plans in my head; if she wanted to refuse him, I could spirit her away to Berlin, then use the connections of Harald's family to keep her out of his grasp. England? France? It was possible, but I couldn't offer her salvation until she asked for it.

"You misunderstand me. It's a good match," Metta said, straightening up and finally looking at us directly. "If I show any hesitation, it is only because I've just met him a few weeks ago. He is very well liked by the Führer himself, and has already built a promising career for himself. His attentions are an honor."

"Of course they are," Mama said. "And that he has chosen you shows he is a man of good taste. You must invite him to dinner as soon as he can be spared from his duties."

"He's very busy, Mama, but I will ask. Even if he cannot attend, I am sure the invitation will flatter him as much as the meal itself."

"Certainly there isn't a hurry to be married," I said, my tone light. "With all that is going on, I would think family is of secondary importance for such a man."

"Quite the opposite, really," Metta said. "He wants to marry as soon as he can get the permission of his superiors. With the world as unsettled as it is, he wants to secure a family and a legacy before duty takes him out of the fatherland. As you say, he's not a young man."

"But he plans to ask for Mama's blessing, I hope?"

"He seems to think such traditions are old-fashioned. And since Papa is gone, unnecessary. That was part of his reason for choosing me. He was worried for me without a male protector, especially with Oskar out of the country."

I bit my tongue against a rebuke of his chauvinist arrogance.

"You've yet to mention if you care for this *Obersturmbannführer* of yours. It might be a sound match, but does he make you happy? Could you possibly know in just a few weeks?"

"In times like these, who can bother with such silly romantic notions? We must look to what is best for the fatherland." She stood and strode off in the direction of her bedroom. I heard her door shut with what seemed to me a resigned click.

I wished to God she'd slammed it shut in fury. If she was angry, we still had a prayer of convincing her to leave. There was nothing we could do with resignation.

CHAPTER EIGHT

ARCHIVING HEARTACHE

BETH

April 28, 2007
Encinitas, California

Lunch had been served and cleared away a couple of hours before, so I made use of the dining table to spread out Dad's photos, postcards, and other war trinkets. The Luger I left at home, guessing the staff would just as soon not have me bring a firearm into the house. He'd not told me what he was looking for or why he wanted to see these things after so many years, but I hoped he would confide in me. Growing up, whenever I'd had to write school papers about the war, he'd always deflected the questions to Mom or the county library, though I knew in my gut he had more insight than either could provide. Different insight at least. But even for me, he wouldn't discuss what he'd been through, apart from an acknowledgment that Paris was beautiful, even when torn by war, and the German forests were as magnificent as any he'd ever seen.

He never went back to Europe, even when Mom hinted at it for vacations. She would leave brochures for Spain, Italy, and Greece in conspicuous spots throughout the house, and he responded with decadent trips to the Caribbean, Australia, and even the Galápagos Islands. And Hawaii—always Hawaii. When they went to Israel fifteen years back, he booked the trip so that the layover was in Toronto rather than London or Amsterdam, so that he wouldn't have to come up with an excuse not to leave the airport. It was the only thing he'd ever denied her, as far as I knew, and I didn't think she begrudged him.

I came armed with acid-free, archival-quality photo books, a fresh notebook and pens to make a record of each of the photographs, and even a mini-recorder in case Dad had stories to tell about the various objects he'd hauled home from his years overseas.

Dad came into the dining room, his walker guiding each step. Kimberly walked beside him, chatting companionably but poised to catch him if his balance faltered.

"You've been hard at work, Bethie," Dad said, observing the organized piles of photos and the carefully placed mementos.

"You wanted to see your things, Dad. I just figured we'd better preserve them after all these years, or there won't be anything left. I hope you don't mind. There was no salvaging the box."

"Fine, fine," he said. "I should have done this years ago, but time plays cruel tricks."

Dad seemed invigorated by the memories before him. He took the packets of photos and organized them into chronological order from basic training to discharge and homecoming. He patiently described the contents of each photo as I wrote copious notes, assigned them numbers, and placed them carefully in an album. He remembered names and dates as clearly as though he'd served last month instead of more than half a century before.

He flipped through the postcards, telling me why he'd chosen them and about some of the sights he remembered. There were quite a number from Paris, though most were from the front in western Germany. He began checking each of the yellowed photo envelopes, making sure they were empty except for the strips of negatives.

I felt a prick of embarrassment, knowing what he was looking for. The picture of Dad with his arm around the blond woman was tucked carefully in my purse. I still wanted to know who she was, but part of me had become afraid of the answer in the days since I discovered it. So long as I didn't know who she was, she wasn't the *other woman* in his life before he met Mom. A Schrödinger's photograph, of sorts. I had pushed away the juvenile thoughts of keeping it to myself, but separating it from the rest of the pile was bad enough.

"Oh, this one fell out of the box when I got home. It hadn't fared as well as the others, so I put it in a protective sleeve." It was a shallow lie, but the kind that parents overlook in their children.

I pulled the picture from my bag and slid it over. For just one moment, his face crumpled, but he regained his composure. His breathing was measured even as he seemed to will his tears away.

"Who was she, Dad?" I asked, deciding that the time for subtleties had passed.

"A sweet girl who was caught up with the wrong people at the wrong time," Dad said, his voice husky. "Smart as a whip and twice as pretty. A lot like you."

"She's lovely," I admitted. "How did you meet?"

He looked back down at the photograph and rubbed his eyes. "Not today, Bethie. It's been a long enough stroll down memory lane, don't you think?"

I just then noticed the bags of fatigue around Dad's eyes. We'd spent a solid three hours poring over the photos, and he looked drained from the effort.

"Why don't you go lie down before dinner, Dad? I'll tidy this up while you rest. I'll stick around to eat if you want."

"I'm sure you have plans, Beth. You've been by a lot lately, and I won't have you giving up your life to look after me."

The reality that I had no plans on a Saturday night didn't sting as much as it probably should have. The blessings of being a homebody, I supposed, but I didn't feel all that compelled to rush back to my empty apartment either.

"I don't mind, Dad. I want to spend time with you," I insisted.

"You go out tonight, Bethie. That's an order. It's not healthy, all work and no fun. You know the saying."

"Are you saying Jane is a dull girl?"

"Never dull, my girl. But you need to be with people your own age and away from work. I'll tell Kimberly to chase you out with a fireplace poker if you give me any trouble."

"It's Encinitas, Dad. You don't have fireplaces. But fine, I'll take the hint."

"Always a smart mouth, this one," Dad said, shaking his head. I took him back to his room and helped him stretch out on the bed. I returned to the dining room and gathered up the newly organized photo album and put the rest of the items in the plastic bin. As I worked, I thought about what to do with my Saturday night. Gwen was out of town with her new boyfriend, so I couldn't impose my company on her, and the thought of going out to eat or to a movie by myself just made me itch. I had never been one to feel uncomfortable in my own company before, but since my split from Greg, I felt conspicuous doing those sorts of things alone. Coupley things. I was a woman of logic and reason. My brain knew that a woman standing alone in a line to buy a movie ticket wouldn't even register on people's radar. Hell, I didn't even have to stand in line in public view if I didn't want to. I could buy tickets online and bypass standing on a busy sidewalk altogether. It was absurd to be even the slightest bit self-conscious, but it was how I felt.

By the time I returned to Dad's room to leave the album and bin for him to peruse later, he was already breathing in the deep, even breaths of sleep. I went to kiss his forehead and noticed that the picture of the blond woman was still tucked in his hands, crossed over his heart.

CHAPTER NINE

Where Loyalties Lie

MAX

September 21, 1944
Hürtgen Forest, Germany

I spent the day in the rear evacuation hospital assisting the colonel as he patched up the men who were shipped to us in scores from the front. I'd sewn up so many bullet holes that day, I'd never again be able to feign incompetence and ask my mother to sew on a shirt button. I wouldn't be surprised if I could perform the task with more skill and speed than she could at this point.

Dusk fell, and I went to stretch out my weary back and breathe in something other than the putrid air of the tent. I lit one of my army-ration Chesterfield cigarettes between my lips and took a long drag, expelling the smoke from my lungs in a slow, steady stream. I heard the snapping of a twig to my right, and dropped the cigarette in the dirt, extinguishing it with the toe of my boot in a quick movement.

I heard another crunching sound from the woods and saw a face peer out from behind a tree. The girl from the night before. She motioned for me to join her away from the tent. I looked around to see if there were German snipers hiding in the trees or bombs hidden in the brush, but the truth was that if she meant to kill me, she wouldn't have gone to the trouble of getting my attention to do it. The camp was its usual bustle of activity, everyone so preoccupied with their work, they wouldn't notice me slip away.

"Are you really so eager to see the inside of an American stockade?" I hissed. "Because it sure seems that way."

"Come with me, please." She took my hand in hers and tugged me deeper into the forest. "The man I tried to treat is still doing poorly. I'm worried he'll die without proper help."

"*I'll* be in the brig tomorrow if I do," I said, not allowing her to pull me farther. "I can't leave my post. This right here is enough to land me in a cell myself."

"You're charged to help men on both sides if the need arises, are you not?" she pressed. "He is a good man. I swear it to you. And he has a chance to live if you come with me."

"You've been reading up on the Geneva Convention," I said with a scoff. "But it doesn't apply if he isn't a soldier."

"Everyone should read it," she said. "If the party members read it and took it to heart, the war would be over. The problem is that they're convinced they're on the right side of things. And he may not be a soldier like you, but he is fighting in this war all the same."

"Everyone thinks they're on the right side of the war until it's over," I said. "How do I know you aren't leading me into a trap?"

"You don't. You'll have to trust me."

I looked into her eyes. They were hardened, no doubt by seeing too much evil at too young an age. They were lined with fear, appropriate given she knew I held her freedom, if not her life, in my hands. But I saw no malice in them. It was exactly the stupid risk my mother begged me—literally on bended knee—not to make while I was away, but I followed this girl into the woods.

We'd walked for no more than ten minutes when the girl made a signal with a rectangular battery-operated flashlight, a bit bigger and bulkier than a pack of playing cards. German army issue. The acid churned in my stomach, but I wouldn't run to be shot in the back like a coward. Another girl, even younger than the one who led me here, emerged from behind a tree. Her eyes widened at the sight of me, and she raised her hands in the air as though I were a police officer in a moving picture.

"Calm down, I won't shoot," I said, barely above a whisper, pointing to the red cross on my armband.

The girl who had escorted me said a few words in German that I parsed to mean *He's come to help.*

The younger girl's shoulders dropped perceptibly, but she still looked at me as though I were a wolf that might devour her at any turn. She waved me over to the base of a tree where a man—more aptly a boy about eighteen—lay gripping his side. He wore plain clothes instead of a uniform, which lent some credence to the other girl's story. His color was that of a freshly starched handkerchief, save his hands, which were stained reddish brown with the old blood from his injury.

Politics were forgotten as I knelt by his side to assess the wound. He didn't have the strength to arch a brow at my uniform but complied willingly with my commands to remove his hands from the wound. I was grateful for the design of my medic's uniform, which made it so that I always carried a small infirmary's worth of supplies on me rather than in a pack that could be left behind. The bandages and antiseptic the girl had stolen would have done their job well enough, but he needed sulfanilamide and sutures if he was going to have a chance at recovering. The wound was more superficial than Davis's, but the blood loss had weakened him enough for concern.

After I closed the wound, I turned to the girl who had stolen the supplies. "What's your name?"

"Margarethe," she replied. "My friend there is Heide, and this poor man is Jonas."

"I'm Max. Why did we shoot him?" I asked, calculating the time it would take for me to get an MP back into the woods. The girls might escape, but there was no way he could move at any speed in his condition.

"Your men did not. It was the goons on our side. They saw our flyers," she explained, pulling a folded square of paper from her pocket. It was a propaganda poster meant to convince the men to surrender to the American and British forces.

"I could see why they'd be upset," I said. "Doesn't seem like the thing that would bolster morale, now does it?"

"The war is all but over," Jonas said more forcefully than I'd thought him able. "We'd do better to surrender while there is something left of Germany to salvage. If we wait too long, the Russians will extend their borders to the Rhine and it'll all be worse than before."

"Rest," I ordered. "If you believe in this cause, you'd do better to heal and get the word out than to martyr yourself for it."

"You believe us then?" Margarethe asked, hope laced in her voice like sugar in coffee.

"There is no way you'd be able to make up a story like this on the fly," I said. "I ought to report you anyway, and I'm risking my own neck if I don't."

"But you won't," Margarethe supplied.

"I won't," I said. "I don't see what good it'll do anyone to have you three locked up in our stockade for the duration of the war."

Margarethe crossed over to me and kissed my cheek. I blinked, shaking my head a bit as I looked down at her. She took a tentative step backward. "Jonas owes you his life. Heide and I owe you our safety. We're in your debt."

"Just keep to your mission," I said. "If it does any good, the gratitude will be mine. But Jonas needs a warm bed and clean linens if you want him to survive."

"You might as well be asking us to give him the moon," Margarethe said. "There is nowhere we could keep him where he wouldn't be found."

"I'll keep him hidden here," Heide said. She was kneeling by his side and looked up at us both with determination. Heide held Jonas's hand, and his breathing had grown easier. The toll of the chill of the early fall weather on his body would slow his healing, but they were right, the cold night air was less of a risk to his health than a German firing squad. "And you need to go, Margarethe, before you are missed."

She nodded. "Thank you for saving his life, Max. You've done a good thing."

Though I ran the risk of being missed as well, I watched her slip into the darkness, back toward the German lines. I considered pressing Heide with questions about the paradox of a girl who spoke better than passable English, as though she'd had a series of British tutors, but who dressed like a street urchin out of a novel by Dickens or Hugo. But the dark-haired imp of a girl looked up at me warily and I knew any questions of that sort would be met with silence.

"Do you have plenty of food? Some blankets?"

Heide blushed in response. Even after a long war, all the people we'd come across were ashamed to admit to the poverty the war had imposed upon them.

"Send Margarethe back to the camp tomorrow morning. I'll see what I can do."

Heide nodded, her expression still guarded but softened. She didn't want to trust me but would stifle her pride for her Jonas.

—

After breakfast, I took a spare field kit and ferreted away two worn blankets and a few packets of hospital rations. A couple of fresh bandages and some antibiotic powder as well. The risk of Jonas developing an infection out in the woods was high, but the powder might help stave it off. The kit wasn't much, though it might see them through a couple of days. But it wouldn't be enough. Jonas needed to be kept warm and dry if he was going to survive. There was a stack of shelter halves among the discarded gear from the wounded, and I took the two kits needed to make a full pup tent.

I left the hospital tent, and as I'd done the previous afternoon, I lit a cigarette as a pretext to dawdling at the edge of the wood. I tried to glance only occasionally at the tree where Margarethe had waited for me, and it wasn't long before I heard the snap of twigs under her feet. I walked in the direction of the tree when I was reasonably sure no one was looking and found her there.

"You're an angel," she whispered as she examined the contents of the bag. "Really and truly."

"How is Jonas faring?"

"Weak," she replied honestly. "But I don't think he's getting any worse."

"That's something," I said. "But he really needs shelter. The tent is only a half step up from nothing. The cold will get to him if the infection doesn't. Surely you know someone who can give him shelter."

She blanched as white as December snow. "Anyone who took him in would pay for it with their lives. And if anyone saw me with him, more than my life would be at stake. The only reason I can keep him as safe as he is is that no one knows they are with me. Truly, I see no choice."

"Let's go see him," I said, not wanting to leave her quite so soon, though I shouldn't have met with her at all.

"That is very kind of you," she said as we began walking deeper into the woods. "You're putting yourself at too much risk."

"I'm just a man who likes to live in fear of a court-martial," I said in return.

"I hope very much it doesn't come to that," she said. "But you're doing a great kindness to the resistance by helping him."

I combed my fingers through my hair. "I'll have to trust you on that. It's really none of my business anyway. I'm not sure why I'm doing this."

"Because you're a good doctor and you care about your patients."

"Don't try to butter me up," I said. *And because I can't seem to leave you alone,* I thought. *Why can't I just pass off the supplies and be done with you? Why am I giving you the supplies to begin with?* The thoughts had plagued me since I'd met this enigma of a woman, but the answers made no difference. I was drawn to her like a drunkard to his whiskey. I worried she was every bit as dangerous. She was German, and I shouldn't trust her for that reason alone.

"I know how you feel about my countrymen, but try to keep in mind that a hungry people will follow the strongest wolf to the hunt. They don't care how ruthless he is, so long as they are fed," she said, as though able to read my thoughts. I looked at her now, wondering if she wasn't some sort of witch on top of it all.

Before long we reached Heide, who emerged from a makeshift thicket that she'd used to hide Jonas and herself that night.

"And how is that working out for your people?" I asked, gesturing to Heide, whose high cheekbones were razors beneath her taut, waxy skin. I didn't need to examine her to know I'd be able to count her ribs from across a fifty-foot-long hospital tent in candlelight. I took the pack from Margarethe and began pitching the tent.

"Have you ever in your life gone hungry?" Margarethe pressed. "Have you seen your own child on the brink of starvation?"

"I can't say that I have," I admitted.

"Then do not hazard a guess at what you might do in our shoes, Captain. People will do horrible things to stay alive."

"Those horrible things included killing my entire extended family. You'll excuse me if I can't be philosophical about it. I can't work out how invading other countries and killing innocent civilians could have brought jobs or prosperity back to the German people in any lasting way."

"I don't see the usefulness of this conversation," Jonas interceded. "We're on the same side, Captain. I think you know this, or you wouldn't be here."

Heide chided him in German, and I didn't need my pocket dictionary to catch the gist of her rebuke. "She's right. Save your strength, Jonas. I'm going to move you inside the tent, and that will take all you've got."

Jonas was a soldier in the truest sense of the word. When Margarethe and I helped him into the tent, he refused to make even the slightest grimace. Back in the hospital, I saw men who were stoic like this too, while others had no qualms about crying out in pain. I didn't think less of the men who couldn't bear their wounds quietly; they were tossed into a war of other men's making. But the men who suffered in silence were those who had formed a close companionship with pain. They'd learned that they could survive it, so they swallowed it like a dose of castor oil and moved on to the next battle. Others gave in to the pain as long as their bodies needed, and then they too returned to their duty.

I wasn't sure if these quiet men were more likely than others to survive the war, but I suspected they might be the first to be broken by it.

"How do you feel?" I asked Jonas once we got him settled with fresh bandages and warm blankets.

"Warmer," he said, a hint of a smile tugging at his lips as he pulled the army-issue blanket up to his chin. "I will repay you for this one day, my friend."

Jonas summoned what was left of his strength and lifted his hand to shake mine.

"You owe me nothing but taking care of those stitches I gave you," I said.

"I need to get back," Margarethe said, checking a gleaming watch on her slender wrist that contrasted painfully with her ragged clothes. It had been months since I'd seen something so decadent, ensconced as I was in a utilitarian world of olive drab.

"So do I," I replied. *Where did she have to get to?*

"I'll walk east with you for a bit," she said, looking over her shoulder. *Who was she looking for?*

She walked by my side for a quarter of a mile or so until the edge of the American encampment came into view.

"You have been extraordinarily kind to us," Margarethe whispered.

"Like you said, I care too much about my patients to let them suffer."

"You're a good man, Max. We need more men like you in this world."

She put her hands on either side of my face and pulled me down to meet her. Her lips lingered on mine for just a few moments and left my own still tingling when she pulled away.

"Be well, Max. I fear we won't see each other again, but I will remember your kindness to Jonas for the rest of my days."

CHAPTER TEN

AN EDUCATION

JOHANNA

January 1940
Berchtesgaden, Germany

"What do you mean, bride school?" I asked as Metta took her place across from me at Mama's kitchen table. "What on earth is such a thing?"

"Just what it sounds like. We learn to cook, sew, keep house, tend children and livestock. All the things we'll have to do when we're married."

"And Mama hasn't done a thorough enough job of this here at home?" I countered.

"Ansel thought it was a good idea," Metta replied, not meeting my eyes.

"Of course it is," Oskar said. "The Führer places great importance on the institution of marriage. He says it is the bedrock upon which our new and glorious Reich will prosper. A man in the *Obersturmbannführer's* position must set an example by marrying a proper Aryan woman who knows what is expected of her by the fatherland. Metta will be a leader among the young housewives of her acquaintance, and much envied. You should be happy for her, Johanna. Not questioning her husband's kindness."

"He isn't her husband yet," I reminded him. Though there wasn't much use in arguing the point. The deed was as good as done as soon as he'd asked the question. His investing a small fortune in her "domestic training" only ensured the inevitability of the wedding day.

"Our Metta has done very well in her local training," Mama said, her eyes piercing me with silent warning.

"Of course she has," I said, aiming to return my tone to neutral. "She was trained by the best housewife in all Bavaria from the time she was old enough to hold a broom."

"So, you simply worry that the school might be beneath Metta's skill, is that it?" Oskar removed a packet of cigarettes from his breast pocket and lit one, despite Mama's strict edicts against smoking in the house. Even Papa's most important guests had been banished to the back patio if they insisted on it. Blizzard or no, Mama never relaxed the rule. In the absence of an ashtray, Oskar used the saucer of his teacup, which was from a set Mama and Papa had been given at their wedding, no less. The muscles in Mama's jaw clenched, but she said nothing. Oskar was home on a short leave, and I supposed she didn't want to ruin his three-day stay with squabbling. That, or she didn't dare countermand him.

"Precisely, brother. In times like these, it is almost criminal to use one's time less than profitably. Is it not?"

"Quite right," he said, his shoulders dropping a bit in appeasement. "But Metta is being trained at the finest school of its kind, right in the heart of Berlin. She'll be seen by the right people. She's demonstrating her skill to people who matter. Proving herself worthy of a match to the *Obersturmbannführer* is one of the greatest things she can do for Germany. And I daresay there will be a few new tricks Metta will find useful when she must entertain her husband's distinguished guests. Few women have the skills you do, sister."

I bit back a rebuke about more women having my skills if they'd been taught mathematics and science with the same rigor and enthusiasm as their brothers when they were girls, but there was no use trying to convince a wolf it was a lapdog.

"Will you mind my staying with you, then?" Metta asked. "Ansel said he could get me a room with some of the other students, but I thought it would be a nice chance for us to spend more time together."

"I'd be crushed if you didn't," I said honestly.

"If Ansel suggested you room with the others—" Oskar interjected.

"He didn't press the matter," Metta snapped, her expression uncharacteristically firm. "And once we're married, when will another such opportunity arise? He understands that camaraderie between women—especially sisters—is important in establishing a family."

Oskar extinguished his cigarette on Mama's saucer and said nothing, but he looked dubious. I was no model wife in his eyes, nor a model German. Like the regime, he tolerated me with civility because I had skills the Reich needed. "Just remember, the first commandment of a good German housewife is to put your husband's needs ahead of your own."

"And she will. Once they're married. Until then, she should take one last chance to do as she pleases. Her marriage will be all the happier for it." I crossed my arms over my chest, daring him to argue. It was dangerous. It was stupid to bait him. But he was my baby brother, after all, and to see him lording over the three of us when he wasn't yet twenty-one was unbearable.

He stood from the table without taking his leave and went outdoors. Within a few minutes I heard the telltale thwack, thwack, thwack of Papa's ax against firewood. He was angry and it was my doing.

"You must treat your brother's temper with care," Mama warned. "It seems to boil very close to the surface these days, and I don't want to see you burned when it spills over."

"I don't think my anger is any less dangerous than his, Mama."

"Oh, I've no doubt about that, my child. But he has the means to exact it in ways you don't have. Think of your husband. I fear Oskar could make life very difficult for him. He could make things difficult for all of us."

"What has happened to my brother?" I asked, not fully aware if I'd spoken aloud.

"War," Metta answered. "It won't be the only change we see."

She stood from her place at the table and retreated to her bedroom.

"Whatever you do, Johanna, protect your sister," Mama said. "I don't know why God chose to call your father home when we need him most, but there's nothing I wouldn't give to have him see us through this."

"I'm afraid not even Papa would be much help in times like these," I said. "And I think this marriage would break his heart."

—

"I hope my coming to stay is a pleasant imposition for you," Metta said as I made up her bed with my best quilt and she unpacked the contents of her bag. She repeated the sentiments from Mama's table. She'd become positively paranoid about causing offense in the past months.

"Imposition indeed," I scoffed. "How can my sister be an imposition? You wound me."

"Don't tease, Jojo," she said. "Truly, I don't want to be in your way."

"We're both busy women, Metta. I have my work and you have your—school." I cringed at my pause. It would not do to show Metta my distrust of the party or of her prospective husband. There was precious little I could do to change her mind about either. "And in our free time, your being here will keep me from missing Harald so terribly much. I couldn't be happier, my dearest girl. I hope you know that."

"It may sound silly to say about a sister, but I was hoping it would give us the chance to get to know each other better," Metta said, still not meeting my gaze.

"It makes sense. We've always been in different phases of our lives. When I was a schoolgirl, you were in diapers. When I went off to university, you were making your way through primary school. We've had little in common besides our upbringing until now."

That truth had just occurred to me as I spoke the words. We'd been living disparate lives, but age is a great equalizer, and she would join me in the duties of work and matrimony. Perhaps motherhood in the coming years, if it was meant to be.

"We'll make good use of our time," I promised. "I'll take you to all my favorite places in the city, and we'll stay up late gabbing as often as we can. We'll be like university chums, won't we?"

Metta came over and embraced me. "These will be the happiest months of my life," she proclaimed.

"I truly hope not, darling. I hope that when your days end many, many years from now, you'll look on your time here as a pleasant interlude before years of real bliss."

Metta said nothing but placed her now empty suitcase in the closet below her row of new dresses. Ansel had apparently given her an allowance for new clothes so that she would look the part of the fiancée of a high-ranking official before she entered this bride school of hers. It was a kindness, to be sure. Mama kept her clothed well, but she could hardly afford to keep her in the latest fashions. But in my gut, I knew Ansel's gesture was meant to improve appearances for himself far more than it was meant to give Metta any pleasure.

"I think I'd like to take a nap before supper," she said, clasping her hands at her waist. "The train ride wasn't particularly pleasant."

"Of course," I said. "I'm going to go put in a few hours at the office, if you have everything you need."

"I'll be fine," she said, the corners of her mouth forcing themselves up into a thin smile.

There were clouds of worry in the sky of her eyes, and it tormented me for the duration of my ride to the DVL. I wasn't expected that day, so Louisa had taken up the plane I'd been working on. It was just as well, as I needed a few more hours with the schematics for the landing gear. The systems in place weren't bad, but a smoother landing would take less of a toll on the aircraft and lead to fewer repairs. Difficult as she was, Louisa was a gifted pilot, and a fifteen-minute conversation with her after her flight would be as valuable as a full-day diagnostic.

"*Flugkapitän* Schiller *Gräfin* von Oberndorff, Herr Gerhardt wishes to see you in his office," Peter said as he knocked on the jamb of my open office door. His expression looked serious. Summons from the head of our department were rare and usually not pleasant.

"Have a seat, *Flugkapitän*." Herr Gerhardt didn't word it as a request. He gestured to the spartan wooden chair that sat opposite his desk. He was the orderly sort who would be able to tell if a pen were a few centimeters off kilter before he crossed the threshold to his office. So long as I wasn't charged with tidying it, I much preferred Harald's merry chaos with his endless stacks of papers to mark, research notes, and heaven knew what all. My own work area fell somewhere between the two. "I trust your tests are going well?"

"Not badly at all, sir," I replied, knitting my fingers to keep them from betraying any sign of nerves.

"Good," he said. He removed his wire-rimmed glasses and rubbed his eyes, which looked red with fatigue. I cocked my head and waited for him to continue. If he'd wanted a status report on my progress with the landing systems, he would have come to my office to see my schematics and calculations. "I've been notified by my superiors that some of your paperwork isn't quite in order. I'm sorry to trouble you with such things, but they do insist on keeping a tidy ship."

"Of course," I said. "But what paperwork could they possibly need? I've always made sure all my files were up to date with my credentials."

"It's to do with your ancestry. It seems there isn't any proper documentation on your father's side to ensure your lineage is—"

"Is what, sir?"

"'Pure' is the word they use. Aryan," he supplied. "They don't want anyone working on sensitive projects who isn't loyal to the fatherland, you understand."

I nodded. I worked in defense and had access to sensitive information that enemies of Germany would dearly love to have. We'd all been quizzed and given forms to complete ad nauseam, and I had been expecting more of this since I transferred to Berlin. I squared my shoulders and forced them to drop a couple of centimeters, back to their normal, relaxed position. I would have him believe this was of no more concern to me than him asking after the health of my mother or the condition of the roads. "I'm afraid quite a few records were lost before my father moved to Berchtesgaden as a boy. I've been told there was a terrible fire in the town where he grew up and there wasn't much to be done. The lack of records caused my father more than a few headaches in his life, I assure you." The lie was a well-rehearsed one. It was the story Metta and Oskar knew from Mama and Papa, and I further embroidered it with Harald's coaching. He'd once suggested that I consider leaving my work aside until the tide changed in the political climate and fewer questions would be asked. It would have been the safer course of action, I was certain, but to give up my work would be to forgo myself. I'd be like the shepherd dog driven mad with boredom when he's separated from his flock.

"That is unfortunate, but I will see what can be done. As scrupulous as the regime is, they can't expect you to produce records that don't exist. I imagine they'll need a statement from you attesting to all of this." He spoke as though the missing records were a trivial inconvenience, but the furrow in his brow told me otherwise.

I smiled as I left him to his paperwork and returned to my own office, determined not to let a soul see how shaken I was. At some point, I feared, the lies would cease to suffice, and the truth would come to light. My freedom, if not my life, would be the cost.

CHAPTER ELEVEN

Under the Sun, in the Mist

BETH

May 1, 2007
San Diego, California

The espresso shop on the edge of campus was as quaint and smug as a college hangout could hope to be. I took my scone and tall Americano with an extra shot from the barista while Gwen accepted her frothy mocha-cappuccino-extra-foam concoction, and we claimed a table under the trees outdoors.

"Why don't you just order ice cream and get it over with? I swear you're secretly eleven years old posing as an adult."

"It's why the world loves me. Everyone is drawn to my youthful exuberance. Like so many flowers straining to reach the sun."

"Or mosquitoes drawn to a bug zapper. Whichever metaphor you prefer."

"Jerk. I shouldn't even tell you why I dragged you here. Aside from getting you out into the sunlight. You have the complexion of a bottle of Elmer's glue."

"Gawd, what would I do without friends like you to keep my spirits up," I said, removing the lid from the paper cup to release the steam.

"I know a great guy for you, Beth," she said, ignoring me. "Tall, handsome, and doesn't work for UCSD. I showed him your picture, and he'd love to grab dinner on Friday."

"Gwen, you're the best, but really, I'm happy being single for now." I slowly twirled the plastic lid on the table with my finger.

"You like staying home every night and falling asleep in front of the TV at nine fifteen?" She sat back in her chair and gave me an exasperated look.

"Oh, young Padawan, don't you think that's 87 percent of married life? I'm just sticking with what I know. The only difference is that now I don't have to agonize for an hour with anyone about what to have for dinner. I just mull it over by myself until I'm too hungry to do anything but pour a bowl of cereal."

"That's really sad, Beth," she said, shaking her head before taking a sip of her coffee-adjacent confection.

"Yeah, yeah . . . give marriage two years and you'll see I'm right. And when you come to that conclusion on your own, I'll be sitting at home watching Food Network and waiting for your heartfelt apology."

"And that's what worries me," she said, her tone now serious. "Promise me you'll get out. Do something other than work, sleep, and watch food porn?"

"Now you know that's not fair. I went to Ross and bought three new work dresses yesterday," I said, folding my arms over my chest.

"Alert the press. We have a party girl on our hands," she chided. "Seriously. Get out of the house. Have some fun."

"*Seriously,* I will. It just may not involve a guy for a while yet. I honestly don't miss being in a relationship, and I don't feel the need to go seek one out." I felt a weight lessen in my chest as I realized the words were true. Mostly true, anyway.

"Who said anything about a relationship? I'm talking about a fun night out. Drinks. Dinner. Maybe a tour of his condo. And don't you dare roll your eyes at me."

I rolled my eyes, simply to be contrary. "I'm not interested in touring real estate."

"Don't be dense," she said.

"I'm not being dense, Gwen. I need time."

"Do you even have a pulse? You left Greg over eight months ago. Aren't you climbing the walls?"

"I'm fine," I said. I didn't mention that sex had become less and less a part of my marriage as the years went on. As close as we were, I let her believe that he and I had drifted apart, but didn't make her privy to how cold things had truly been. Countless times, I thought his having an affair would have been worlds easier. People don't blame women for leaving cheaters. Losing the spark? That was chalked up to laziness. Many more marriages die in the icy chill of lovelessness than in the fire of anger and passion.

"OK, girl. Just don't waste your life waiting to be ready. Sometimes you have to jump into the fray, you know?"

"What would appease you? Archery? Horseback riding? Kayaking?" I took a tentative sip of the still-steaming coffee from my cup. There was something to be said for adding a pint of milk, sugar, and cocoa to the drink, I supposed. Gwen didn't have to wait for the coffee to cool down from the temperature of freshly erupted lava.

"I wasn't thinking you should enroll in summer camp, for God's sake." She placed her cup down with enough force that the couple at the next table glanced over at us before resuming their conversation. "I really am trying to be serious with you."

"I know, Gwen. And I promise I'll do something outside of work. Something fun."

"Something social," she added. "Get out and meet people."

I nodded, though I was at a loss for something that would be enjoyable for me and wasn't mostly a solitary endeavor. I'd not been particularly introverted as a kid, but it set in during college and took hold during my marriage with the voracity of kudzu vines.

I feigned a glance at my watch and made an excuse about needing to prepare notes for my next lecture. I was more than prepared, but I'd come to the end of what I could handle of Gwen's relentless meddling. She accepted my excuse and let me go with her usual bear hug.

Though I loved Gwen like the sister I'd so wished for my entire childhood, her solution to getting over my divorce was simplistic. For some women, a quick roll in the hay would be healing enough, but the thought of opening up to anyone else made me shake.

She didn't know about the countless nights Greg rolled to his side, rebuffing my touch. She didn't know about the hundreds of conversations I wanted to have with him that he shut down with generic advice, though I tried to explain to him how I wanted to work through whatever the issue was on my own. He didn't understand the need for a sounding board and some empathy.

Every time I pictured going out on a first date and the first date progressing to something more, I worried about the inevitable moment when a perfectly nice guy would take me out for an above-average dinner on the third date, ask me back to his place, and look at me with those hopeful eyes. Would I be able to summon the courage to follow him inside and let one thing lead to another, or would those countless rejections from Greg come roaring back to fill my senses and steal my enjoyment? There was only so much *no* a person could handle before they began to feel something was wrong with them.

～

I honored my promise to Gwen as I drove up to Encinitas on Saturday and considered what I could do to get out more and meet people. I was an avid swimmer and thought about re-devoting myself to it, but it was really more of an individual sport. Joining a book club was too close to my daily grind to hold much appeal. The opportunities swirled in my head as I went north to help Dad continue wading through all the photos and souvenirs. They were now in a better semblance of order, but there was still plenty of cataloging to be done. The pregnant blond woman came to mind, Dad's arm wrapped protectively around her. *A lot of questions yet to be answered.*

Instead of Kimberly, Dad greeted me at the door of the care home. His hands gripped his wheeled walker tightly, but his face was more exuberant than I'd seen since Mom passed. I supposed the prospect of spending some time back in the days of his youth invigorated him.

"We can use the dining room again," he proclaimed as I leaned in to kiss his cheek. "It's good to see you, Bethie."

His voice was stronger and his gait steadier as he ushered me back to the gleaming wooden table where the artifacts of his past were already laid out for us to go over. I took out the album and my notepad to take down his descriptions of all the photos.

"Good heavens but Stu Phillips looks young in that one," he said, pointing to a rather baby-faced soldier whom Dad had captured in an open-mouthed laugh with a handful of other medics. "I saw him ten years ago at one of the regimental reunions. If it weren't for the dimples, I'd never have recognized him. He died just a few years back. He was one of the last ones left. We stopped having those get-togethers after that one."

"I'm sorry to hear that."

"It's the price of living to be an old man. You end up outliving almost everyone you ever knew. And it's a hefty price tag, I'll say that much."

"I'm sure it is, Dad. I always found it funny that you'd never talk about the war but would never miss a reunion," I said.

"Well, the boys knew which subjects to talk about and which ones to avoid. I know it doesn't make sense if you haven't been to war. And I'm damn glad you'll never learn what I mean by it."

I squeezed his hand and went back to taking notes about the subjects in the seemingly endless pages of photos. After two hours, I felt as though I knew the men from his regiment as well as he'd known them sixty years before. He remembered their names, their professions, and even the names of the women they married and the children they fathered after their service. He was always that way, whether with friends, patients, or family. I remembered the massive stack of holiday cards he and Mom would send each year. They'd sit at our dining room table, not unlike the one where we sat with his photos now, every day after dinner for a full week to get them all written and addressed. No simple "Best wishes from the Blumenthals" would do. Dad insisted on a handwritten note for each person. He would prompt Mom to ask after ailing relatives and new babies as she worked her way down her half of the list. Mom had met most of these people, but Dad *knew* them.

Mom kept close tabs on who would receive cards with the header *Merry Christmas, Happy Hanukkah*, or the more generic *Season's Greetings* in scrawling script letters superimposed above a family photo. Dad's clients were a diverse lot, and he wanted their cards to honor whatever traditions they celebrated. The photo was the same each year. Mom would shop the sales to get my holiday party clothes in late October, I'd be scrubbed within an inch of my life, and we'd snap the photo even before I'd carved my jack-o'-lantern for Halloween. Mom would always look perfect—straight from the hairdresser and with a fresh coat of lipstick. Dad's smile would always be toothy and full of sunshine and truth. Either Dad or I would end up displeasing Mom with a less-than-flattering stance or a peculiar expression, but Dad always preferred the outtakes. As soon as I surrendered the holiday clothes to be wrapped back in plastic and hidden in the deepest corners of Mom's closet for the next two months, she'd have the photos off to the printer to ensure they'd have plenty of time to get them out the week after Thanksgiving. The whole of our acquaintances could have kept their calendars by the regularity of the Blumenthal holiday cards, until the last batch had gone out two years before.

"We made good progress today, Dad," I said, proudly marking our spot in the photo album. We were nearing the halfway point and would have it finished in another couple of sessions. I kept my eyes on my notes as I worked up the courage to ask the question I'd been burning to. "You kept one of the photos last time, Dad. Do you want to put it in the album, or should I look for a frame or something? It doesn't seem smart to keep it unprotected."

He produced the photo from his breast pocket as if he'd been waiting for me to ask.

"She belongs in the book," he said. "On the last page. I'm just not ready to paste her in a book and put her on a shelf just yet."

"I understand," I said, though the words weren't true. I couldn't understand until I knew who she was.

"She was a lovely girl," he said. "I wish you could have known her."

"Me too, Dad," I said, though I suspected that if she'd played a larger role in Dad's life, I wouldn't be alive and sitting with him.

CHAPTER TWELVE

ANGEL IN THE ASHES

MAX

September 26, 1944
Hürtgen Forest, Germany

Max Blumenthal, you are the dumbest piece of shit that ever walked the earth.

I cursed myself with each step I took into the forest, stealthily as I could, trying to avoid detection by the Germans. All I had was a vague idea of where they'd camped from the direction we'd walked from the hospital and how long it had taken the blond waif of a thing—Margarethe—to take me there. Other men in my platoon had grown up in Scouting, in groups that took them on camping trips in the backwoods armed with nothing more than a compass, a map, and their wits. They learned how to read a landscape, tell time by the sun, and other survival skills that the son of a Los Angeles tailor simply wouldn't have gained in his formative years. I was more convinced with every step I took into the woods that I was going to end up lost or in enemy hands, all in the attempt to deliver food and supplies to the injured man and the two women who fought to keep him alive.

I told myself I was going for Jonas's benefit, but the memory of the kiss Margarethe had given me in parting was a stronger lure than I wanted to admit.

"You shouldn't be here," a voice said. Margarethe emerged from behind a tree and holstered a small pistol under her jacket, her movements practiced and graceful. "You're lucky I didn't shoot you."

"Lucky for both of us. I brought food," I said.

"I can loot bags after I shoot their owner," she said. From her wry tone it was clear that it wouldn't be the first time she'd had to perform such an office. How this reedy woman who so easily disguised herself as a schoolboy could have found herself in this situation, I didn't know, but I felt myself choke on the idea that she willingly put herself in harm's way. Seeing the adept manner in which she handled the gun, she was probably deadlier than I was by a margin I didn't want to consider.

"I'd appreciate it if you made an exception for me, then," I said. "Considering I saved your friend's life and all."

"This once," she said, but flashed a wink and motioned for me to follow her. "I could take the food and send you back on your way if you'll be missed, but I suspect you want to check in on Jonas."

"Yes, I'd like to see how he's doing," I said, though her lack of alarm on his behalf was as telling as anything I'd see in person.

"The forest has been busy lately. You have to be more careful. I could have heard you from a mile away."

"I was trying to be quiet," I protested.

"Well, it's not your strong suit, Max. Stick to caring for your patients."

"I plan to," I said. "I'd never planned on anything else, but this war seems to have gotten in the way."

"It got in the way for a lot of us, didn't it? Anxious to get back to doctoring in America?"

"I'm not a doctor, I'm a dentist," I said. "Or almost. Just graduated from dental school, but haven't set up my practice yet. I should be back in Los Angeles filling cavities and telling children not to eat so many sweets. Not dodging bullets as I try to collect dying men off the battlefield."

"You brave soul. I think I'd rather face the bullets than put my hands in someone's mouth."

"It's not that bad," I said, my shoulders shaking with a chuckle I couldn't restrain. "There's something gratifying in keeping a child's mouth healthy or helping someone learn to like their smile again."

She stopped in her tracks and looked up at me. "You're a good man, aren't you, Max?" she asked.

"I like to think so," I said, shrugging. I didn't consider myself much better or worse than the average man. Like all of us, I was just trying to get by in a world that seemed to have gone topsy-turvy. "I try, at any rate, and I hope that's good for something."

"You *are* a good man, Max. Just be careful. Good men don't last long in war."

"You seem to know a lot about me after only spending an hour or so in my presence," I said.

"I've had to become a quick study of human nature," she said. "I live too close to the den to not be able to tell the difference between a lion and a sheep. One slip would mean my life and more."

"Don't you have someone to take care of you?" I asked. I wished I could bite the question back as soon as it fell from my tongue. "I mean, doesn't your family mind that you're out here alone? Your father? Your husband?"

I felt my mouth sour on the word *husband*, but lord knew it would be a miracle if she hadn't been snapped up already.

"My father is dead," she said, no emotion leaching into her voice. "And I don't trouble anyone else with what I do. They're safer that way."

"You're probably wise," I said. "Though I'm sorry about your father."

"I'm not," she said, rancor seeping into her words. "I'm glad he died before he saw the worst of this. He worried for Germany when I was young. He saw the rise of these thugs, but always trusted that reason would prevail. I'm grateful he never lived to find out how misguided he was in his faith in his own people."

"I would think he'd be proud of you and what you're doing," I said. "He just might wring your neck if he knew how dangerous it was."

She actually tilted her head back and gave a full-throated laugh. One more genuine than I'd heard in ages. "He was always one to make sure we didn't grow up too fearful of danger. Cautious, yes, but never afraid. My sister got that message plain enough—she's a test pilot."

"Do you ever think that maybe he was too thorough in his teachings? Your traipsing about these woods is closer to suicide than bravery."

"First of all, sir, I do not traipse. And secondly, I'm still alive after four years working for the resistance movement, such as it is. I'm many things, but reckless isn't one of them."

"There's truth in that," I conceded.

"Of course there is," she said. "I don't mind taking risks, but I won't throw my life away if I have a choice. I can do a lot more for the resistance alive than I can full of bullets."

We reached the camp where Jonas and Heide had camouflaged the tent I'd set up with branches and debris to make it look like part of the landscape. They'd done a convincing job of it, and I felt better seeing how well they'd managed to secure themselves in such a vulnerable location.

"Your color looks good," I pronounced as I saw Jonas.

"This is the closest I've had to a roof over my head in weeks," he said, gesturing to the small tent. "I'm able to sleep better when I'm not shivering all night."

"I just hope you're able to get out of here soon," I said. "When winter sets in, that tent won't do much good."

"We'll do what we can," he said. The furrow in his brow showed that this thought had already occurred to him. Winter set in early here, and was merciless.

Jonas allowed me to examine his wound and change the dressing. Heide had done an excellent job keeping it clean despite the challenge of doing so in the middle of the forest. She blushed furiously when I praised her efforts.

"I'm going to take the good doctor back toward the hospital so he doesn't accidentally wander into Berlin. I won't be back tonight," Margarethe warned them.

They nodded solemnly, and again I wanted to ask where she was going, but I knew my query wouldn't be met with a real answer.

"Max, promise me you'll stay away. It's too dangerous for you here."

"I think I can decide for myself which risks I'm willing to take," I said, though I didn't fully feel the forcefulness I'd given my words.

"Someone could follow you. How would you explain things to your superiors? Though to be honest, it might be better if they did catch you. You'd spend the rest of the war in a jail cell, but at least you'd be safe."

"Why are you so concerned with my safety?" I asked. "You brought me here in the first place."

"Jonas would have died if I hadn't. That was different. He's going to live, thanks to you. But he'd not be happy you'd done it if you end up sacrificing yourself on trips like these."

"I thought you'd be grateful for more food and supplies," I said. "It's a poor doctor who doesn't see his patient through convalescence. You don't have to try to protect me."

"Max, there are precious few people in this world with a good heart like yours. It's worth protecting. More than almost anything else, it's worth keeping safe."

⁓

The explosion was so violent, it rattled the teeth in my head. The men near me either dove for cover or protected the patients nearest them, sometimes shielding them with their own bodies. When the initial shock wore off, some bore a terrified look, wondering where the next bomb would hit. They weren't wrong—whenever one bomb hit, there were usually plenty to follow. Others assessed the damage with the intent to determine the need to evacuate the hospital, salvage equipment, or do whatever else was necessary to get back to the business of treating the wounded. Every second the hospital ceased to function meant lives were lost. We quickly judged the hospital itself had suffered no worse than toppled supply stations and upturned cots. One sergeant broke his wrist, but that was the worst of the casualties.

Within fifteen minutes, the chaos had subsided enough that I noticed the earthy scent of charring wood and the tang of smoke in the air. The explosion had turned the trees into burning pillars of death, but if anyone noticed me running toward the blaze instead of away from it, they were too concerned with their own skins to fret about mine. Jonas and Heide might have been in the middle of the blast.

Margarethe might have been with them.

In my mind I saw a flash of her lithe frame trying to run through the burning trees, so easily injured or trapped by a falling limb or a blocked pathway. I couldn't just stand by and wish idly for her safety. My legs carried me, though my head knew it was foolish. My heart had no such concern.

I ran with all my strength, uttering all the prayers I'd learned at my mother's side and a few of my own invention. *Please be alive, please be alive* was as elaborate as I could muster, but grace could be sacrificed in the name of efficacy.

By the time I found their camp, my legs were screaming from the sprint over uneven terrain, but I could barely register the pain. The small clearing they used for a camp was empty, save for Margarethe, who burst forth from the thickest part of the woods. Her clothes were black with soot and her hair was wild as she scanned the clearing for signs of her friends as I had done.

"Where are they?" she demanded.

"I got here just a few seconds ago," I said. "I know as much as you do." The camp looked untouched. The tent and their things were still there. They didn't dare have a campfire, so I couldn't check to see if there were still warm coals. I didn't see any footprints in the mud, but they may have been smart enough to cover their tracks. Likely the case, given that they'd stayed alive this long.

"It doesn't look like they fought anyone," she said, voicing the thought I hadn't. No Nazi alive would have left the camp in one piece. They left nothing but ruin in their wake. The longer the war went on, the truer it was.

I registered that Margarethe was dressed in fine clothes, despite their being covered in soot. A wool suit and heeled shoes. How she managed to cross the woods without breaking her neck, I didn't know. "You've left your boy's costume behind," I mused, still scanning the landscape for signs of where they might have gone.

"I didn't have time to change. I'll come up with an excuse for my ruined clothes later."

"There's a war on. Plenty of excuses to go around."

She folded her arms over her chest. "Where could they have gone?" she asked. "You don't think they're hurt, do you?"

I bit back a platitude, knowing that it might well not be true. I barely knew this girl, but I found the idea of lying to her, even in an attempt to comfort her, as distasteful as a mouthful of the ashes at our feet. "I don't know," I said honestly. "But they're cunning and they seem to know these woods. If anyone has a chance, it's them."

She sat down on the ground. Heedless of her clothes or the cold. She put her head on her knees and wept. It wasn't the terrified sobs of someone who feared a looming danger, but the heartbreak of someone who had seen so much of it, she was no longer scared by it—she was simply past all reasonable limits of exhaustion from it. I knelt by her side and wrapped my arms around her.

"Why are you so kind?" she asked. "I'm on the wrong side of all of this."

"You didn't have a choice where you were born," I said. She was in her early twenties, I guessed. Possibly as young as her late teens. She didn't want the war. She was blameless but didn't have the luxury of being isolated from the war like the women and children back at home.

"I don't deserve it," she said. "I don't deserve kindness."

"Nonsense," I said, sitting fully on the ground now, pulling her closer. I pressed my lips to the top of her golden head. She stiffened at the brief contact, but I felt her muscles loosen against me almost as quickly. "You're exhausted. Why don't you go lie down in the tent? Going to look for Jonas and Heide would be a remarkably bad idea until the fires have died down."

"Do you think we'll be safe from the fire here?"

"The wind is headed the wrong way," I said. "I'd be more worried about troops coming to put out the fires, but it would take your side a good long while to get things under control before they find us. And my side isn't likely to shoot before asking questions. I hope. You'd be fine to take a nap."

"Stay with me?" she asked, her voice small.

"I can't stay long," I whispered. "But I'll lie with you awhile."

"Thank you," she said.

We both clambered into the tent. I wrapped her in my arms, then pulled Jonas's blanket over us. She shivered for several minutes until my warmth began to envelop her. After a few more minutes, I felt her inch closer. Her breathing seemed more relaxed and I felt her lips brush almost imperceptibly against the skin of my neck. I might have dreamed it, though I couldn't be sure if this nymph of a woman wasn't a dream herself. Rather than respond in kind, I tightened my embrace just enough to let her know the kiss, if it had been real, was welcome.

She placed a hand on my cheek and drew my lips to hers. The post-school-dance embraces, the chaste kisses at the door after the third date with the nice girls my parents encouraged me to date, all were nothing but prim handshakes compared with one timid kiss from Margarethe.

"I knew you would be different," she whispered.

"From whom?" I asked.

"Don't worry about it," she said. "Would you kiss me again?"

I rolled her over and braced my weight on my forearms so that my torso was perched over hers and lowered my lips to hers once more. The kiss grew from tentative to emboldened in moments as she matched each of my caresses with one more ardent than the last.

"This is crazy," I whispered. I was vaguely aware that there was a battle being fought outside the flap of the tent, and it might be miles from us. Or yards.

"It is," she said. "But please, don't stop."

Her fingers worked nimbly on all the buttons of my uniform, while mine quickly divested her of her soot-covered suit.

"You're sure?" I asked, not knowing what I would do if she had a change of heart.

She nodded in response, pulling me against her once more.

And for a short while, at least in that tiny corner of the forest, even the enormity of the war ceased to matter.

—

Only a thin beam of sunlight intruded on the solitude of the small tent that was the center of my universe. The grumbling of the guns was, for once, far in the distance, and the only thing that mattered to me was the rise and fall of Margarethe's chest as she breathed the even breath of one succumbing to sleep. I wanted to hold her for hours more, but the forest was a dangerous place, and the longer I was gone, the more I risked trouble with my superiors.

"I have to go," I whispered, kissing her brow. I wanted to swallow the words as her eyes fluttered open, but we couldn't delay much longer.

I had no idea how long I'd been gone, but I had to hope that things had been chaotic enough at the hospital that my absence had not been noticed, and yet not so much that my help had been missed.

"Thank you, Max." Her breath, sweet as sugared dates, perfumed the tiny enclosure. There was nothing I wouldn't have given to lose myself again in the softness of her porcelain skin and the alluring curve of her hips.

"Don't thank me, sweetheart. You've given me the best hour of my life, just now." Somehow, I mustered the wherewithal to sit up and begin to dress. She sat up as well and took over, buttoning my shirt and brushing my skin with light kisses as she helped me back into my uniform. She was unabashed in her nakedness, and I loved her for it. I'd never been with a woman before, but I knew from the way the others kissed, even the way they held hands, that they would never allow themselves to be so unguarded with me. I admired how the dim light bathed her breasts as she straightened my jacket, and she wasn't fazed by my attentions.

"You look ready," she pronounced at last. "Like a proper soldier." She hastily threw her spoiled suit back on and smoothed her hair.

"And you look like an angel," I said, then crawled out of the tent and offered her a hand. I pulled her to my chest and cradled her in my arms for a few moments, then wove my fingers into her blond tresses as I bent down for a kiss.

"I can bring more food and medicine tomorrow. In case Jonas and Heide return," I said, offering up a prayer that they were hiding and safe somewhere.

"I don't think that would be wise," she said, leaning her forehead against my chest. "I'll do what I can to find them supplies elsewhere. I don't want you to have trouble. I will likely have enough of my own without worrying about yours. Supplies may be growing sparse on our side, but we aren't depleted yet."

"What troubles?" I asked, holding her back to look at her face. "Tell me."

"They are mine alone to bear, my sweet soldier. I won't have you distracted by them on the battlefield."

"I'll be distracted as it is," I said, not letting her escape from my embrace. I began kissing a trail up her neck, but she gently pushed me away.

"Precisely," she said. "And distracted soldiers rarely grow old. Just know that it is a beautiful thing to know that men are still capable of goodness and kindness. I have seen precious little of that since my father died."

She glanced downward before meeting my eyes again. "You two would have loved each other."

"I'm sure we would have," I said. "If he was anything like you, I wouldn't be able to help myself. And I'd tell him I want to spend the rest of my life making his daughter happy."

"We've only just met. You're letting this"—she gestured toward the tent—"cloud your judgment. Once the war is over, you'll go home and fall back in with your schoolyard sweetheart."

"I didn't have a schoolyard sweetheart," I said. "And precious few after. None of the women I've met have anything like your spark. I'd be a fool not to get down on one knee and beg you to come home with me."

"A world away, where I wouldn't know a soul," she said, though her face brightened a moment before clouding over once more. "I'd never see my home again."

"If you're homesick, I'll build you a house just like the one you're leaving behind. Maybe not right away, but I'll fix every aching tooth in California until you have the home of your dreams."

"I believe you mean that," she said, her grip tightening around me.

"Every word. Tell me about it," I said. "Tell me about your house."

"It's just a cross-timbered farmhouse like every other in Bavaria," she said. "Though Mama's flower boxes were the prettiest for kilometers every spring."

"And yours will be too," I said. "We haven't many Bavarian farmhouses in Southern California, but you'll have yours. And you won't have to wait for spring. You can have a riot of blooms in winter if you want. Yellow buttercups and blue columbine to your heart's content. Edelweiss too, if it can stand the heat."

"You make it sound as though you live in a fairy kingdom instead of another country."

"Oh, it's not always paradise, but you'll never be in want of sunshine again."

"That seems close enough to paradise for me," she whispered.

She pulled me close for another kiss, slow, lingering this time. Then she straightened my uniform jacket once more and looked at me, ensuring I looked tidy enough for a rigorous inspection.

"Go now," she said. "Win this war and make the world a better place."

"I'll be back," I vowed. "Whatever your troubles are, we'll figure them out together. I'm not going to leave you here in the rubble."

"It seems foolish to dream of such things, Max. But just this once, I will allow myself to hope."

"Then I know I'm doing something right."

CHAPTER THIRTEEN

Forged in Fire

JOHANNA

March 1940
Berlin, Germany

"We can refashion Johanna's gown, Mama. It's fit for a countess, after all. Or better still, yours. It was simpler." Metta's face turned lily-pad green as the salesclerk showed us her assortment of ready-made gowns. Clearly she had cold feet, but her reaction was one of the strongest I'd ever seen. And it wasn't just with dresses. Every aspect of wedding planning drew out the same response from her to the point where Mama chose not to notice it anymore.

The store was one of the poshest spots in Berlin, but the strain of the war was already starting to show. There hadn't been new inventory in ages, as textiles and textile workers were needed for outfitting the troops. "Or I can wear my good brown wool suit. Most of the girls are wearing something nice they already own. It sets a good example of frugality."

"You will have a gown, my dear," Mama proclaimed. "Johanna may have a daughter who will want her gown, and mine has yellowed terribly. You need your own."

Mama held her tongue about not having the wedding in a church. The regime had little use for religion, and a high-ranking official like Ansel could not be seen doing anything that contradicted their philosophies. But Mama had her limits. If she was going to see Metta married to this man, she would have her in a proper gown. It was an extravagance in wartime, but Mama would not be refused.

"But, Mama," Metta protested.

"Let her have this," I said, placing my hand on hers. "She hasn't any other daughters to marry off, and she can afford to do this for you."

"Very well," she said, exhaling slowly and shaking her head.

"Just try to act like you're having fun," I said, brushing a kiss on her temple. "A daughter should enjoy shopping for her wedding dress with her mother. None of this will matter once you're on your way down the aisle."

Metta changed from garish green to ghostly white in the flutter of a songbird's wing, but she seemed to gather her composure just as quickly. "You're right," she said, screwing on a smile that seemed as sincere as the ones painted on the mannequins' faces throughout the shop.

"How about this one?" Mama had passed by the clerk to look through the rack herself and now held up a gown with meters and meters of Brussels lace. It was a little old-fashioned, but few of us had the time to pay attention to the latest trends—if indeed fashion was still evolving. As far as I could tell, most everyone was either in uniform or simply wearing the most practical pieces from their existing wardrobes until they were threadbare. The gowns that clung so artfully to the mannequins were relics in a museum that honored a gentler time. They were tributes to a grace and beauty that was quickly being sacrificed on the altar of efficiency and utility.

"It's rather a lot, don't you think?" she replied.

"It's your wedding," Mama insisted. "You don't need to be understated."

"It would swallow her whole," I said, coming to Metta's defense. Metta barely came to my shoulder and was about as big around as a quilting needle. "She'd do better with something with clean lines."

Mama replaced the gown, mollified by my justification. She didn't want to skimp, but neither would she have Metta look ridiculous. In the end, I found an oyster-colored satin gown with simple lines and tasteful embroidery, and beading at the shoulders and waistline. It was modest and plain enough for Metta's tastes and elegant enough to satisfy Mama. Best of all, it wouldn't need alterations, which we had precious little time for with the wedding a week away. We added a veil and Mama even conceded the satin slippers in favor of a pair of more sensible shoes that could be worn with a good suit.

Metta looked distant as the clerk wrote up the order.

"Are you all right, dear?" I asked, keeping my voice low, so Mama and the clerk wouldn't hear.

She blinked furiously for a moment, and her smile reemerged as she returned to the present. "Fine," she said. "Of course, I'm fine."

"Pre-wedding jitters?" I asked. She'd always been the shy sort; I suspected the idea of standing in front of a roomful of people was more terrifying to her than the permanence of marriage.

"That must be it," she said, taking my hand for a moment and squeezing it. "I'll be fine."

I bit back the reassurances that she didn't have to go through with it. Each time I'd waltzed near the topic, it had only served to cause her to retreat further within herself. She'd completed her course at the so-called bride school the week before, and she'd gone from reserved to positively shadow-like during her stay with me. There had been far fewer late-night chat sessions than I'd hoped for and far more quiet evenings where she begged off to bed early on account of a headache.

She grew paler and lost weight during our two months together, when I'd hoped the opposite would happen.

I couldn't bear the hypocrisy of offering up a comforting lie, even for her sake. The marriage was as good as done. The only hope I had was that the war would claim him and leave her free.

God forgive me for thinking it.

And God spare her from Ansel's cronies if anything were to happen to him.

I tried to think of something I could say that would ease the nerves she endeavored so diligently to conceal, but everything sounded contrived and trite in my head. I claimed her hand in mine once more.

"I love you, sister. To the moon and stars. Husbands, children, and even wars can't change that."

Her face crumpled for a moment, but she stoically willed the tears away, and pulled me into her arms. She regained her composure and drew me to a quiet corner where we couldn't be overheard.

"You must promise me something, Jojo," she whispered, no more than a couple of centimeters from my ear. "Stay safe at any cost. Dark times are coming. Darker than we can imagine. The moment you see trouble for yourself, do whatever it takes to get out."

"What do you know, Metta?" I whispered back. "I can help. I can try."

"This is bigger than us. The boulder is already rolling down the mountain, and there's no stopping it. You can either get out of the way or be crushed by it. There is nothing else for any of us."

—

Metta's wedding took place a week later. A gentle snow fell on the steps that led to the grand hall that Ansel had rented for the occasion. I'd expected rather a spartan affair, but every surface was decorated with lush fir boughs. Ansel stood at the front of the room just as he would have done in a church, but rather than a priest beside him, a colonel from the SS waited to join the couple in marriage. Oskar, his face glowing with pride, stood beside Ansel. Next to them was a charcoal brazier, which I supposed had some sort of ceremonial significance. I was astounded at the number of people in attendance—a sea of uniformed men, many accompanied by smartly dressed young women. Newly married couples, or those who soon would be, I suspected. All were there to celebrate another union enthusiastically endorsed by the Reich that would no doubt lead to more healthy German children and a solid future for Hitler's Germany.

A sweet-faced girl from Metta's bride course, designated as her bridesmaid, walked gracefully down the aisle. Eight children appeared; four girls lit the way with torches, while the boys sounded the arrival of the bride with a jubilant trumpet fanfare. The trumpets gave way to the hired string quintet, who played Metta down the aisle with strains of Wagner's "Bridal Chorus." She was the very picture of German beauty. Each step she made matched the crisp notes played ardently by the skilled hands of the musicians. She did not fight back tears, nor did she smile like a giddy schoolgirl. She was as demure and composed as any high-ranking official could hope for in a young bride. The oyster satin gave her skin a healthy glow. Her blond hair shone even more brilliantly than the satin of her gown under the warm flickering light from the numerous candelabras.

Though the men's ranks were evident from their uniforms, one could have easily parsed the hierarchy from the seating arrangement and the way underlings deferred to their superiors. The women all fell into the same ranks as their men, so Metta would soon take her place near the top of the social order gathered in the room, though she had to be among the youngest women there. Mama and I were the only exceptions, with two seats reserved for us at the front left-hand side of the aisle. I was certain Ansel would much rather have ceded those places to his comrades in arms but knew that slighting the few members of his bride's family would reflect badly on him.

I'd met Ansel only twice before, and my impression of him wasn't improved the longer I was in his company. He was a tall man and cut a fine figure in his uniform, to be sure, but he was too lean by half and had a long, humorless face. His piercing blue eyes enveloped everything in his gaze with the warmth of an arctic glacier. His neutral expression looked truculent, his lips permanently twisted in a disapproving scowl. I hoped my view of him was colored by my general dislike for his presence in Metta's life, but I couldn't imagine finding him pleasant even if he weren't marrying my only sister.

The ceremony went on for quite some time, talking far more about the plight of the Reich than the union of the couple, but the entire assembly sat transfixed by the readings. They spoke endlessly of fire. The fire from which the struggle emerged, the fire that would purify Germany so that the Aryan race would be free to rule overall. Metta kept her eyes on the colonel and the readers as they spoke, and she looked appropriately solemn. I clasped my hands in my lap, hoping I looked attentive rather than petrified.

Rather than a traditional recessional, the entire assembly sang the national anthem. We gathered in a separate room where a feast awaited us. There was roast chicken, glazed duck, spiced hams, and any number of delicacies along with fine wines and an endless supply of beer. How Ansel had managed to procure all this while rationing was so strictly enforced, I didn't know, and I suspected I was better off in my ignorance.

As at the ceremony, Mama and I were seated near the bride and groom at the front of the dining hall. I picked at the succulent pheasant, crisp fried potatoes, and perfectly braised brussels sprouts, but could not find the stomach to enjoy them.

"We're so glad to have you in the family," Mama said to Ansel, attempting to make conversation. "I feared your duties might have taken your attentions away from our Metta."

If only they had. I fiddled with my napkin to release some of the nervous energy that coursed through me like voltage through wires.

"You assume correctly that my duties increase each and every day, *Mutter* Hoffmann, and that is precisely why I wished to have the wedding as soon after Margarethe had finished her bridal course as could be arranged."

"Margarethe," I said. "My goodness, for a moment I wasn't sure of whom you were speaking. She's always been Metta to us."

"I have a dislike for nicknames," Ansel said. "I believe in calling things by their proper names."

"You were never Ani as a boy?" Mama asked.

"No," he replied without further elaboration.

What a pleasant father he'd make. He'd have them marching in lines instead of playing ball.

"Ansel has done very well for himself," Oskar interjected. "He's been given a command in France."

"Oh, how unfortunate you'll have to leave Metta—Margarethe—so soon after the wedding," I said, hoping I sounded sincere. "She'll be sad to be parted from you so quickly."

"I could not marry her just to leave her behind," Ansel said with a nod in my direction. "Margarethe will accompany me on my assignments. I've secured her a post with *Frauen Warte*; she will be able to write articles about our successes in France and elsewhere to keep up women's morale here at home."

The expression on Metta's face betrayed that this was new information to her, but she did an admirable job of keeping any displeasure from showing. Mama and I had begun to receive the magazine at home, and I suspected Oskar was responsible for our subscriptions to the biweekly magazine for women in the party. It contained not only such innocuous things as recipes and sewing patterns, but also parenting advice for raising children who would be prepared to defend Germany to the death and other such cheerful content.

"I didn't think the party approved of married women working," I said, not meeting Metta's eyes.

"Her contribution to the war effort will be invaluable, not unlike your own," he said. Of course, Ansel knew about my work for DVL. He would have researched every detail about Metta's background before extending her an offer of marriage. Thank God Papa's father's records had been "conveniently lost," or Metta's fate might have been even worse than what had already befallen her.

"I look forward to it," Metta chimed in. "It will be good to be of service."

Ansel's dour face broke into a smile, and the effect was even more chilling than his scowl. "You will be a credit to us all, my dear. I am sure of it."

CHAPTER FOURTEEN

STARTING A SEARCH

BETH

May 5, 2007
Encinitas, California

"So, who was she, Dad?" I pressed, sliding the photo in front of him. I wasn't going to pretend I was indifferent any longer.

"She was the first woman I ever loved. The only one aside from your mother—and you, of course. Her name was Margarethe. I would have stolen her away and married her in a heartbeat when the war was over, even if it would have killed your grandmother for me to marry a Gentile girl. But there was no finding her once it was done. I can't tell you how long I searched for her."

"And the baby?"

"Mine," he said, as though warding off an argument I didn't have cause to raise. Was the child's parentage uncertain? The look on Dad's face let me know it wasn't a question to press.

"I wonder whatever happened to them." The question sounded lame to my ears as soon as it rolled off my tongue. This was my half sibling. My stepmother of sorts. People I would have loved if they were in my life. That I might not have existed if this woman had remained in my father's life was unimportant. I was here and he loved me. But had Dad been nursing a broken heart for this woman and child for more than half a century? Why hadn't I ever known?

"Bethie, I've wondered that every day for over sixty years."

I took his hand. "I know, Dad." And I did. There was no way this man could have fathered a child without longing to be a part of their life. He wasn't built for anything else. I felt myself blinking against tears.

"Are you all right, Beth?" he asked, seeing the brightness in my eyes.

"You're telling me I might have a brother or sister, Dad. It's a lot to process."

"I hope you're not too upset by the news," he said, squeezing my hand. "You've been the center of my life for forty years. A miracle your mother and I thought would never happen. No matter the news, you'll always be my girl."

"Dad, I've wanted a sibling since I understood what one was. Though I always expected her to be younger."

"Convinced it was a girl?" Dad asked, his own eyes growing bright. "So was her mother."

"Well, I always pictured a sister. It would be lovely to have one after all these years."

"You know what's funny, Bethie, I've lived for more than sixty years consoling myself with the idea that I'll learn the answers soon enough in the next life, but I still can't bear the thought of not knowing in this one."

"Then let's do it, Dad. I'll help you. If there are answers to be found, we'll find them."

"I said it once already, Beth. I won't have you give up your life to take care of me. You need to be going out and having some fun."

"Dad, maybe what I need right now is a project. Something constructive to do while I figure out what's next for me. Think of it as a stepping-stone between moping at home and going out clubbing every weekend."

Dad straightened up for a moment and gave me a look as though he were seeing me for the first time in clear light. "That makes an awful lot of sense, Bethie. You see what you can dig up. I won't stop you. I figure the answers are long buried, but you can try."

"Thankfully your daughter has a world-class research facility at her disposal. If there are answers to be found, I'll find them."

"I've no doubt you will, sweetheart." Dad looked out the window over my shoulder rather than directly at me.

"I just have one question, Dad. Why didn't you tell me any of this sooner?"

"Well, when I married your mother, I promised myself I'd not make her feel like she was playing second fiddle to someone else. To talk about Margarethe seemed plain disrespectful in my book. Some women might have understood, but not her." Dad exhaled a long breath. "And what's more, I wouldn't have you thinking poorly of me."

"For loving another woman? Dad, it was ages before you married Mom, and as your generation is so fond of saying, there was a war on. I'm glad you were able to steal a few moments of happiness in the midst of all of it."

"Not that, Bethie. I worried you'd never forgive me for leaving them behind."

⌒

"My God, sweet old Max. Who would ever have thought he'd have such a secret?"

"You see him as he is now, Gwen. Look at his old war photos. He could have left behind a string of broken hearts if he were a different sort of man."

"So, what are you going to do?" she asked. "Go knock on every door in Germany and ask if anyone knew someone by the name of

Margarethe back in 1945 who looks like the woman in the photo? You don't have a lot to go on."

"No, I don't," I admitted. I'd spent the better part of an hour asking Dad all the questions I could think of about the woman in the photo that might give me something to research. He didn't know her birth date, any previous addresses, or even her last name. All he knew was that she was named Margarethe and was about twenty-four years old, and that the baby would likely have been born sometime in June of 1945, if indeed Margarethe had survived that long. And aside from the photograph, that was all I had to start my search. "If you were me, where would you start?"

"Probably by banging my head against a wall, honestly."

"OK, after you finished with that and took some Advil for the resulting headache, what would you do?"

"I'd probably go talk to James Fletcher at the main library on campus. He's a research wizard. He's not the man with all the answers, but he sure knows where to find them."

James's reputation was good enough; I'd heard of him, despite never having had to avail myself of his services. My work dealt most often with current affairs, which rarely gave me cause to fall down a research rabbit hole. Gwen had far more need to delve into the archives about the history of feminist political theory and the like than I ever did. She'd worked enough with James to have his cell number in case she needed help in a pinch, though I couldn't imagine any emergency research needs so dire she'd require after-hours help. I suspected he'd been one of the many men to slip her his number in hopes that she'd call him up for a date. She was the sort of attractive woman that men flocked to, and just approachable enough for them to try their hand. She was off the market at the moment; her current boyfriend, Gabe, seemingly had more staying power than the last few.

I called, not really expecting him to pick up for a strange number, but a deep baritone responded on the second ring. I fumbled my way through the call, explaining that I was Gwen's friend, a professor at the university, and looking for a long-lost relation. I'd expected to set up a time to meet on Monday or later in the week, but he insisted on meeting at the library that afternoon despite my protests that I didn't want to impose on his weekend.

The Geisel Library, named for Theodor Geisel, better known as Dr. Seuss, was one of the most beautiful buildings on campus. Its stone trunk sprung from the earth and sprouted into five glass-paned levels, making it vaguely resemble one of the whimsical trees from *The Lorax*. I found James at the research desk on the main floor of the library. He looked much as one would expect a research librarian to look: an unkempt mop of dark-blond curls, two days' worth of stubble on his chin, and wire-rimmed glasses. But he had a deep tan and board shorts that suggested I'd pulled him away from the beach or a hike in the mountains instead of the stacks at the library.

"I'm so sorry to drag you away from whatever it was you were doing," I said, reaching to shake his hand.

"No problem at all, Dr. Cohen," he said, flashing a quick smile. "It sounds interesting."

"Blumenthal," I corrected, realizing I'd finally reached a decision on the question of my name. It was Blumenthal on most everything official anyway, but I'd gone by Cohen conversationally out of deference to Greg. And my mother's insistence that women who kept their own names or who hyphenated weren't truly invested in their marriages. "And Beth, if you don't mind," I added.

"James," he said, accepting my handshake. "So, given the parameters of what you have, this is going to be quite a hunt."

"I figured as much," I said.

"Without a last name, I can't verify that we can find anything of use, but I do have a few tricks up my sleeve."

"I'm willing to give it a shot," I said. "I think it will mean a lot to my dad if we just try."

"It's not hopeless," he said. "You'd be amazed at how much can be found with a shred of information, a fistful of determination, and a dollop of luck."

I smiled at the optimism that reminded me so much of Gwen. "You sound like a baker," I said as he escorted me to one of the study rooms. It was equipped with several sleek desktop computers and a large table perfect for spreading out documents.

"I make some of the finest focaccia in Southern California," he said with a wink as he fired up a machine.

"A bold claim, sir," I said, crossing my arms over my chest. I'd never made focaccia, but it couldn't be that big of a challenge after my mother's challah.

"Fortune rarely favors the faint of heart," he said. The machine had booted up, and I waited as he entered his credentials and navigated through several databases. We searched for women named Margarethe born in Germany between 1918 and 1922, and thousands of records were returned. We filtered the searches to exclude those who had died before early 1945, the last year we knew she was alive, which eliminated a decent number, but not enough to consider the field narrowed in any respect. We looked at hundreds of the entries for Margarethe, but nothing seemed to mesh quite properly with Dad's story.

"What if her name wasn't even Margarethe? What if she gave Dad a false name to protect him?"

"Then that makes our job here exponentially harder," he said. I exhaled and rubbed my temples. He patted my hand. "Harder, but not impossible. I've found more with less, so just keep the faith."

CHAPTER FIFTEEN

RELUCTANT RETREAT

MAX

December 16, 1944
Hürtgen Forest, Germany

After nearly three months of slaughter, the brass finally conceded that there was no taking the territory from the Germans. We'd lost thousands of lives during the invasion of Normandy and the days after, but though the sacrifice was great, we could see that each step farther on those beaches was taking us a step closer to liberating France. There was nothing gained from three months in the Death Factory of Hürtgen Forest aside from irrevocably broken souls. We could have continued slogging on amid the shattered trees, but in my bones I knew they needed us elsewhere. I could only hope we'd have better luck at making advances, wherever it was we were going.

It had been almost three months since I'd seen Margarethe. Each day since our tryst in the woods, I went to the clearing to give her supplies. I prayed she'd leave a note or something to indicate she'd been there. I occasionally took the supplies in a pack from a deceased soldier—there were plenty to be had—and left them in plain sight in various spots in the forest in hopes that she would find them. They were always waiting undisturbed the following day. My only consolation was that it was possible she'd found a safer place to hide Jonas.

I worried for Jonas and Heide too. I hoped the battle that churned around them hadn't claimed them in the middle of his convalescence, but mainly I thought of Margarethe. I didn't even know if she'd made it back home after our afternoon together. I would have died happy if that sweet hour had been my last, but it shouldn't have been hers.

It was the last day I'd be able to look for Margarethe, and I knew that if I didn't find her, she'd be lost to me forever. That very thought bore through my soul as cruelly as a German bullet. I went to the clearing. I felt my heart hammer against my rib cage when I noticed a female form hiding in the bushes.

Heide.

She looked terrified but seemed to relax as I approached. She didn't trust me fully, but she knew I posed less of a threat to her than any other soldier—American or German.

"F-for you," she stuttered, handing me an envelope with her shaking hand.

It was simply labeled *Max* in a perfect formal script.

"She wants you to be safe," Heide said in stilted English. "You must be very careful, please."

"I will," I promised, pronouncing my words carefully for her benefit. "Why couldn't she come?"

"Her husband—is a very bad man," Heide said, growing paler as if the words would somehow summon him where we stood.

"Husband?" I said, disbelieving.

"Yes." Heide's face scrunched up in frustration at her lack of vocabulary. "You please not think bad of her. She was young. She had no choice."

"No," I said solemnly. "Never."

"Read her letter. Be safe for her."

"Yes. How is Jonas?" I added as an afterthought, embarrassed I hadn't thought to ask sooner.

"Better, I think. Still sore. Slow."

"Are you safe?" I asked.

"Do not worry. You go. I will worry for Jonas. I must go." As if to punctuate her words, the boom of artillery shattered the relative quiet of the woods.

I returned to camp, the unopened letter in my pocket. The site was chaos as the army prepared to move the remaining troops to another area on the front. We hadn't been told where we were going, and it didn't seem the higher-ups knew all that much more than we did. They did what they could to act like everything was orderly for the sake of the younger men, but no one was terribly convinced by the charade. Trying to look absorbed in official business, I opened Margarethe's letter and secured the page to a clipboard. Her careful script looked as though it belonged on the page of a Shakespearean folio.

> *My dearest Max,*
>
> *If you are reading this, Heide has found you, and that makes me a very happy woman. I wish the world had granted us more time together, and I hope deep in my heart that we may yet have a chance to be together. I pray my work to end the war is enough to absolve me of being born on the wrong side of it, but only time will tell. I will try to find you again if ever I can, but such a thing will not be easy. My husband is a powerful man, and I cannot risk him learning what I've been doing. More than my life would be at risk. I am being watched constantly as it is, and I fear that his reprisal would be brutal if he knew even the merest details of my work, let alone of our time*

*together. Please know, your sweetness and kindness will
remain one of the fondest memories of my life. No matter
what happens, I will carry you in my heart always. Win
this war, my darling. For all our sakes.*
    Metta

Metta. She'd never used the nickname with me before, and its simplicity and elegance suited her. Margarethe belonged to a matronly woman clucking over a classroom full of children. It wasn't for someone who had so recently left behind the mantle of girlhood herself, still so youthful and vibrant. Yet she called herself Margarethe and that's how I thought of her. She may have had her reasons.

"Blumenthal, you're needed in the hospital tent. Those supplies won't pack themselves." The voice was attached to one of the medical staffers, though I didn't bother looking up to see who.

"Yes, sir," I said, forcing myself to stow the letter and walk in the direction where the ordered chaos of moving a hospital was underway. I threw myself into packing away the vials of medicine as carefully as time would allow, not letting my mind wander back to Margarethe and the hell she might be facing.

CHAPTER SIXTEEN

PARACHUTES

JOHANNA

May 31, 1943
Berlin, Germany

One system is the same as another.

I told myself this time and again as work on strengthening landing gear and improving fuel efficiency evolved into perfecting targeting mechanisms and bomb-release techniques. I was there to make the aircraft the very best it could be, and it was not for me to decide which systems took priority. And moreover, there were men and women in offices just like mine in England and France—and now America—who were doing the same thing for their aircraft. The harder I worked, the safer Germany was. The sooner the war was over, the sooner Harald could come home. Oskar and Ansel too. And Metta.

I had never liked Ansel, but I would never forgive him for dragging her from battleground to battleground. I'd taken solace in the idea that she could stay with me in Berlin. I thought she would bide her time making a nest for Ansel to come home to, but would be mostly free to do as she pleased, provided she made a good enough show of helping out the war effort. She could roll bandages and knit caps with the other wives for a few hours each week and be pleased with what she'd done. But no, he had to keep her under his thumb. She was too young and beautiful to be left alone. He didn't need to say it. I could read as much in his smug expression.

She'd written only once since she was taken to the front, and there was no mention of where she was. She reassured us that she was safe, but she'd never have been at liberty to say otherwise. I tried to decipher if there was fear behind her words, but I couldn't find anything that signaled genuine alarm.

But even more unsettling than Metta's bland missive was the total absence of any letters at all from Harald. Before now, he'd managed to write each week without fail, and though the delivery was sometimes delayed, I was never left with more than an extra few days of worry. Mama, who now stayed with me in town rather than face the solitude of life on the farm by herself, tried to convince me that there was no need to worry in earnest until bad news was certain. She, however, had the perspective of having lived through sending a husband to war and seeing him safely home. I didn't have the benefit of that perspective, and though I'd always been proud of my ability to remain detached until I had reason to do otherwise, I was failing now.

I was sketching my ideas for improvements to the bomb-deployment mechanism on the Junkers Ju 88, though my mind was only on my work in the most superficial sense. The city itself was constantly under threat of Allied attack these days. The bombing mechanism I was perfecting would be doing the same thing to Allied cities and camps within weeks. Only the mechanism would function better and be even more deadly than it had been in the past.

"Are you here to work or daydream, *Gräfin*?" Louisa crowed as she walked by my open office door. "Planning your next dinner party? I expect your supervisors would rather you do that on your own time."

"Oh, would you rather design this yourself?" I asked, turning the sketch to face her and sliding it across my desk. "Be my guest if you think you can."

She rolled her eyes and crossed her arms over her chest. "Some of us prefer to do the real flying instead of worrying about that dry stuff."

Aside from the fact that I had logged close to twice the number of hours that she had over the past six months, her willful ignorance of the engineering behind the aircraft set my teeth on edge. "This dry stuff is what wins wars. Go brush your hair, show pony. I'm sure some journalist is here to snap your photo. I have work to do."

She opened her mouth to retort and snapped it shut with an audible click of her teeth, then stalked off to the field to clamber into her plane. It was her standard response when her feelings were piqued, which they were with increasing regularity.

"You'd think the only two women in the office would get along," Peter said, entering to place a stack of mail in the tray on the corner of my desk.

"Why would you expect that?" I asked, looking up from the drawing I'd already repositioned in front of me. "Aside from our sex and our occupation, what else have we in common?"

"I should think that would be enough to start with," he said.

"Does every man who works in this office get along?" I queried. "Would you expect them to?"

"No," he admitted. "But there are far more of us. We have the luxury of choosing friends from among our colleagues, I suppose."

"And Louisa and I have the luxury of finding friendship outside the office instead of inflicting our company on each other, since it isn't appreciated."

Peter simply nodded and limped out.

I set aside the sketch with a sigh, no longer willing to keep up the illusion that I had the slightest interest in my project that day. It would mean late nights soon, but there was no forcing my attention now. On top of the mail pile was a large, crisp envelope. Inside was a certificate with an official seal printed on thick parchment paper.

> *Frau Johanna Schiller Gräfin von Oberndorff is hereby granted status equal to Aryan. She is entitled to all the rights and privileges afforded to a person of the Aryan race . . .*

My eyes blurred as I read the rest of the text. This paper was my parachute. I would be free to work and would be protected from the roundups that were happening with more frequency.

I was sure Metta's marriage to Ansel, as well as Oskar's party involvement, had helped with this. I was torn between relief and disgust at the document in my hands. I had mine, but how many others were left without theirs?

The rest of the mail was of the uninteresting sort, but there was a crumpled letter stuck to the back of the newspaper.

It was from the war department.

I opened it, a ragged breath forcing itself from my lungs.

> *Frau Schiller Gräfin von Oberndorff:*
> *Your husband, Harald Schiller Graf von Oberndorff, Leutnant in the Wehrmacht, has been wounded in service to his country. We will apprise you of his condition as soon as possible.*

I gathered up my belongings, taking special care of my certificate and the letter, and left the sketches forgotten on my desk. If I had to track down Ansel on the front lines and guilt him into using every connection he had to find Harald, that's what I would do.

~

I mounted my bicycle and pedaled as fast as I could to the nearest post that had a telegraph machine. I would have rung Ansel on the phone if I'd had any idea of his number. I suspected they were close enough to the fighting that they wouldn't have a phone of their own in any case. I'd send the telegram to the military outpost nearest the last address I had for them and hope that one of the men in the office would forward the information to him. I scribbled my message on the card and handed it to the clerk.

> *Harald injured, status unknown. Unsure of location,*
> *please assist so I may join him.*
> *Johanna*

I pedaled home, this time much more slowly. Once I arrived back at our little lakefront bungalow, I'd have to tell Mama the news. This grief was certainly my own, but she was left with nothing but worry for her children, so she would bear it along with me, just as she bore her concerns for Metta's marriage and Oskar's proximity to the front lines. She didn't need this worry for her son-in-law added atop her shoulders too, but there was no keeping the news from her.

She was sitting at the kitchen table with her afternoon coffee and her latest issue of *Frauen Warte* when I walked in. She looked surprised to see me and stood immediately to fetch me a coffee of my own and some pastry, acting as though she'd been caught dozing on the job. She wasn't used to leisure, and though she took more of it in my home than elsewhere, she hadn't yet made friends with it.

"Metta's article was very good this week," Mama said. "It sounds like things are going well for our men and that spirits are high."

"I'm glad to hear it," I said. There was no chance they would allow her to say anything else, but I let Mama cling to the idea. If Metta was able to write, she was likely safe. For now, that was enough.

"You're home early. I'm glad. You put in too many hours. It's good for you to take an afternoon off every once in a while."

I had, in fact, cut down my hours since Mama moved in so we could at least have time together in the evenings. If she were still in Berchtesgaden, I'd work until I was fatigued enough to worry I was making errors in calculations. With Harald gone, I had to keep myself occupied as much as possible. Having Mama home meant that it didn't always have to be work that filled my hours, and that was likely much better for my constitution.

She placed the cup and plate in front of me and brushed a kiss on my cheek. I took her hand in mine and kissed her palm before releasing it. God, how good it felt to be mothered in that moment. She reclaimed her place at the table and took a sip from her own mug.

I waited until the mug was safely back on the table and endeavored to calm my breath. "Mama, Harald has been injured. I don't know how else to tell you."

"My darling girl, I'm so sorry. What's to be done?"

"Right now? Nothing. I've asked Ansel to help."

"Do you think he will?"

"I've no idea, Mama. All I can do is hope. I don't expect he'll be all that anxious to use his position to help me out. I'm only in the party's good graces because I'm useful to them and keep my head down."

"But you *are* useful to them, my dear. That must count for something."

"I'm going to hope he sees it your way, Mama."

"There's no reason to think he won't."

For now. The unspoken words hung heavy over the table like an iron chandelier in a medieval banquet hall.

Mama did her best to distract me. We had a light dinner of soup and bread and spent the rest of the afternoon knitting socks for the men, using one of the patterns from *Frauen Warte*. At least while my hands were occupied, I wouldn't be wringing them, contemplating all the fates that might have befallen my Harald.

Dark was nearly upon us, and I set to closing all the heavy curtains to comply with the blackout regulations. I nearly jumped out of my own skin as a knock sounded at the door. I looked through the peephole to find a man in a delivery uniform.

Harald.

I accepted the telegram from the man, hands shaking, and removed it from its envelope. In the space of a few seconds I managed to recite every prayer in my repertoire that the news wasn't the worst.

LEUTNANT HARALD SCHILLER GRAF VON OBERNDORFF CURRENTLY CONVALESCING NEAR SALZBURG. STATUS STABLE. HE WILL BE SENT HOME WITHIN THE WEEK. ANSEL ZIEGLER, OBERSTURMBANNFÜHRER

"He's safe," Mama breathed, having read the note over my shoulder. I took her in my arms for a weary embrace.

"Thank God," was all I could say.

"Perhaps Ansel is kinder than we feared." Mama's face brightened at the prospect.

"We can hope so, Mama." It was true. If Ansel had a spark of genuine kindness in him, Metta had at least some chance of finding happiness with him.

"Harald is so close to home, it's a wonder they sent him so far from the fighting," Mama mused. None of us had much concrete information about where the fighting truly was, but it was certainly kilometers from Salzburg. Last I knew, we were well entrenched on Soviet soil and still pushing eastward. But I mistrusted the reporting and wondered if in fact Salzburg wasn't much closer to the front than we feared. Then again, the loss of most of Austria would have been known to us. Even Hitler couldn't keep something that horrific from us.

"You'll have your husband back home," Mama said. "What a wonderful thing in such awful times."

"Truly," I agreed, forcing my lips into a grateful smile. "We must say a prayer of thanksgiving."

Mama bowed her head, and I did the same. Mama prayed, I am sure, with a heart full of gratitude for her beloved son-in-law's safe return.

I, however, had seen my share of wounded men returned home from war. The only reason men returned home was because there was absolutely no chance of their being useful on the front. One-legged men could still shoot Russians, after all. My prayer was that there was enough of my husband left to rebuild into the man I loved.

CHAPTER SEVENTEEN

NEEDLES AND HAY

BETH

May 8, 2007
San Diego, California

James messaged me several times with a few leads, none of which panned out. While it was certainly not what he was paid to do, the challenge of the project seemed to be motivation enough for him to squeeze in research time between his regular student consultations and courses on research methodology. I'd taken to visiting him at the library between classes, and it seemed that each time, he was sitting in front of records from the National Archives from World War II or some ancient scrap of microfiche from the 1940s.

"You're very good at this," I said, admiring the pages of notes he'd taken.

"Just think of me as an academic Sherlock Holmes. I might not be solving crimes, but I have a knack for finding answers."

"Very well, Mr. Holmes. Just don't get yourself in trouble on my account."

"They wouldn't dare reprimand me, my dear Watson," he said with a wink. "No one else here knows the collection like I do. They'd be lost without me."

I cocked a brow at the boast but got the feeling it wasn't far from the truth. I'd seen a dozen students approach him asking for a specific title, and in all but two cases, he was able to direct them to the very shelf they needed without the use of the online catalog.

"Have you never wanted to work in the National Library or the Ivy League?" I asked. "With your skills they'd snap you up."

"I've considered it, but there's not much surfing in DC. Plus, I grew up in Minnesota. I've done my time shoveling snow."

"That seems fair," I said. My own encounters with snow were always on vacation. And deliberate. After my first ski trip in middle school, I fostered a deep pity for anyone who couldn't escape the stuff for an entire season. "Where should I look?"

"I'd say you should focus on birth records for 1945. Narrow down by mother's first name."

"Hello, needle, meet haystack," I said, taking my place at the computer adjacent to his.

"It's not that bad," he said. "You can filter by the year of the mother's birth too."

"Sure, but all this assumes the baby was born alive, and in Germany."

"It's what we have to work with," he said. "And even if it doesn't get us anywhere, it will eliminate some possibilities."

"You're quite the optimist."

"I have to be in this business. If I were daunted by the sheer amount of information at my fingertips, I'd never find anything. To use your metaphor, I have learned to accept that some needles are buried in a lot more hay than others."

"This one seems to be an entire field's worth," I retorted.

"Which makes the sorting all the more rewarding, once we find it."

"Dad wasn't able to tell me her last name," I said. "He only knew her as Margarethe. It just doesn't seem like him to have a relationship and not even know her last name."

"It was another time," James said. "We're lucky to live in uninteresting ones, comparatively."

"I suppose that's true. What are you working on?" I asked, looking over his shoulder.

"I scanned in the photo, and I'm going to call in a favor from a friend in DC. I'm hoping his facial recognition software can place her. It's imperfect tech, though, and we're dealing with a very old photograph, but it's worth a shot."

"Don't use up favors for me," I said.

"It's fine. He lives for this cloak-and-dagger stuff. He's in the right field."

"I just don't want either of you getting in trouble for me."

"Don't mention it. Email sent. It's too late now, anyway."

"So long as the Feds don't come knocking down anyone's doors."

"The Feds? What is this? A 1920s gangster novel?"

"Ha. Maybe."

"So, would you be interested in grabbing a coffee sometime?" His eyes never left his computer screen, though it was obvious he wanted to turn his head to assess my reaction to the invitation.

"That's extremely tempting, James, but I'm very freshly divorced. It just doesn't feel like the right time."

"I totally get it," he said. "I'm sorry to hear that."

"It's OK. Nothing cataclysmic. We just grew apart." Harmless answer. Close enough to the truth.

"It still sucks. Been there. If you need to talk, just let me know."

I looked over at his profile, as his eyes were still locked on the screen. I wondered who his ex was and what exactly went wrong. From his subtle hesitance when asking me out, I was guessing the split was fairly recent. He didn't lack confidence so much as practice. His left ring finger was an even bronze color, but the indent from the ring was still visible. Months, I'd guess.

"Thanks—that's incredibly sweet of you."

"What can I say, I'm not just a research ninja, I'm also a good listener with an endless supply of tea."

"Tea and sympathy, is it? My style has always been more alcohol and sarcasm."

At this he let out a full-bellied laugh that turned the heads of several of the students nearest our computers. He shot them an apologetic look, but his shoulders still shook.

"That works too," he said. "I like your style."

"Thanks," I said, feeling the color rise in my cheeks a bit.

"Seriously, though, any time. And when you *are* ready to date, I would really appreciate a phone call, if you're interested."

"You've got a deal," I said, offering a hand to firm up the agreement.

I wondered if I'd ever be bold enough to make the call. I'd never been bold before, but perhaps I should have been. I'd seen men in the past to whom I was attracted and assumed that they were out of my league or uninterested in me for one reason or another. What opportunities had I missed out on because I wasn't willing to show *my* interest first?

I thought about my mother and her insistence that ladies never initiated a date invitation. She'd married Dad in the late '40s, when women were not meant to be bold. Of course, other kids didn't follow their mothers' advice, but that was something she'd hammered into my psyche. *Only the most desperate girls ask boys for dates. If they're interested, they'll ask you.* She held that tenet to be as ironclad as if it were carved into stone on the mount by Moses himself. Even in a situation like this, where James had already shown his interest, she would have advised me to let him reach out again. I understood her point about not appearing overeager, but I didn't see much use in making myself completely unapproachable either.

For close to two hours, I waded through dozens of entries in the database, finding nothing of import, but saving the search so I could continue where I left off. James was there most of the time, searching at twice the speed that I was, given his years of practice.

"If it weren't for the picture, I'd wonder if she existed at all," I said. "She hasn't made herself easy to find."

"No, she hasn't, but we're still early in the search," he said. "I have some other ideas. In the meantime, ask your dad to remember whatever he can. Even the smallest detail might loosen a key part of the knot we're trying to untie here."

"Will do," I said, and left the library. I found myself in the San Diego sunlight on the long concrete path that led through a lush grove of trees. There couldn't be much resemblance to the forest where Dad fought the Nazis and met the woman who bore his firstborn. If indeed they'd survived. Despite thousands of active students and faculty, the groves of trees always felt peaceful. It was hard to imagine this peace being shattered by the roar of artillery and the rattling of guns as the forests of Germany had been. It could happen here as well as any other place on earth, but for a few moments, I gave thanks for the tranquility these woods enjoyed, and gave a small prayer that they would never know otherwise.

CHAPTER EIGHTEEN

APPARITION

MAX

March 8, 1945
Near Remagen, Germany

"You'll never get better if you don't get up and walk," I chided. "Come on now, you don't want to be stuck in a bed for the rest of your life, do you? It'll make you an old man twenty years before your time. Forty even."

"It's no use, Captain. I can't manage more than two steps without collapsing." The young private couldn't have been over twenty-two years old. He'd taken a fair amount of shrapnel to his left thigh, which was bad enough, but he'd also contracted a cold. If he lay in bed with no exertion, it would sure as sunrise lead to pneumonia. He'd beaten the odds—making it to the hospital in time to have the shrapnel removed before infection set in. He'd avoided gangrene once the healing began. To lose him to a common cold would be nothing short of infuriating.

"Then take two goddamn steps, Private Jenkins, and in a few hours, you'll try for three," I ordered. The humor I'd been known for grew thinner as the war went on, and it seemed like Jenkins was the sort who needed orders more than he needed a laugh.

"You're a real sonofabitch. You know that, Captain?" Jenkins muttered as he sat up. I didn't care for the wheezing sound in his chest as he exerted the effort to move.

"More than you could possibly imagine," I said, deadpan. Jenkins managed to sit fully upright and swing his legs over the side of the bed. He tentatively slid to put his weight on his injured leg and blanched in pain immediately. I was at his left side, ready to act as a crutch and let him wrap his arms around my shoulders.

"It hurts too much." He grimaced. "Let me lie back down."

"You will not lie back down until you have taken two steps," I said, gripping him a little tighter so that he wouldn't have to bear his full weight on the injured leg. "You faced the huns; you can do this."

"Fuck you," he muttered under his breath.

"What was that, Private?"

"Yessir," he said, louder.

"That's what I thought."

Jenkins managed his two steps, and I prodded him to take five, which meant ten to get him back into bed. More than I'd hoped for, but he was sweating and pale when he lay back down.

"Again in three hours, Private. No excuses," I said.

He gave me a wary look but nodded as he pulled the blanket back up. I patted his chest and moved on to the next patient.

I should have been relieved to be in a field hospital that was now miles from the fighting, but the farther I was from the front, the farther I felt from Margarethe—Metta—that enigma of a woman. When the American troops pushed across the Rhine, there was an undeniable surge in morale—I felt it too. But with each push forward, I worried that Margarethe was caught under the wheels of the war machine.

"Jenkins?" my commanding officer asked as I placed Jenkins's record back in the file.

"Leg is healing fine, but a patient at more obvious risk for pneumonia I've never seen."

"Is he safe for transport to a convalescent hospital?"

"If he gets up and moves every so often, most likely, sir."

"Then I'm shipping him back to France as soon as the next hospital train arrives," he said. "Safer for him, more beds for us."

"If you think that's best, Major," I said. Clearly his decision was made, and I'd learned from others in his position not to bother taking a contrary position. Certainly, I'd feel more comfortable keeping Jenkins here where I could oversee his care myself and help keep him from getting sicker, but he was one injured man out of tens of thousands. I couldn't rehabilitate them all. Jenkins didn't seem likely to attempt to exercise without coercion, but back home, I wouldn't be able to force my patients to finish the antibiotics I prescribed or even brush their teeth as often as they should. I could only parent them so much before they had to take responsibility for themselves.

I thought of Ma and Dad, about the dental practice I'd start when I was back stateside. I'd always thought I'd stumble across the right girl once I got my practice off the ground and have a gaggle of kids for my parents to spoil. Too many years of hunger and adversity in the old country had left Ma unable to bear more than just one child. I'd honestly given little thought to the woman I'd share my life with, and had always assumed I'd know it when I saw her. And, of course, the perfect girl would come along precisely when I was ready for her, when the practice was well established, and I had money for a home. She wouldn't have to endure scrimping and saving at the supermarket, asking for the cheapest cuts of meat with her head bowed. She wouldn't have to be ashamed of her clothes at temple. In fact, she'd have the finest wardrobe in the Fairfax district. She'd set trends in the neighborhood with her smart dresses and would be the envy of all her friends. We'd have a modest home and hired help, so she'd have the days to do as she pleased. Lunch with friends, charity work, whatever she wanted. She could leave the work to me and enjoy life. All I'd ask for was a cheerful greeting, a pleasant evening together, and a warm body next to mine in bed.

But Margarethe shattered everything about that dream.

Lovely, gentle Margarethe, who had disappeared months ago. I was certain I'd never hear from her again and had resigned myself to praying for her continued health and happiness wherever she was. There was precious little else I could do for her. And as hard to admit as it was, Margarethe didn't fit into the picture of domestic bliss, however naive and idealistic it was, that I'd painted for myself. How would that lovely creature find her place in our old neighborhood? Her accent would raise suspicion. Her blond-haired, blue-eyed beauty wouldn't be admired, it would be scrutinized. And even if she proved herself the kindest neighbor and dearest friend, she'd never be fully welcomed. Would she even want to be? Taking her from Germany to Los Angeles would be like taking a lion from the grasslands of Africa and moving the beast to the arctic circle. Try as it might, it would never adapt.

And yet, for all the heartache our relationship would bring about for our families, our friends, and ourselves, I would take the chance in a heartbeat to make her my own.

I'd tried to keep my mind off the contours of her lovely face, the soft curve and the downy skin of her hips. The way her hair caught the sunlight, so brilliant I expected it to reflect rainbows like a prism. The constant barrage of patients certainly helped, as well as our descent into the depths of Germany. We seemed to be accelerating toward Berlin at a breakneck pace. But still, as I worked, I could see her face emerge in the sea of dirty men clad in olive drab who all looked as though they needed six months of rest on a beach with their mothers' cooking served at regular intervals. Nearly every day I saw her face in the shadows. But today, it spoke.

"Hello, Max. I've missed you."

CHAPTER NINETEEN

MENDING THE BROKEN

JOHANNA

June 6, 1943
Berlin, Germany

"*Liebling*, that can't be you." Harald's voice was a raspy shadow of itself. He'd been home for six hours but was still in shock. He faded in and out of consciousness—mostly out of it—but I was relieved to have him home where I could watch the rise and fall of his chest with my own eyes all the same. I kissed his brow and put a moist towel on his forehead, though I didn't sense a fever. I had him stretched out on our bed, hoping my ministrations were helping his healing rather than slowing it down.

"Don't speak, *Knuddelbär*. Save your strength. Just nod or shake your head. Would you like some water?"

Nod.

I'd set out a pitcher of cold water and a glass on the nightstand, along with whatever else I thought might be helpful to nurse him. I cursed myself for not having the forethought to take a basic nursing course, but no one truly expects Armageddon to break out in their own backyard. I poured him a glass and handed it to him, not releasing it until I was sure he had the strength to lift it to his lips. He drank greedily, as though he'd been wandering through the deserts of Africa for days with no water in sight.

"Easy, love. Don't make yourself ill." He looked pained at the prospect of not downing the entire glass in one long series of gulps but indulged me by slowing his pace.

Information was scarce, but it seemed he'd been close to a bomb blast of some kind and had fairly extensive bruising and lacerations. Walking was next to impossible for him, but the doctor I'd summoned, one of the few still left practicing who hadn't been drafted, assured me that none of the damage to his spine appeared to be permanent.

"Are you in any pain?" I asked. I had precious little to offer him by way of relief, but if I had to go to the black market for medicines that would help him, I would do so without hesitation.

He shook his head, but not with much enthusiasm. He was in pain, but he was coping. That was my Harald, more stoic than was good for him.

"Don't suffer needlessly," I said, but did not press further. The more I pushed on that score, the less likely he would be to accept help.

"Would you like some food?" I asked. At the prospect of a home-cooked meal, his eyes lit up like a boy's at Christmas. While our soldiers seemed to fare well enough at the front, I got the impression that care and feeding was haphazard at best on the medical trains. He nodded with as much enthusiasm as I'd seen him express about anything since the war broke out.

"Good," I said, and smiled. If he wanted to eat, he wanted to heal, and that was as much as I could hope for.

I exited the room with another kiss to his forehead to find that Mama had already anticipated the need in the kitchen. She stood in front of a massive stockpot, stirring with rapt attention. Wafts of steam danced up from the surface of the soup, encircling her face as she bent her neck to taste her creation. With a deft hand, she added a pinch of salt and continued stirring.

I walked up behind her and kissed her cheek. "Whatever you've concocted there looks wonderful, and your son-in-law would very much like some."

"I've not heard better news in months," she said, patting my hand that rested on her shoulder. "Potato soup with sausage. It's not what he grew up eating, but it will put meat on his bones."

"I'm sure he'll enjoy every bite. Thank you."

"Thank me by eating your own portion once he's had his," Mama replied. She removed a bowl from the cabinet and placed it on a tray. She ladled the soup into the bowl and placed a good-sized hunk of brown bread beside it.

I hadn't thought about food since Harald arrived, but Mama was right. There was no sense in wearing myself down to the point where I was of no use to him.

"Of course," I said, taking the proffered tray from Mama.

Harald had managed to scoot himself into something closer to a seated position in anticipation of his meal. I placed the tray on my nightstand and helped him finish what he'd started. Once he was fully upright and his pillows were fluffed, I began to spoon the thick soup into his mouth slowly. It was just as well he wasn't in any condition to feed himself. I could see the impatience in his eyes as I offered him spoonfuls at slow intervals to ensure I wasn't going to cause his system any distress. I broke off a chunk of bread after the fourth spoonful of soup and handed it to him. He placed the entire piece in his mouth and only chewed as an afterthought.

"You'll choke if you keep that up," I warned, but doled out the soup a little faster once he showed that he could handle the viscous liquid without too much trouble.

His color was improved dramatically by the solitary bowl of soup, and there was something of the usual sparkle in his eyes once I helped him recline back into a supine position.

I wanted to question him. The list I had for him could have gone on for hours, but his need for rest was the only thing greater than my need for answers, so I limited myself to one.

"Tell me what hurts, *Knuddelbär*. Let me help you get well."

"Everything, *mein Liebling*," he replied with a stronger voice. "From my hair to my toenails. Everything hurts, but nothing so much as my heart. If I were more of a praying man, I would use every prayer to beg that you never have to see the things I saw in that hell."

CHAPTER TWENTY

The Garden Path

BETH

May 10, 2007
Encinitas, California

I took Dad outside to enjoy the sunshine. He always grumbled that I shouldn't go to the trouble, as he had to be escorted with every step he took. He stooped forward to relieve the pressure on the nerves in his spine, which made walking perilous, even indoors. The paving stones in the garden, no matter how well maintained, still made the journey nearly impossible for him. But at the end of the slow, arduous walk was a chair in the sun to welcome his weary bones. Each time we ventured outside, I saw the tension fade from his face, and he looked at least fifteen years younger. When I was a girl, I used to joke that my father was part cat. He was always seeking out the sliver of sunshine in the house on the rare cloudy days. On lazy Sundays, he preferred to nap on a lounge chair in the backyard instead of on the sofa or in bed. It probably contributed to some of the lines on his face, but I didn't think he'd have traded those lines for a single moment of his sun-filled past.

Especially now, when venturing out into the sun took as much effort as a considerable hike used to.

"You really loved her, didn't you?"

Dad nodded. "And even if it was just a boyhood infatuation, there was the baby. I couldn't bear the thought of the child being fatherless. Growing up and resenting me for my absence."

"I'm sure Margarethe explained things," I said, wondering if Dad had been worrying over people who had no chance of being found. So many civilians died and were never accounted for that it was beginning to seem like the most likely scenario.

"That doesn't make it right," he said, as though this were explanation enough. And to him, it was. Dad had always been the most involved father at school. Every concert, recital, science fair, or school play, he was there in the front row, even when none of the other fathers were. It occurred to me now that his involvement in my life growing up wasn't just out of devotion to me. He was also parenting the child that was lost to him. There would never be any convincing Dad that he hadn't shirked his duty.

"We'll find them, Dad. And when we do, I'll tell my brother or sister that you parented me enough for the both of us." I hoped the promise wasn't an empty one, but James and I would certainly explore every road that we thought might lead to Margarethe.

Dad patted my hand, but his expression didn't relax with my assurances.

"Thank you for doing this, Beth." He pulled his wrap tighter around himself despite the summer sun. "It means more than I can express. Please don't spend too much of your downtime on this, though."

"It's important to me too, Dad," I said.

"Even so," he said, "I ought to have dug around on my own when the internet became so popular. I shouldn't have left this up to you. But I knew it would upset your mother."

"You do realize that if the baby survived, he or she is likely my only family after you're gone, right?" I replied. "You've actually given me a gift, Dad. The hope that I might have an honest-to-God relative after you pass away." It was a long shot that I'd find my half sibling, but having some sort of biological tie in the world was a comfort.

"I never wanted to leave you alone, Bethie," he said. "I really hoped you and Greg would have been able to work things out."

"Dad, if there's one thing I learned from my marriage, it's that it's perfectly possible to be married and alone. Lonely. Even when he's in the same room."

"I'm sorry that's a lesson you had to learn." Dad looked solemn, though he leaned back to absorb the sun. "I can't say your mother and I didn't have our moments . . . but it was never like that."

"I know, Dad," I said. I'd seen them live almost forty years of their married lives together. It was like watching a well-choreographed dance. Each one knew their steps; each one knew when to lead and when to follow. Like the best dancers, they highlighted each other's skills rather than showcasing their own. They might have missed a beat in the music every now and again, but no one watching them go through life together would think that their dance was anything less than beautiful to watch.

"So, forgive a busybody, but what is this project you two have been working on?" Kimberly asked, swooping in beside me after I took Dad inside to use the facilities.

I explained about the missing love and the baby.

"I was just talking with Naomi over at the care home on Vine Street," she said. There were several care homes like these owned by the same organization. The caretakers were often in communication and covered shifts for one another frequently, so I'd come to know quite a few staff members. "There's an older German lady who spent a lot of time hunting for her sister. Her sons have helped her a lot. Maybe she can give you some help?"

"Anything would be worth a shot," I said. "Who knows what resources they might have."

"I'll get ahold of Naomi and see if we can't arrange a visit. If nothing else, the visit will do them both a lot of good. I worry about Max. He's been withdrawing, and that's never a good sign. Maybe reminiscing over the old days will bring him back to himself."

I was doubtful but didn't want to quash Kimberly's hopes. If nothing else, he'd be cheered at the prospect of new company. "You're wonderful, Kimberly. We're lucky to have you."

"There's more to my job than bandaging wounds and serving dinner, honey. And it's a happy day when I get to remind myself of that."

CHAPTER TWENTY-ONE

FOUND

MAX

March 8, 1945
Near Remagen, Germany

"My God," was all I could think to say. Margarethe's face was like a holy apparition in the midst of grime and death.

"Max," she breathed once more.

In ten strides, I crossed the hospital to her and scooped her up in my arms. Regulations, orders, and good judgment be damned. I lowered my lips to kiss her, and she didn't pull away from the embrace.

"I never thought I'd see you again," I murmured into her halo of blond hair once I had resurfaced for air. "You're alive. You're safe."

"Alive," she corrected. "None of us is safe. I thought the same, though I looked for you whenever I managed to come close to a hospital. It was rare, but I always hoped."

I held her tighter as I considered the risk that entailed. "I'm just glad to hold you. Where have you been?"

"Working as much as I can for the cause without raising suspicion. It's getting harder now that our side is beginning to see the truth. There is no path to a German victory with the Americans and British to the west and the Russians to the east. And thank God for that. I just fear that Hitler will have us fight to the last man, woman, and child."

"It seems his style," I admitted. "But enough of the damn war. Are you all right?"

"As can be expected," she said.

I stepped back a pace to look at her. The swelling at her midsection registered with me. She gazed intently at my face as comprehension flooded my expression.

"How far along?" I whispered.

"Five months or so," she said. My mental calculations must have been plainly visible on my face.

"Is it mine?" I asked.

"I pray nightly that she is," she said. "It's possible. Probable, if my instincts are right. Though there is enough possibility that my husband is the father to keep us safe."

I flinched at the idea of her in another man's arms but was perversely glad that he didn't have reason to suspect her of this. Between Heide's warning that he was a "bad man" and Margarethe's few references, I felt like I had the measure of him. Power hungry and controlling, he was the sort to see his beautiful young wife as a possession to be guarded jealously. He would not be the kind, tolerant type who would sympathize with a woman who was too often left alone in uncertain times. I sensed there would be a lot of husbands returning to the States who would have to manfully pretend a child had been born too early or didn't bear too close a resemblance to the mailman or the plumber. It wasn't just the soldiers who found comfort in the arms of a convenient lover.

"She?" I asked. "How can you know?"

"It's more of a hope, really. I can't bear the thought of mothering a soldier. You must do me a favor and write to your mother. Often."

"I write weekly," I said, holding up a hand as though making a solemn oath. "I'll write to her again tonight and tell her all about the beautiful woman who will make her a grandmother in a few short months. She'll be thrilled."

"Truly?" Margarethe's brow arched in disbelief.

"She might prefer that you were a Jewish girl, but she won't let her disappointment get in the way of loving her grandchild. She doesn't have enough family left to cast any aside willy-nilly."

"Is it possible to *become* Jewish?" she asked. "So many have disappeared . . . having one more in the world might be a small step in the right direction. Two, actually."

I blinked, taking in the massive sacrifice she was suggesting. It meant coming to Los Angeles, marriage, spending a life together. Joining my tribe at the cost of the only family and home she'd ever known.

"It's not impossible," I said. The process to convert wasn't an easy one, but I knew Rabbi Rosenberg was a good and reasonable man, and a patriot. He would be sympathetic under the circumstances. "You'll like our rabbi. He'll be kind to you for my sake. No reasonable man could refuse free dental care for his four children, besides."

Her eyes sparkled as she laughed. "It is good to know I can still laugh."

"What are we going to do?" I asked. "How can we keep you safe?"

"There is no such thing," she replied, her face growing stony. "And I must continue my work. It's more important now than ever. It can only be a matter of months. Weeks or days, if there is a merciful God."

I wanted to share in her optimism, but I'd seen too many successful drives fall short of their objectives. I'd seen too many missions that were supposed to take hours take weeks. It was the way of war. It was a beast that feasted on time and flesh.

"Margarethe, you have to think of the baby. I can't have you putting yourself at risk knowing that you carry our child," I said. "Please. Let me see if I can get you sent to France. Maybe as a volunteer for the

Red Cross. I don't have much clout, but I can use what I have to keep you safe."

"I can't just abandon my work," she insisted.

"I'm not asking you to abandon your service altogether," I insisted. "You can still help the war effort. You're smart. You could be trained up as a nurse's aide in no time. You'd be providing an invaluable service to the war wounded."

"What I do is too important. Every man we convince to lay down his arms is another gun that isn't pointed at your head, Max."

"It is important," I agreed. "And therefore, too dangerous for the woman I love. I beg you, Margarethe. Don't leave me to wonder again if you're alive or dead. I can't bear it. I'm not asking you to go sit in my mother's living room and knit socks. I know that isn't who you are. For God's sake, think of our baby. There have to be others who can take over your work for you."

"I will think about it," she said. "But unless I can find someone I trust to continue my work, I cannot leave. I may be risking two lives, but it's for the chance to save thousands."

I inhaled and counted to ten. I wanted to argue. I wanted to put her in the first truck headed west with instructions to keep her safe, even if it meant locking her in a prison cell until the last bullet was fired. "That seems reasonable." I nearly choked on the words, but there was no use in trying to keep her from doing what she felt was right. What I knew was right.

"I should go, my love," she whispered. "I will be missed if I am not back by sunset. I am expected home tonight."

"Your husband," I said, remembering Heide's last words to me. I swallowed back bile at the thought of Margarethe in another man's arms.

She nodded. "And I better not hear of you trying to seek him out. He's not worth getting killed for."

I wasn't sure her assertion was true, but I let it pass. "Before you go, I have a small favor to ask of you."

"Anything, if I can manage it," she said.

I took her to the edge of the camp and dashed to my barracks, where my Kodak was wrapped in a spare shirt. I disentangled it and returned to where she waited.

"Miller," I called to a young medic who looked in need of a reprieve. "I need you for three minutes."

He set his clipboard aside and joined us. He assessed Margarethe, who was clearly German, but had the good sense not to ask questions of a senior officer.

I handed him the camera with a brief tutorial, then looked for a small chunk of the world that wasn't littered with the paraphernalia of war and that sat in good light. I positioned Margarethe against a plain house that was now being used for convalescent care. The sun bounced off her curls and made her already radiant glow look all the more resplendent. What I wouldn't have given for color film to capture it properly. I wrapped my arm around her, gave Miller the order to snap the photo, and smiled.

"There, now when I find someplace to develop my pictures, I can send my mother proof that I'm in love with the most beautiful woman in the world and am in good health all at once."

"She will be grateful for the latter at least," she assured me.

"I have no idea how long I'll be here," I warned her. "Likely a few weeks, but I can't be sure. You need to find your replacement fast. I can pull whatever strings I have to get you sent to France, but it will need to be soon, or we risk losing contact again."

"I'll work as fast as I can, my love. I swear it. Now kiss me before I go so I have something to keep in my heart until we see each other again."

I obliged, drinking in a long, sweet kiss before I reluctantly let her go back into the weak late-afternoon sunshine. My arms felt empty as I watched her walk away, always cautious to look over her shoulder for those who wished her ill. She should never have known such fear, and I swore then, I would never allow her to know it again.

CHAPTER TWENTY-TWO

LION IN THE DEN

JOHANNA

June 13, 1943
Berlin, Germany

"*Liebling*, you mustn't try to do too much," I chided, seeing Harald working to sit up in bed as I entered with his morning meal. He'd been home for only one week, and while he was much improved, he was not in good enough health to risk overexerting himself. I placed the tray with his supper on the bedside table and rushed to help him finish getting into position.

"I can manage," he said, his tone dry and humorless. He winced as he adjusted his position so he could sit closer to upright.

"Please let me help," I said, sitting on the edge of the bed and placing my hand on his thigh.

"It's maddening," he said, leaning his head back against the headboard. "I feel useless. I hate having you wait on me hand and foot like a housemaid."

"It's what a loving wife does for her husband in his hour of need. And if the situation were reversed, I know you'd do the same for me."

He didn't reply, but his expression relaxed into one of resignation. "How are things at work?" he asked, steering the conversation away from himself.

"Strained," I said. I had all but stitched my Aryan equivalency papers to my forehead per Harald's instructions. I always kept them on my person, in a breast pocket rather than a handbag whenever possible. It wasn't the question of my status that created the tension, though, but the war itself. The lines on the commanders' faces grew deeper each week, their conversations more curt. Though I was told little, I sensed the war wasn't going well for us now that the Americans were truly in the fray to bolster the beleaguered British and French troops.

"To be expected," he said. "I only saw one small slice of the war, but if it was representative of what's going on elsewhere, we're in trouble. We'll need to dominate the skies if we have any prayer of saving our skins."

"The papers don't make things out to be so dire," Mama said, coming in to place a helping of cake on his tray. Rations were getting sparser and sparser, but Mama still managed to make miracles from flour, eggs, and sugar and iced them with hope.

"Well, the papers aren't interested in reporting the truth, are they?" Harald retorted. "They have to report what the party says, or they'll be shuttered in a heartbeat and half the staff never to be heard from again. They only exist to serve the party now, and never think otherwise."

"You've got to keep comments like that to yourself this afternoon," I warned. "Metta may be bringing Ansel with her."

Harald rolled his eyes at the mention of the visit we'd all been equal parts thrilled for and terrified about. "I'll have to watch my mouth even if he doesn't come. Metta can't be trusted any more than he can. He'll pump her for information about us and our beliefs the minute he sees her."

"That doesn't mean she'll tell him anything," I said loyally. She was my darling sister, after all. I could sooner imagine a spotted tiger or a striped leopard than her betraying us.

"You must assume that she will," Harald said, employing the stern voice he used for university students who had failed to meet his expectations. "Our lives may depend on it."

I pursed my lips but said nothing. What he was saying was unthinkable. But also the most prudent course of action.

Had Ansel succeeded in converting Metta over to the party's way of thinking? Would Ansel be able to turn her so completely against us? The question was too terrible to ponder, so I set about tidying the house with the energy of a restless hummingbird.

Metta and Ansel were set to arrive at noon for lunch, though given the nature of Ansel's position, they warned us that his plans could never be more than tentative. I was torn as to the outcome I desired. I wanted to have some time alone with Metta to see how she was doing but also wanted to see how she and Ansel had settled in together. Seeing their reactions to each other might be more telling than her words.

At noon precisely, both Metta and Ansel were on the front stoop. Metta greeted me with a bottle of French wine, a basket of cheeses and fruit, and a long hug. She seemed stronger than she had the last time we embraced, and I considered that a positive for her relationship. She was being well cared for, at least in the physical sense.

Ansel greeted us with formal handshakes, as he had done at every prior meeting. He wore the same serious expression as always, but there was a palpable air of exhaustion that extended from the dark rings under his eyes down to the tips of his weary toes stuffed into polished uniform boots.

The conversation never went beyond mundane matters like the weather as we shared the pork chops and fried potatoes that Mama and I had made. Harald kept to his bed, but we left the door open so he could listen in on the conversation if he chose to.

"You don't seem to be suffering with the new round of rationing," Ansel said with satisfaction. He'd taken notice of our comfortable food stores and our clothing, which was still in good repair.

"Oh, it was just the two of us until Harald came home," Mama said. "Two resourceful women can run a comfortable household on precious little if they've a mind to. I certainly wouldn't object to an extra fifty grams of sugar now and again, but sacrifices must be made."

"Well said," Ansel said approvingly. "And I'll see what I can do about getting you a bit of extra sugar and flour. We must be careful with our supplies, of course, but you are doing the Reich a great service by caring for Harald at home."

"That's very kind of you," I said. I glanced over at Metta, whose expression betrayed nothing. Was this a gesture she had expected? One he had made to others? "Speaking of Harald, why don't we take our coffee in with him? I know it's a bit unusual, but I'm sure he'd love to see you both."

Ansel would have preferred to take his coffee at the table, it was clear, but he gave an impassive nod. I'd moved three chairs from the sitting room into the bedroom, leaving barely enough space to maneuver, but it at least gave Harald a chance to be part of the visit.

"You look like you're being well looked after, *Leutnant*. This is good news," Ansel said, shaking Harald's proffered hand.

"I have the two best nurses in all Germany," Harald boasted.

"Naturally your wife and mother-in-law are the most attentive caretakers possible," he said. "I hope this means you'll be ready to return to duty soon."

"We shall see what the doctors say next Thursday. They seemed to think it would be weeks," Harald cautioned.

"For active service, that is quite right, *Leutnant*. But I have been inquiring after other opportunities that would be better suited to your skills. My superiors agree that your talents would be put to better use as an educational adviser. It would keep you out of harm's way, but you would still be of service to your country and the Führer. Does that seem agreeable to you?"

"That seems like a good use for your talents," I interjected despite my better judgment. Anything that would keep him away from the front lines. Anything to keep him kilometers from artillery fire.

Harald shot me a warning glance. Such an appointment would put him directly in the path of some of the biggest names in the party. His every move would be scrutinized for as long as he held the post. It might have seemed safer on the surface, but in truth it was no less dangerous than the vast territories to the east that tried to repel us back to Berlin. But to refuse Ansel's offer would be tantamount to suicide.

"I would consider it an honor, *Obersturmbannführer*, when the doctors think I am equal to the work."

"I knew you were a sensible man, *Leutnant*. I am pleased to be proven right."

CHAPTER TWENTY-THREE

WAVES

BETH

May 12, 2007
San Diego, California

An hour or two after dawn, I lowered the hatchback on my Prius, beach bag and umbrella in tow, and padded off toward Scripps Beach. I'd wrestled with what to do with my weekend for hours the night before and kept circling back to the lure of the beach. It had been so long since I'd lain out on the sand or swum in the ocean, I actually had to stop at a big-box store for a proper beach towel and flip-flops. I still had a two-piece suit and a sarong from the cruise Greg had taken me on a couple of years back, but I'd not worn them since. It was cliché . . . the New Yorker who never went to the theater, the Denverite who didn't ski, and me, the San Diegan who never went to the beach.

The sand rubbed between the soles of my feet and my newly purchased purple flip-flops that clashed horribly with my red suit and blue towel. Just as well—if everything looked coordinated, it would be obvious that I never went to the beach. It was enough that the crowds hadn't amassed yet. Only a handful of the most dedicated beachgoers had begun to converge.

I laid out my towel and pitched my umbrella, then fumbled for the paperback I'd bought as an afterthought at the checkout aisle. I'd agonized between a popular zombie novel and a Tudor historical with the omnipresent lavish-dress cover, bypassing altogether the romances with Regency-era belles draped in the arms of open-shirted men. I selected the historical, trusting that the political intrigue would overshadow any flowerier aspects of the story line.

For fifteen minutes, the book lay unheeded by my side as I absorbed the sun and listened only to the gentle rumbling roar of the waves. I let go, for a precious few moments, of all that had held my mind and body captive for the past months . . . Dad's health, Mom's passing, the search for the mysterious German woman, work, and all the mundane details of daily life. There was nothing but the gentle breeze lapping over my skin like silk and the occasional cawing of some far-off gulls. It had been too long since I had let myself simply be.

I opened my eyes, now toying with the notion of taking up meditation and yoga on a regular basis and wondering if a more Californian idea had ever been thought. I reached for the book and decided to see if it could captivate my attention.

"You looked so peaceful, I didn't want to disturb you," a voice said from my right. James had perched in the sand a couple of feet from me, and I hadn't even perceived his presence. Instead of trunks and flip-flops, which were the unofficial uniform of men on the beach, he was in a blue wet suit that accentuated his strong chest.

"I was," I said, grateful that he hadn't startled me out of my trance.

"It's nice to see you out of the library," he said. "I got the impression you weren't much of a beach person."

"I used to be," I said, thinking of all the summers in Hawaii and the countless beach trips closer to home. "I fell out of the habit."

It was more or less the truth. Greg was so fair that he didn't care for spending hours in the sun worrying about his next application of sunscreen. He also loathed sand and would spend a solid hour vacuuming his car after each trip. He never complained, but I could see it wasn't all that enjoyable for him, so I stopped suggesting it after a while.

"Do you surf?" he asked.

"Never have," I admitted. Dad didn't know how, and Mom wasn't keen on me learning.

"Care for a lesson?" He motioned to a group of people closer to the waterline, all of whom had boards in tow. "The waves are perfect for a beginner."

"I don't have a wet suit," I said. "And you're here to have fun. Don't slow yourself down with a newbie like me."

"You'll always be a newbie unless you learn," he reasoned. "And how else will I get you to come on a surfing vacation with me someday? Watching from the shore won't be fun for you. I'm sure one of my friends has a suit you can use."

I felt the color rise in my cheeks at the intimate implication but managed not to stammer something offhand and embarrass myself. I looked out at the water where several of his friends had managed to catch waves and were riding them with a skill that must have taken years to acquire. It was mesmerizing to watch them glide over the waves as though the boards were extensions of their feet. I wanted to voice a refusal, that I'd make a fool out of myself in front of his friends and take away from his enjoyment of the day, but I nodded yes in spite of myself.

"That's the spirit," he said, offering me his hand. Before I knew it, my stuff was gathered up and I was integrated into a circle with his surfer friends, who were all discussing the conditions for surfing as seriously as stock traders discussing dips and surges in the market. One woman, probably ten years younger than me with a toothy smile, lent me a spare wet suit. I wrangled my way into the suit, and James took a step closer to slowly pull up the zipper. Our eyes caught for a moment, but I looked away before I could read into his expression.

"You'll want to use my longboard," he said. "They're actually easier for beginners than the short ones."

It seemed contrary to logic, but I trusted in his expertise. He had me lie on the board in the sand to practice form and how to pop up once I caught a wave. Once I mastered that, we paddled around in the shallows. He called instructions for me to move forward and back on my board to get the proper balance, and despite my newness to the sport, I didn't feel completely inept.

"Think you're ready to try catching a wave?" he asked after an hour or so of coaching.

"No time like the present," I responded, sounding more confident than I felt.

"Attagirl," he said. "Let's do it. I'll be as close as I can safely be in case you fall."

I nodded and paddled in the direction of the wave. I popped up at what I thought was the correct moment and managed to stay standing for a few seconds before wiping out. The sensation was unsettling and surreal . . . and positively breathtaking.

"You OK?" James called as I pulled on the tether to recover the board.

"Fine," I said. "It was amazing for the two seconds I managed to stand."

"You stood on your first wave. That's pretty damn amazing, actually."

As we waded back into the shallows, he held his hand up for me to slap.

"I understand why you like this so much," I said. "It's quite a rush."

"I hope you'll come out with me often, then. I think the ocean and you get along nicely."

I flashed him a smile and couldn't disagree.

CHAPTER TWENTY-FOUR

As Light Returns

MAX

March 10, 1945
Near Remagen

I tasted the metallic tinge of fear on the tip of my tongue but kept walking forward. She had to come. If I missed her today, we might never have the chance to smuggle her out again.

The possibility of Margarethe being watched was too great for us to risk any sort of real contact. I began to calculate the probability that she would be detained by her husband or somehow kept from the rendezvous point I'd jotted down in a note two days ago. My chest tightened as though caught in a steel vise. It was a battle to keep my breath even and my expression calm.

At length, not long before I was due to return to my post in the hospital, Margarethe approached. She wore her best coat and a traveling suit that made her look like a smart young matron embarking on a European tour. Not a hair out of place . . . a far cry from the impish girl in a dirty boy's costume I'd seen in the woods. Her lips were pressed in a firm line, and I guessed that she was gathering the courage to make her departure. Though it was clear she had no desire to stay with her husband, she was leaving others behind.

Margarethe spoke so rarely about herself that she was still a mystery in many respects, but she had mentioned her family several times. Not individual family members, but her family as a unit. She'd spoken about her mother but no one else in detail. She might have brothers and sisters, nieces and nephews, that I never would. Perhaps even a beloved aunt or uncle that it would break her heart to leave behind. Not to mention dear friends. My parents had done the same, and I knew the pain it still caused them decades later. I would spend the rest of my life trying to repay her for that sacrifice. I would do what I could to reunite them, if such a thing were possible. I wished I could protect them all for her sake, but I was risking my career and my freedom, perhaps even my life, to see her safely away from her husband and the rest of the Nazi thugs he yoked himself to.

I walked north along the cobblestone street as she headed south. There was little left, aside from bombed-out ruins and haunted-looking people. We slowed as we reached each other, pausing just long enough to speak a few words as we got within earshot.

"Good morning, sir. Do you need to see my papers?" she asked in English, her accent thicker than it was by nature. Her brow was creased, and she bit at her lip, adding to the illusion that she was merely a worried German citizen who'd encountered an Allied soldier.

"Yes, please," I said. She fumbled with her handbag and produced her identification. I made a show of examining it thoroughly, then reached into my pocket for a small notebook.

"What is your business in this area?" I asked, opening to a blank page and taking notes, as though I were making an official record.

"Simply hoping to buy some rations. They're harder and harder to come by, sir." She sounded convincingly like a frightened citizen of an invaded country.

"Captain," I corrected. "I don't think you'll have much luck in this area, but you're free to go."

I handed her back her identification papers, discreetly passing the travel papers I'd secured for her along with them. "Tomorrow afternoon," I whispered. "Bring those and the rest of the information to the base."

The plan was a simple one. I'd secured travel papers for her, but those could still be rejected for nearly any reason. Our safeguard was information. Given Margarethe's access to a high-ranking SS guard, we'd decided she would find some bit of information in his files to present to the American authorities. It didn't have to be anything especially incriminating, but interesting enough to make protecting her worthwhile. The end of the war was in sight, all but won unless Hitler had a hidden army lurking in Berlin. Any German citizen who offered reasonably credible information that might end the war even sooner was almost a certain case for amnesty. Margarethe was to report to the authorities at the border and, with any luck, be granted amnesty and refugee status. It might be an uncomfortable few months for her, but she would be safe.

She nodded, her jaw set firmly. She offered no farewell.

I longed to kiss her. To tell her how much I loved her and how well I would take care of her.

Instead, I let her pass and continue on her way.

A week later, a letter was delivered to my bunk covered in Margarethe's familiar script. It hadn't gone through the post, so I had no idea who had left the note. Hastily, I tore into the envelope, praying it spoke of her safe arrival in France.

Max,

By the time you read this letter, I will be gone. Someone else who needed your government's protection far more than I do has taken my place. Know that I am safe and well. I will do all I can to find you before long. I will keep our child safe for you in hopes that we can raise her to be a force for good in a world given to evil. Forgive me, darling. I will find you when the long night ends and we are all returned to the light.

All my love,
Margarethe

CHAPTER TWENTY-FIVE

BACK TO BATTLE

JOHANNA

July 5, 1943
Berlin, Germany

Once again, we stood in our tiny bedroom in our little cottage on the lake, and I had to play the dutiful wife sending her husband to war. Harald was summoned to report for his new assignment, just three weeks after Ansel made the offer. Though he was ghostly pale and winced when he walked more than twenty paces, the doctors cleared him for duty. No doubt they'd been ordered to do so. Harald was ashen faced as he donned his new uniform, and my cheeks matched the starched linen of his shirt.

"Perhaps you can effect change from within. Maybe some of these men are more reasonable than we fear." It was a grasping hope—like trying to cling to blades of grass in a hurricane—but it was the closest thing to comfort I could offer him.

"Your optimism seems to have given way to foolishness, *Liebchen*," he said as he buttoned the calves of his pants that fit snugly inside the requisite jackboots. "They are nothing but meat-headed thugs with only enough brainpower to march over innocent people."

He spoke the unvarnished truth, and I admired him too much to refute it.

"All the same, there isn't much choice." I busied my hands folding a spare shirt and adding it to his case, for fear I'd begin wringing them and make this all the worse for him. "Do what you must to survive, Harald. Just do all you can to come home to me."

"There's the sensible girl I know and love. A glimmer of candor." He pulled on the gleaming black boots, though he never looked directly at them. He stood, and I barely recognized the man I married. Gone was the man of grace and elegance, and in his place stood a man who was dressed to be part of the war machine. The uniforms were designed to be sleek and evoke a sort of nobility. The effect on Harald, a man who wore nobility as gracefully as a bespoke suit, was just heavy and brutish.

"I'm just sorry it has to be this way," I said, unable to look at him as he adjusted his various pins and medals. "You ought to be back in the classroom doing what you were born to do."

"That's the last place they want me," he said. "I'm as dangerous to them in the classroom as the Allies are to them in a tank. They've given me this position to keep an eye on me and to keep me under their boot."

"Better under their boot than in front of a firing squad," I said, mustering the courage to look up. "Just get through this and we can set about mending what these brutes have done after the war is over."

"As you say," he replied, examining his uniformed reflection in a mirror, grimacing. "Though God knows what will be left to mend. At some point, even the most skilled tailor will abandon tattered trousers to the scrap heap."

"Germany is still worth saving, my love. She isn't ready for the scrap heap just yet."

"I pray nightly that you're right, *Liebchen*. If that is true, then there is still hope. Where there is hope, there can still be peace."

I smoothed the shoulders of his uniform and kissed his freshly shaved cheek that still smelled of the spice and leather of his good soap. He wasn't a soldier; he was a poet. A philosopher. He had as much business being sent to war as a cabinetmaker being sent to design airplane engines.

As I kissed him goodbye, I could see tears looming in the corners of his eyes. He didn't need to speak to tell me what caused his heart to ache in this moment. It had been defensible in his mind to serve in the Wehrmacht. No matter who was in power politically, Germany was still worth defending. But to be part of Hitler's SS guard, as he was now, was tantamount to wholesale approval of the Führer's politics and methods. He was now forced to abandon his principles to save his very life.

"Don't forget who you are, Harald," I said. "You're a good man."

"We'll see how long they allow that to last, *Liebchen*."

⌇

The one blessing about Harald's new assignment was that he was able to come home most nights, though rarely in time for dinner. He'd taken to casting off his uniform at the door, unwilling to pollute more of the house than the entryway with it, falling into bed for a few hours of restless sleep, then stumbling back out to the entryway to dress and return to work at first light. I could feel him growing leaner as I held him in my arms each night. The layer of flesh over his ribs grew more meager with each passing day, but there was no convincing him to take a meal when he returned home, nor even a proper breakfast in the morning before he left.

"He refused my fried eggs and good sausage this morning," Mama said, shaking her head. "It was almost as good as a breakfast before the war. I had thought certainly it would tempt him."

Mama fretted about him every morning over coffee, lamenting that he wouldn't accept so much as a slice of toast with butter and jam before he left. It was the same refrain each morning, and while she only echoed the sentiments of my heart, to hear her speak them aloud did nothing to ease my worries. It only served to make me feel more useless in finding a solution to them.

"Eat the eggs, save the sausage," I ordered. After a month of his service, I no longer had the heart to commiserate with her on the matter. "I'm going into the office."

She looked at the clock on the wall. Not quite seven in the morning. To Mama's credit, she swallowed her rebuke at the hour. The long days I was putting in were scarcely less demanding than Harald's. The office was the only place where my mind could take proper refuge from the distress I felt about Harald and the state of the war in general, or whether I even felt I wanted Germany to win it. She clicked her teeth around her censure and tucked into the eggs I'd refused.

I stowed my bicycle at the entrance of the office. It was so early that there was no hum of activity. Only the soft footsteps of the cleaning crew who had come to ensure the facility was gleaming before the arrival of the commanding officers and a few mechanics who worked the earliest shifts. Louisa was the only other member of the senior staff on site. Her eyes widened a moment upon seeing me, but she bit back any derisive comment she might have had. Perhaps she knew Harald was serving again and understood my need for refuge in my work. Perhaps she'd grown a tad kinder over the course of the war. In either case, I wasn't going to risk encouraging her barbed tongue by taking notice of the change in her demeanor.

"I was hoping you'd arrive early again today. I'm glad to see you, *Flugkapitän*." She walked over to the entrance where I was shaking the dust from my boots.

"Well, that's a turn of events for you," I said, immediately regretting the words. I shook my head at my own tongue. "Forgive me, what can I do for you, *Flugkapitän* Mueller?"

"I was hoping for a private word in your office," she said, her tone low.

She stood straight, almost at attention, as she made her request. Whatever the matter was, it was important, at least to her interests. I led her to my small corner of the complex and motioned for her to take the seat opposite mine.

I leaned back in my chair and threaded my fingers in anticipation of what she might possibly want to discuss.

"Johanna," she said, using my given name for perhaps the first time in our acquaintance. It sounded absolutely strange coming from her lips. "This war has been exacting an enormous toll on Germany. On all of us. I fear that the path to victory has been growing ever narrower and that we cannot sustain a series of drawn-out battles long enough to reach that objective. If Germany is to win, we must strike definitively. Hit as many key military targets as possible in a short period of time— less than twenty-four hours if it can be managed. It would have to be perfectly choreographed, and there would be no room for error."

She wasn't wrong. If Germany had any chance of winning, we would have to end the war soon. It was merely a question of numbers. We might have technology that was the envy of the world. We might have the keenest strategic minds on the planet. But America and Russia still had men. A seemingly endless supply of them. "Very well, Louisa," I said, her name sounding equally awkward on my own tongue. "I'm not sure why you're bringing this up to me of all people. I'm an engineer and test pilot. If you have suggestions for strategy, take them to command."

She had the ear of Hitler himself. How I could be of any use to her I didn't know.

"Well, first, I will need your expertise to make sure the bombsights on our aircraft are as close to perfect as we can make them. That's something I cannot do. For another, your dive-bombing techniques are the best in the Luftwaffe. I want you to train an elite force of men for this mission. And most important, your support will be imperative in getting this plan approved. You have more clout than you realize, and an endorsement from you could mean the difference in getting this plan off the ground—excuse the pun—or not."

"So, what precisely do you have in mind?" I asked, an ache forming at the top of my gut. She wouldn't be hedging if the plan were a simple one.

"There would be no room for error," she repeated from her earlier speech. "We would coordinate an attack against all the key military targets—all of them—in short order. We would have an elite team of volunteer bombers who would ensure that their targets are destroyed. It would create such pandemonium that the Allies and Russians would be paralyzed. Once they're weakened to such a degree, victory just might be within reach again."

"An ambitious plan," I said, thinking the upper echelon would be enthusiastic to hear the specifics. "But how would you ensure that each run is successful? Even the best bombers miss their targets at times."

"If the pilot flies his plane into the target, there will be much less room for error. The only way the pilots would fail is if they're shot down before they reach their objective. In which case we could send several planes at once to ensure that at least one is able to complete the mission."

I sat, unable to do more than blink at what she was suggesting.

"I know it sounds horrific, Johanna. But it would be a sacrifice for the fatherland. These men would give their lives to save thousands, if not millions, more. We wouldn't recruit madmen or radicals. We would find good and true patriots willing to give everything in Germany's hour of need. The same sacrifice every soldier is prepared to make."

"You're just providing them with a great deal more certainty on the subject."

"You think I'm a monster, don't you?" she asked.

"I think you're pragmatic," I said diplomatically. "Ruthlessly so."

"All that matters is a German victory, Johanna. And I'm willing to fly with these men myself if command will approve the plan."

There was sincerity in the icy pools of her blue eyes. She meant to give her life in service to Germany, and I admired her commitment to the cause she held so dear, even if I didn't share her ideals. I'd become quite adept at doing my work while pushing aside its aims. I loved my country and her people, but I hardly recognized either.

"I will only say this, Louisa. I won't speak against it. And if the orders fall on my desk, I will follow them. I can promise you no more."

"That may be enough," she said, drawing her lips in a firm line. It wasn't the endorsement she wanted, but she didn't have to count me as an adversary. She extended her hand and I shook it firmly. She exited to the complex, which was finally beginning to show signs of life.

I wondered if I shouldn't have taken a stronger stance with Louisa. Endorsed her plan or condemned it. But the decision was now in the hands of others, and being absolved of responsibility offered me more comfort than I ought to have admitted.

CHAPTER TWENTY-SIX

Vigil

BETH

May 20, 2007
San Diego, California

"Dad, please wake up," I muttered, perhaps for the millionth time in the space of an hour. Kimberly's call had come at three in the morning. I'd dashed out the door in my pajamas and flip-flops. Greg dozed in the large comfortable chair in the corner, but I pulled up one of the flimsy plastic numbers next to Dad's bed and held his hand, careful not to disturb the alarming number of tubes and wires that seemed to be attached to every inch of exposed skin. The whirring, buzzing, and beeping of the machines kept tabs on more bodily functions than I could name.

"You should try to get some sleep, Beth," Greg mumbled from the chair. I looked over at him and regretted my hasty decision to text him that Dad was in the hospital. My judgment at three in the morning wasn't as sound as it usually was. In my groggy state, I thought he'd want to be present for the ex-father-in-law that he'd held in such regard.

He'd come without complaint, but it was clear from his demeanor that he didn't see much point in being here when Dad was unresponsive.

"I can't," I said. "Not while he's like this."

He sighed and adjusted his position. Within three minutes he'd resumed the deep, even breathing of restful sleep. It was all I could do not to throw a pillow at his head.

Dad had pressed his call button in the night, and the night nurse had found him unresponsive just a few seconds later. The doctors said his blood sugar was dangerously low and spouted on further about other test results that meant little to me.

Around seven, a doctor entered and looked at Dad's chart. He shook his head, replaced the chart in the slot, and examined a few of the monitors Dad was strapped to.

"He's stable for now," was all he said, and turned to leave, never having made eye contact with us.

"Excuse me, Doctor," I called. He turned back, his expression harried. "Do we have any sort of diagnosis? What are you doing to help him?"

"He's ninety years old," he said. "His systems are just wearing out. Nothing much that we can do apart from keeping him comfortable."

"Surely there's more you can do. He was fine yesterday morning," I said. "This seems pretty sudden."

"Sometimes it happens that way. It's better than lingering."

It took every ounce of my restraint not to pull the doctor by the lapels of his pristine lab coat and shake him. "Excuse me, that's my father you're talking about. He's not just some old man."

"You'll forgive my wife, she's tired," Greg said, now sitting up in his chair.

The doctor nodded and headed back out the door to younger patients more worth his time.

"How fucking dare you?" I rounded on Greg. "First of all, I'm not your wife, so don't call me that. Secondly, don't dismiss my concerns in front of medical staff ever again."

"Come on, Beth. You're exhausted and stressed. The doctor is right. And you know Max wouldn't want heroic measures."

"Third, don't you dare presume to tell me what my father would have wanted. Wants," I corrected. I'd convinced him to stay on a few of his more essential medicines as we continued our search for Margarethe and the baby, and his mood had been far more optimistic since we began looking.

"Fine, Beth. Of course you know better." Greg threw off the hospital blanket and slipped his shoes back on. "Clearly you have everything under control here and you don't need me."

"No, I don't. I texted you in a moment of weakness, and I'm sorry to have disturbed your sleep," I said, not bothering to look at him. I had my gaze fixed on Dad's face and willed his eyes to open.

"Look, Beth, I'm sorry. I don't want things to be like this between us. Don't be mad at me."

"I *am* mad, Greg. And I'm not going to accept your apology. You might be sorry that I'm angry, but you don't think you did anything wrong. That was always one of our problems. You were never sorry enough to actually fix what wasn't working."

"And you were in no way to blame here? You weren't being the least bit irrational with an overworked doctor?"

"Demanding care for my father and wanting a real update on his condition isn't irrational. And right now I don't give a fuck if he's overworked, so let's save the debate about the state of our health care system for another day."

Greg shook his head in equal measures of defeat and exasperation and walked out.

"To hell with him," I said, still looking at Dad. "I'm not ready to let you go. You need to wake up, Dad."

I wiped the fresh tears from my cheeks and kissed his knuckles.

I wondered if I was sitting my last vigil with Dad as I had just barely managed to do with Mom the year before. I'd screeched into her room about twenty minutes before she passed. I had been drained from a round of mediation with Greg, and I'd wanted to ignore the call altogether. When I answered, and they warned me that her time was close, I sat, unable to react until a nurse made a second, more frantic call, insisting that the situation was more dire than I was allowing myself to believe. It was only then that I had the courage to get in the Prius and make the trip to Encinitas. The looks on the nurses' faces were stormy as they saw me enter the room. *What could have been more important than this?*

I held her hand as she died, though I couldn't know if she was aware of my presence. Her passing was as calm and dignified as she would have wanted, and that made me happy for her. But she'd been alone so much in the weeks prior, the grief I carried was interwoven with fine strands of guilt. It always would be. I would not bear that same burden with my father.

CHAPTER TWENTY-SEVEN

WHAT REMAINS OF HATE

MAX

April 29, 1945
Near Dachau, Germany

We were ordered to drive our jeeps and tanks northeast of the town of Dachau. The ache in my gut let me know that there was no quaint village or relieved welcome waiting for us. The fighting had all but ceased, but there were still the risks of ambush and guerrilla attacks that were in some sense more terrifying than the monstrous direct attacks we'd faced for the past months. None of us rested well. We were all in dire need of our mothers' cooking, hot showers, and proper beds, and the knowledge that the German war machine was slowing to a halt made the longing for creature comforts all the more acute. We were close enough to victory to see them in our futures.

We were no longer warriors; we were liberators.

The mission was to explore what was happening at the old munitions factory on the outskirts of town. I was hoping for an empty skeleton of a building, but we all worried about an ambush or a fully functional factory pumping life back into the Reich.

The first thing we happened upon was a train stalled in front of the massive factory complex. There was no movement from inside. The silence was heavy, oppressive like the worst humid day in summer where the air is so thick you can hardly breathe. Without being given the command, the men held their rifles at the ready. It was always silent before the worst happened. Major Dawes, our commanding officer, descended from his jeep and took the initiative to open one of the boxcar doors, rifle aimed at whatever awaited us inside. He stumbled back and covered his face with his sleeve.

"Medic!" he screamed.

I stumbled down from my own jeep and dashed forward, a steel band constricting over my heart as I ran. Perhaps he'd taken a blast of some chemical weapon to the face. A booby trap seemed a fitting trick for an army in retreat. Snare a few last victims before defeat.

"What is it, Major?" I said, pulling his sleeve away from his face to assess the damage. His face was intact, though he coughed and sputtered, obviously fighting back the urge to vomit.

My adrenaline subsided as I realized he hadn't been injured. The stench coming from the train finally processed, and I could see why the men within fifteen feet were doubled over. Some were retching, the others on the point of it.

"Clear out," I ordered. The men willingly complied, scattering from the train like bullets spilling from a dropped box of ammunition.

Being unarmed, inspecting the train car meant risking my very life, but the smell of human misery could not go without investigation.

I was rooted to the very spot, my knees locked as if anchored by pillars of concrete. The car was filled with dead bodies. Dozens upon dozens of them. If not hundreds.

"Keep the men at bay," I advised the major. "I don't know how long these poor people have been dead, nor what killed them, but whatever it was might take the rest of us down too."

Major Dawes, now more collected, along with a half dozen other men, opened the doors to the rest of the train cars. Each and every one of them was the same picture of carnage.

"Blumenthal, take your crew and examine the bodies. See if you can get a cause of death. Then we'll see what else is to be done."

I nodded and entered the first of the train cars, having fastened a mask around my face. It was about as effective at blocking the smell as a silk parasol would be at keeping you dry in a typhoon, but it might protect me against any diseases.

There were men, women, and children of all ages in the car. Some appeared to have suffered bullet wounds, while others simply looked too emaciated to live, whether from malnutrition or disease, I couldn't say. None seemed to have been dead more than a couple of days. If we'd reached the camp that much sooner, they might have lived. I began to count the bodies as best I could, given how they were piled on one another. If the other cars were as full as this one, there were over two thousand dead on the train alone.

"Anything conclusive?" Major Dawes asked as I descended from the train.

I shook my head. "Nothing beyond what you can surmise with your own eyes. I'd need a proper lab to determine if any of the ones who weren't shot died from disease."

"Typhus," Captain Richardson called out from across the crowd. "The camp is lousy with it."

We explored the area, unable to take in a full breath, wondering what other horrors awaited us. It wasn't long before we discovered a horde of people staring at us from behind barbed wire fences. They looked frightened, like antelope that had just spotted a lion lying in wait. They had been trained to act like prey animals—that's all they had been to the SS guards that penned them in.

We set to work isolating the ill prisoners from those yet to be infected. There wasn't an inch of camp that was clean enough to be fit for providing medical attention, but we would have to improvise to save the people we could.

We'd heard the news of these death camps. The Russians had liberated several in the east. There was nothing they could have said to prepare us for the grime, the stench, the utter horror of it all. I suspected the poor souls on the train were bound for another camp farther from the advancing Allies. The Germans didn't want a single one of their prisoners liberated by us. Given enough time, no doubt they would have executed them all.

A boy, no older than fourteen, was burning up with fever. Uncomfortably hot to the touch and racked with shivers. He collapsed at my feet, but I had no bed or covers for him. I knelt by his side, reaching for my kit. I pulled out my stethoscope and listened to his chest. The crackling sound of fluid in his lungs was clear as church bells in my ears. That they were still taking in air was miraculous. Advanced pneumonia, likely as a result of the typhus that had swarmed the camp and laid waste to it like clouds of hungry locusts.

"What can we do for them?" Hansen, a junior medic fresh from basic training, asked.

"Nothing," I told him. "Keep them separate from the others and pray it doesn't spread further. This lot will either get well, or they won't. There isn't much else to be done."

The young medic looked horrified at his own uselessness. He was maybe four years older than the boy who lay before me, probably having joined up with the delusions of becoming a hero in the last moments of the war.

"You can comfort them," I said. "Be with the ones who aren't going to make it. God only knows they could use a bit of compassion after the hell they lived."

The medic knelt on the other side of the boy and began reciting the Lord's Prayer. I looked into the face of the dying boy and recognized one of my own tribe. He needed the words of his people. Though I'd not said my prayers in many years, the words of the Mi Sheberach flowed back to my memory as clearly as the days when I'd learned them in Hebrew school.

May the one who blessed our ancestors, Abraham, Isaac and Jacob, Sarah, Rebecca, Rachel and Leah, bless and heal those who are ill . . .

There was no telling how many had been left in this squalid camp on the cusp of death, or the number who had spent their last terrified moments in its confines. Was this how my parents' families were killed in Riga? Crammed together like animals, tortured, and left to die? The ones butchered in the streets were probably the lucky ones. I remembered the look on my mother's face when she read the letter from her cousin. She had seen something of this evil before she'd left Latvia, and it was only this evil that had allowed her to give her blessing for me to take up arms.

I was too late for these people. Too late for my own family. But God help me, I'd not live to see this tragedy happen again in my lifetime.

"Captain Blumenthal, some of the prisoners are scattering from the camp. We fear they may be sick with typhus like the others." It was one of the junior medics who had joined the company straight out of boot camp. The sort who complained about joining up after the *"fun"* was all over. They stopped saying that after a few days. "What do we do?"

"Let them go die in whatever way they see fit," I said. "They weren't given the opportunity to live as they pleased, so they can at least have the honor of dying on their own terms. A few lucky ones might pull through."

"But what if the disease spreads to the villages?"

"They knew what was happening here, Lieutenant. They knew and did nothing to stop it. If the typhus claims a few souls, I won't feel a mark on mine over it."

CHAPTER
TWENTY-EIGHT

Vows and Ignorance

JOHANNA

June 18, 1944
Berlin, Germany

Harald sat at the dinner table in pajamas and his dressing gown, as had become his custom. After he shucked his uniform at the door each night, I would collect the pieces and hang them in the coat closet, where he wouldn't have to look at them for the scant hours he got to spend at home. Rather than soil fresh clothes, he took to wearing his nightclothes to the table and falling into bed almost immediately after his meal. It was an odd custom, and one that I feared didn't sit well with Mama, but neither of us said anything to him.

"Louisa's plan is not unique," he said after I divulged the contents of the latest conversation Louisa and I had had on the subject. "More and more, the people in the highest ranks are looking at last-ditch efforts like these. They see that we're losing, but Hitler and his closest cronies will hear nothing of it. They press forward as though our supplies and men are limitless."

Louisa hadn't succeeded in convincing our superiors of the merits of her idea, so my lukewarm promise not to speak against the scheme was no longer enough for her. She wanted my full and unconditional endorsement to help sway our commanders. Though I was a scientist and she a glorified stunt pilot, our sex mandated that we suffer comparison to each other. I'd always had the reputation of being less impulsive than Louisa, though occasionally more reckless behind the throttle. I would grant it to Louisa that she was never one to take unnecessary risks with her aircraft. A moment of showboating could cost her a record, which would do little for her reputation, or that of Germany's aviation program. Because I was behind the curtain, I could test the limits of the equipment without risking more than my own neck.

"How would you have me move forward? I can't bear to think of supporting this atrocity, but I'm not sure it would be wise to be seen opposing any plan the party thinks might stand a chance of working." My honorary Aryan status had been approved, but it would take a mere flick of the right wrist to revoke it.

"You're right on that, Johanna. You mustn't make a fuss. Best to wait and see what's decided before speaking your mind. If they ask you directly for your opinion, be as noncommittal as possible."

"As you say," I replied, though the words were bitter on my tongue. Would I ever be free to have an opinion again that didn't take the party into consideration? Would I ever have the liberty of disagreeing with anyone without fearing for my freedom and safety? My very life?

The air hung heavy over the table, and none of us could find words to lighten it. Asking Harald about his day would be met, quite rightly, with a sullen grunt as he stabbed his food a little too ruthlessly with his fork. He didn't have the energy to inquire after ours, and neither of us could fault him for it.

Mama shooed me from clearing the table when Harald stood with a murmured thanks for the meal. I could hear the dishes clinking in the sink as I joined Harald in bed. For the first time in ages, I felt his arms coil around me as his lips sought out mine in the dark. Gentle, then insistent as I felt his weight shift on top of me. It was not the slow, passionate lovemaking from our past, but something more desperate. He held me down so tightly, I could barely move, so I didn't try. I looked into his eyes, but the Harald I loved was gone. There was no affection in his embrace, only physical need. He found his release after only a few minutes, and I realized that I was, in that moment, completely disinterested in finding my own.

"My God, Johanna. I'm sorry," he whispered a few moments later as he wrapped his arms against me anew and pulled me tight to his chest, tucking me under his chin. I could feel the warm, wet proof of his remorse on the top of my head.

"No need to apologize, my love," I said, kissing his neck.

"It was selfish," he said. "I can't bear being that way with you."

"Don't trouble yourself with such worries right now. I know you love me. It can't be fireworks and champagne every time."

"Don't try to make me feel better, *Liebling*. I deserve to feel horrid. Taking things without regard for others is their way. Not ours. Not mine. You should be furious with me."

"No," I said. "I will do as you ask and not offer you sympathy, but I won't be angry with you. You can't command that, Harald. Even if I were a good, obedient sort of wife. Which I'm not."

"Thank God for that," he said, a throaty chuckle finally rattling loose from his chest. "How dull that must be."

"Deathly," I said. I breathed him in, not that his steel-hard embrace left me much choice. The same clean scent of vetiver soap and new leather that had always clung to him. There was something precious about the things they couldn't steal from us.

"I swear by all I hold dear, I am going to keep you safe from all this," Harald said, his voice already sounding as though he were drifting off to sleep.

"Just keep yourself safe, my love, and I'll fend for myself," I replied.

"There are thousands of dead who thought the same," he said, sounding more alert. "Maybe millions. Something must be done. And if no one else will, it must be me."

"Harald, you're frightening me."

"Don't be frightened," he said. "I will say no more, but if I send you word to hide or run, you must do so. Get in a plane and go to the very ends of the earth if you must."

"Never without you."

"You must promise me, Johanna." He sat up in bed and pulled me up to look him in the eye. "Promise me," he repeated.

"You have my word," I said, reluctant to give it. I wanted so much to demand Harald include me in his plans before consenting to them, but I knew him well enough to see he was on the brink of losing his composure. I acquiesced out of compassion.

He exhaled and relaxed visibly. Within moments he drifted to sleep, less troubled than I had seen him in weeks.

But though this nonconfession of his gave him a measure of comfort, it robbed me of mine.

Harald had a plan, perhaps as unthinkable as Louisa's, and though he tried to protect me with ignorance, I feared it would only serve to make us both more vulnerable when the wolves came to the door.

∽

The order to begin the training necessary for Louisa's plan came down almost immediately after I made my promise to Harald, and I'd lived on a diet of coffee and anxiety in the four weeks since. My opinion hadn't been sought, so at least I hadn't been forced to lie or risk my neck over the horrific endeavor. I was to do all that she required when it came to design work and testing, but she would be training the men herself. Thank heaven for that small mercy. But I was at her beck and call when it came to design and testing. My clothes hung on me like wash on a line, and my cheekbones looked razor sharp, but I managed to make an appearance at the office each day.

"The planes have been delayed," she said in lieu of a greeting, shutting my office door with a loud bang.

"I'm sorry to hear that. I sent the specifications for the alterations to the factory in Thuringia almost a month ago. I hope there haven't been any problems with them." I'd sent the plans in the earliest days of the operation, at Louisa's request. There wasn't any reason the plans themselves would have been at fault.

"Not that I was made aware of," she said. "Not that they told me much."

"The factories everywhere have been inundated," I said. "They simply can't keep up with demand. I'm sure it's just that."

"You're more charitably minded than I am," she said. "I'm half convinced they're scrapping the whole idea."

"I wouldn't worry about that until they tell you otherwise," I said. "There's a war on. It's impossible to know what their priorities are."

She sucked in a breath and crossed her right leg over her left knee in an unladylike slump. She didn't dare criticize their choices . . . it was unpatriotic to speak against the decision-making at the highest levels.

"I don't see why they would scrap the plan. It's a good one. I am choosing only willing men," Louisa assured me. "Men who fully understand what they are signing up for and who understand the sacrifice we are asking of them."

"You have the endorsement of the highest sort," I said, knowing full well that the Führer had given her his consent. "I don't know why you continue to try to persuade me of your plan's merits."

Her eyes didn't reach mine but seemed to focus on the edge of my drafting table. She played with a loose splinter of wood on the edge where the varnish had worn.

"Because yours matters more," she said.

"Nonsense," I replied. "I'm an engineer. How could my opinions possibly compare with those of the head of the entire country and his closest advisers?"

"I've never liked you," she admitted. "You've always acted superior. As though your work were more important than mine."

"First, I don't see how that's a logical response. Second, that was never my intent. My work is different from yours, that's all. If I ever implied that mine was more important, it wasn't intentional."

"I know," she conceded. "You're still a countess. You came from a comfortable family even before you met your husband. My parents worked in a factory and we scraped by day to day . . . but despite all that, you know what an uphill climb it is to get where we are, even if you started up a rung or two higher on the ladder than I did."

"Well, I can't deny that," I said. There were stories from the east that said the Russians had women fighting in the infantry. Women in the air force even. More than a few, from what I'd heard—and they were fierce, according to Harald. The eerie sound their planes made as they zeroed in on their targets was something like the wail of a banshee. And no matter if they made their mark or not, there wasn't a soul asleep in a camp once they found it. How different their policy of women's emancipation was from our own, though I wondered truly if Stalin's policies resulted in any real freedom for the women under his control. Here, Louisa and I were the exceptional women who proved the rule. We'd never been heckled by our male colleagues once they saw what we were capable of, but they considered us like spotted tigers. Permitted to continue with our work but made to understand that we were in no way typical of our sex.

"Do you think me mad?"

"I think you're committed to your cause," I said evenly.

"My cause?" she asked. I saw her straighten. "I hardly consider this war to be my cause alone."

I held my breath. Slips like these cost people their lives. "I meant for your . . . plan. The war is the cause we all serve, naturally."

"The two aren't unrelated," she reminded me.

"Of course," I said. "I will say that I think the plan will be effective and that you've thought it out well."

"But?" she pressed.

"What will you have me say, Louisa? We will lose men and aircraft. It's not a risk, it's a certainty. Whether it makes strategic sense, I cannot say. It's not my area of expertise. I am ordered to help you see your plan through, and all you need to know is that I will carry out those orders to the best of my ability without complaint. If you want me to assure you that I have no reservations, that I cannot do, but I can assure you that any reservations I might have will not preclude my ability to do my duty."

"You speak like a politician," she said, crossing her arms over her chest.

"As you're so keen to point out, I married a count. The jobs aren't dissimilar," I replied. "We just don't have to bother with the hassle of gathering votes."

Louisa threw her head back and gave a full-throated laugh. "Well put."

"Louisa, it shouldn't matter to you what I think of this plan," I said.

"I know," she said. "But it does all the same. You're a good pilot, though it pains me to say it."

"I think the same of you," I said.

"Thank you," she said, shifting in her seat. "Do you promise you'll tell me if you hear that someone is sabotaging the project?"

"I hardly think that information will come across my desk, but if it does and I'm at liberty to tell you, I will."

"Thank you," she repeated. "I know you must think I'm being positively mad about this, but I just want to do something more for the war than set records and have my picture taken. I want to contribute something real."

"I understand your drive and admire it, though you shouldn't think those contributions are somehow lesser than anyone else's. You've given your gifts for the cause, and that's all anyone can ask."

She looked satisfied and left with a lighter step than she'd entered with. The delay at the factory might have been a massive setback in Louisa's eyes, but it felt more like a blessed reprieve for me. I hoped that perhaps someone in the higher ranks had knowledge that proved such drastic measures were beyond what was called for, though even the most optimistic corners of my heart could not convince the more logical side of me that there could be any truth in it.

CHAPTER
TWENTY-NINE

A GLIMMER

BETH

May 31, 2007
Encinitas, California

Kimberly introduced Mrs. Patterson and her sons, Stephen and Nick. She was still shapely and graceful with a head of gray hair that still bore thick swaths of chestnut brown. Her boys were tall; both had their brown hair trimmed short, and they had perfect, even teeth that I knew Dad was taking in with approval. All-American boys like the ones who landed on the beaches at Normandy. I fought the urge to pace nervously as Kimberly saw everyone settled in the living room before rushing off. Mrs. Patterson took in her surroundings, assessing the situation.

"Hello," she said, offering Dad and me a formal nod. Any trace of a Germanic accent was now gone, replaced by one fit for a California newscaster. I imagined she'd worked hard to get rid of her accent in the years after the war so she would find a readier welcome in her new home. "You look like you're doing well, Mr. Blumenthal. I am glad to see it. I heard you gave everyone a scare."

For two days, I'd sat vigil by my father's side, preparing for the worst and holding out hope for the best. I washed his face and combed his hair. I read to him from the tattered hardcover of one of his favorites, *From Beirut to Jerusalem*, that Kimberly had tossed into a bag with some of the personal items she thought might comfort him. The gesture was such a sweet one, I'd pulled her into a hug and gotten the shoulder of her top soaking wet with my tears, but it wasn't the first time she'd had to provide a comfort to a family member of one of her residents.

On Tuesday, she visited again. "Just be strong, honey," she said, gently swaying as she held me in her arms. "He's a tough old cuss. Don't give up on him yet."

It was almost prophetic. Just a few hours later, Dad's eyes fluttered open and he began to respond to the world around him. He stayed a week in the hospital and was still pale and feeble, but he'd moved back to the care home and seemed happy about it. If nothing else, Kimberly's cooking was infinitely preferable to the bland diet the hospital had forced on him.

"Well, I wasn't done with this rock just yet," he said, offering Mrs. Patterson a wink. "Still a few things left to do." *A wink*. The old coot still had it in him. It had been so long since I'd seen him with new company. He was a natural-born charmer and couldn't help but turn it on even now. He wasn't practiced or smarmy as so many men are; his charm was simply an authentic part of who he was.

"Good afternoon," I said, offering her a smile. "How are you today, Mrs. Patterson?"

"Quite well, my dear. I needn't ask how you are, for you're the picture of good health."

"Thank you," I said, feeling some prickling at my cheeks.

Kimberly came into the room with five glasses of lemonade and a full pitcher on a tray. "You're both supposed to stay hydrated, hot as it is. I'm going to trust Beth here to enforce that for me."

"You've got it," I said.

"Good. Your dad is still recovering, and I don't want Mrs. Patterson getting poorly on my watch."

Kimberly bustled back to the kitchen to prepare lunch. Mrs. Patterson obediently sipped from the glass. She was prim, almost elegant, in her movements.

"Kimberly says you're looking for a relative in Germany?" Nick stated as he topped off his mother's glass, which was only short an inch or two. "We've been looking for Mom's sister for the past two years. It was something we wanted to do for her before it's too late."

"We're looking for Dad's old war flame," I said, slipping Dad a wink. "He wants to know what happened to her as well."

"So many stories like these," Mrs. Patterson said with a knowing shake of her head. "So many families spending decades praying to be reunited. So few prayers answered."

"That's the truth," Dad said, solemnly nodding his head in agreement. "An ugly truth about war, no matter what the outcome."

"I spent a year looking for my sister before I came to America," Mrs. Patterson explained. "By that time, there seemed so little for me left in Germany that I saw no reason not to follow the handsome American lieutenant to California."

"And we're glad you did, Mom," Stephen said, raising his lemonade as if toasting her.

"I should say so, rascal," she said affectionately. "But even from Monterey, I spent all my spare time writing to whomever I could think of that might be able to lead me to some hint of her whereabouts."

"It was the same for me," Dad said. "If there was an organization, foreign or domestic, that I thought might have a lead on her, I sent them a letter. English. German. French. I learned what I needed to write a passable letter in all three and sent them everywhere. Kept my secretary, bless her, busier with that than my dental records."

"Tell us about your sister," I urged, shifting in my seat. "Did she have a job? Was she married?"

"Yes to all of that," Mrs. Patterson said. "She was married, though the brute isn't worth mentioning. She wrote for a women's magazine for a time. Drumming up support for the war movement and other such balderdash. But she was cleverer than that. She used her connection to the SS to spread antiwar propaganda for the resistance."

"She sounds incredible," I said. I couldn't imagine my mother doing something so audacious. She wasn't one for subterfuge, no matter what other skills she had.

"That sounds a lot like my Margarethe. She was doing something with propaganda, it seemed, though she wouldn't tell me much about it. She figured the less I knew, the safer I'd be."

"That was practically my family credo during the war years. You say your sweetheart was called Margarethe? My sister was Margarethe, but we called her Metta. She was the most gorgeous girl. We all loved her so."

"Margarethe used that nickname once or twice in letters. She was about as big as a minute and had a gift of disguising herself as a boy. She was probably brilliant at doing secret errands for the resistance. No one would have thought it of her."

"How curious . . . Did you know her last name?"

"No," Dad confessed. "She didn't want me to know. It was her trying to protect me again."

"There must have been lots of women named Margarethe then," Stephen chimed in.

Mrs. Patterson nodded. "It was fairly common. And I have to say, if you were looking for your sweetheart without the help of a last name, you had even more of an uphill battle than I had."

"Needle in a haystack doesn't even come close," Dad agreed.

"Do you have a picture of your sister?" I asked, inspiration coming to me.

"Unfortunately, most everything I had was lost. Either before coming here or in a fire when the boys were small. The dangers of living in California and all."

"We have one of our Margarethe," I said, darting to Dad's bedroom. I found the picture on his bedside table, where he'd kept it next to a picture of Mom and me when I was younger.

Panting, I handed Mrs. Patterson the photo of Dad and Margarethe, and her soft brown eyes grew watery. She pressed her fingers to her lips, then pressed them on the glass over the image of Margarethe's face.

"I can't believe it," she managed to say. Nick put an arm around his mother and looked ready to snatch the picture away to keep her calm. "How did you find this?"

"It's mine. I had one of my staff snap it," Dad supplied. "That was my Margarethe and me, one of the last times we saw each other."

"Her name was Margarethe Hoffmann. Later Ziegler. She is my sister," she confirmed. "Though you called her Margarethe, we called her Metta."

Her shoulders began to rack with sobs. I felt a breath catch sideways in my chest until it wedged its way free, seemingly raking daggers across my lungs as it finally escaped. I gripped the arms of my chair, trying to steady the room. I didn't know how I'd expected the answers to come, but this certainly wasn't what I'd envisioned. Dad had gone pale, manfully swallowing back sobs of his own. I felt pricking at my eyes and tried to fight tears back as well.

This mystery woman from the photo, this enigma of a woman, was real. And not just to me and Dad. Mrs. Patterson composed herself, aided by tissues readily supplied by her sons.

"She stopped using her nickname after she married that awful man. He wasn't fond of nicknames and the like." She looked past me, gazing at the wall, as though a projector replayed those moments from her past on the obliging surface. Her voice had grown husky, but she'd mastered her tears.

"Can you tell us anything?" I asked, taking her hand in mine. "If we work together, we stand a better chance of finding out what happened."

"The last time I saw her, she had me turn myself over to the Americans in France to keep me safe. She had me go ahead so that if he sent his goons after her, I still might get away. She was going to join me a day or two later, but I never saw her again. I wrote. I sent inquiries. I did everything I could think of. If I couldn't find her then, I don't see how we can find her now."

"We've told Mom that the tech is so much better now, but it's her German stoicism talking. We wanted to do this for her," Nick said. "We knew that not knowing what happened to Aunt Metta always bothered her."

I peppered her and her sons with questions. Being her sister, she knew Margarethe's full name, date of birth, and a few other facts that would make finding some answers a much simpler affair.

"I always wondered who the American was who helped her get papers. She told me so little."

"That was me," Dad said, looking distant for a moment.

"Well then, Max Blumenthal. I owe you my life. I never dreamed I'd get the chance to thank you in person."

"Well, I can't regret anything that led to saving your life, but I only wish I'd managed to do the same for Margarethe—Metta." Dad seemed to be making friends with the nickname, but wasn't wholly used to it. She'd been Margarethe to him for half a century, after all.

"No one wishes that more than I do, Max. I'd have never let her stay behind if I'd known it was her only chance. I've lived with that regret for more than sixty years."

"I believe you," Dad said, taking her hand. "And if I know anything, she wouldn't have risked the safety of the baby if she thought it was her only chance to leave. She wasn't sacrificing herself for you intentionally."

"You knew about the child?"

"Well, there's a good chance it was mine."

"Thank God for that, Max. That might be the only blessing in this whole sad affair."

CHAPTER THIRTY

BEYOND THE BREACH

JOHANNA

July 19, 1944
Berlin, Germany

The dark circles under Harald's eyes grew more cavernous with each passing day. His words were fewer, and his face became gaunt. The war ate at him like a cancer for which the only cure was peace. He was now coming home in the middle of the night most times, and Mama couldn't keep herself awake even long enough to bid him good night. I'd taken to eating my dinner with her at a normal hour but fixing myself a little plate of something so that Harald wouldn't feel like he was dining alone. I placed sausage, potatoes, and fresh greens before him, but he only moved the food around the plate with his fork. Though he didn't speak of it, the tide of the war had changed. Whether there had been a major advance by the Allies or some catastrophic loss, I didn't know yet, but the general tenor of anyone in service had become far more strained in recent weeks.

"Please eat," I begged him as he picked at his meal. "You'll get sick."

"Please don't, *Liebchen*. I know you mean well, but I can't bear the coddling."

"Very well," I said, crossing my arms over my chest. "But such waste is unpardonable in times like these."

He heaved a deep sigh and took a few bites of sausage in earnest. It was gristly and greasy, but there wasn't any better to be had. It was at least warm and restorative, so long as you didn't think about what might be in it.

He cleared half his plate before shoving it away. I put the leftovers into a bowl and placed them in the icebox for later. Rationing was becoming strict enough that we didn't dare waste a scrap. He was never much of a drinker, sipping coyly at the same glass of champagne for an entire evening during social occasions, but tonight he poured a generous tumbler of the brandy we kept on hand for illness.

"Johanna," he said, staring at the wall rather than me and taking a deep drink from his glass. "Do you think you could confiscate a plane?"

I only just managed to keep the dishes from clattering into the sink. "How do you mean?"

"Take one on a test flight and simply not return." He took another drink from his brandy glass and removed a pack of cigarettes and a lighter from his breast pocket. Another new habit. I handed him a saucer to use for his ash, as we weren't in the habit of keeping ashtrays in the house.

I'd been waiting for a question like this for weeks. Either that or a troop of jackbooted thugs at my door ready to haul me in for inquiry. I wasn't sure which I feared more.

"It's possible, I suppose. Though it would cost me my wings, my clearances, and possibly my honorary Aryan status," I said, reminding him of what was at stake.

"Would you do it if I asked?" he pressed.

"If it was a matter of life or death, yes," I said.

"It is," he said.

"Harald, what on earth is going on? Tell me what you have planned. I know you've been plotting something for weeks now, and I'm tired of you not trusting me with it."

"You're safer not knowing. I promise you."

"You're asking me to help. Don't you think I'd be better off knowing what you're getting me involved in?"

"No, the less you know, the fewer questions you can answer if things go badly."

"Perhaps I feel like I need to know what you're doing before I agree. Did you ever consider that possibility?"

"I need you to trust me, Johanna. I haven't asked for blind faith from you very often, but this is one of those times."

I bowed my head and rubbed my eyes with the tips of my fingers. It was true. He consulted me far more than many other husbands thought to do with their wives. He didn't think of me as subservient or lesser in our marriage—he referred to it as a partnership of equals even when it wasn't politically prudent to do so. If he needed to withhold information from me now, it wasn't without reason.

"I'll do it," I said.

"Do you have any flights scheduled tomorrow? I don't want you to schedule anything new or do anything out of the ordinary."

"I have one on the books for tomorrow at two in the afternoon. A few later in the week."

"Tomorrow will have to do," he said. "Probably best to have it done with as soon as possible now that you know something is going on."

"I wish you'd tell me," I said, though with no expectation that he would change his mind.

"All you need to know is that I'm doing what I hope will end the war sooner rather than later. And don't expect to return to this home. Perhaps ever. We'll have to leave everything behind."

"What about Mama?" I said, my eyes flitting to the door of the room where she slept completely and blissfully unaware.

"Send her back to the farm first thing in the morning. Get her on the six a.m. train if you can get a ticket. Tell her nothing other than that you think she might be safer up in the mountains with all the air raids we're having. Invent a story if you must. You're creative and she'll believe whatever you tell her."

"What about Metta and Oskar?"

"Not a word. Not a single word or this will all be for nothing. Do you understand me?"

"Yes," I said. The pang in my chest was so strong it was almost crippling, but I didn't let him see me flinch. The thought of never seeing my sister or brother again was beyond any pain I could articulate.

"This is the only way, Johanna. I wish it were different, but it isn't. You have to trust me that this is the only way for us."

"Of course I trust you, my *Knuddelbär*." I crossed from the sink to kiss his temple. "Just tell me what to do, and I'll be waiting."

He patted my hand and we climbed into our bed. In my bones, I knew it would be for the last time, and even as Harald's breathing grew even and deep, I could not find it within myself to succumb to sleep.

~

It was just as well I was unable to sleep. I had breakfast ready by four in the morning and was able to get Mama ushered to the train station with most of her belongings in tow in time for the six o'clock train. Harald left for work as we were packing, his face set in concentration thick as concrete. Mama wondered why I insisted she take the sentimental items like her photographs and a vase of her mother's, and yet urged her to leave behind some more practical items like her heavy winter boots and coat. To her credit, she did not question why I sent her from the house.

She'd have a much easier time replacing those items come winter, as she wasn't likely to see this house again. I considered asking a neighbor to post the rest of her belongings to her, but even such a small maneuver could be enough to attract attention. It was best that Mama look as though she were just going home for a few weeks to check on the farm and her personal affairs.

I went to the ticket counter and purchased a return fare, which would have her back in two weeks. Again, a one-way ticket might alert suspicion if anyone took the trouble to investigate it.

I pulled her close as though in a farewell hug. "Do not come back unless we send word and you are *certain* that word comes from Harald or me. Understand?"

Mama's eyes widened but she nodded curtly.

I wiped a few tears away as the train departed, wondering when I might see my mother again. God willing, the war would be over soon enough, and we'd be able to come back home and figure out how to build a life once again. Harald would never be the same man, but I would endeavor to walk with him on his path to healing.

I considered going directly to the office after I dropped Mama at the train station, but that would put me to work a solid two hours before I usually arrived, which would be more concerning than a train ticket or scheduling a last-minute test flight. I decided to bathe and style my hair to look as polished as I could. Looking harried, apart from being out of character, would also be a signal that something was amiss. I dressed in a sturdy navy pantsuit and comfortable shoes as I did most days, though my hands shook as I tied the laces. I was leaving this house, this life, and perhaps my family, forever.

I ran to the restroom and emptied the contents of my stomach into the toilet. I had no idea where Harald and I were headed or what to prepare for. We couldn't bring our possessions, of course. We'd have to buy clothes and necessities wherever we went. It seemed likely we'd be on the run, perhaps for some time, and would need the means to start over.

I found the old canvas rucksack that I occasionally took on longer-haul flights. I gathered up every small object of value I could cram inside: the cash Harald had in reserve, the gold coins he kept to protect us from the devaluation of the mark after the war, the jewels that served as a reminder of when my social duties as the countess von Oberndorff were the biggest headaches of my week. Passports, identification, bank account information, and more. I wanted to cram the rucksack full of everything I could stuff inside, but arriving with a bag I rarely used was risky enough. To have it stuffed to brimming would be alarming even to those who paid only casual attention.

I arrived at three minutes past eight, just casually late enough to look nonchalant.

The biggest challenge of my day would be to fill the next six hours with enough activity to keep myself from running mad. I placed the rucksack under my desk, reassuring myself of its presence by resting my calf against it.

I sketched designs for changes to the throttle in the Me 328 per Louisa's request. The changes were straightforward and uncomplicated and gave me just enough to do before my flight.

Harald said he would meet me before I was to take off, but that if he did not show, I was to take off and fly someplace safe.

Switzerland was the closest I could think of, and there was a good chance I could manage a landing there without getting shot down. The same wouldn't be true for France or England or most anywhere east of here.

Louisa knocked on my office doorframe and entered before I bade her.

"I'll take the Me up at two for you," she said. "That way you can continue to work on the plans."

"I'd prefer to do the flight myself. The dive systems are tricky."

"I'll give you a detailed report when I return. That will suffice. I want to get a feel for it."

"I'm not comfortable signing off on the changes until I've flown it myself."

"Listen, *Flugkapitän*. This is my project and I want to test the new designs for myself."

"And that's your prerogative, *Flugkapitän*. You can take a run after I've landed. Schedule it now. They'll accommodate you. But I will not sign off on the changes until I've made a test run. Do I make myself clear?"

"Do I have to remind you that I'm the head of this project?"

"You wouldn't allow anyone within ten kilometers to forget. The fact remains that if *my* name is on the plans, *I* will take the test run myself. Today at two in the afternoon. If you have an issue with that, find another engineer to work under you."

Louisa turned on the ball of her foot without another word. No doubt to speak with a supervisor to see if she could have my decision overridden. Thankfully, the engineers were seen as somewhat like doctors on a ship, and their commands were to be obeyed.

But thanks to her outburst, my concentration was shattered. The crew would be readying my plane by now, and I would be there to get in the cockpit as soon as it was ready. I could well imagine Louisa taking off on her own if I were even seconds late, and I wouldn't risk losing Harald's and my one chance at escape to her brash maneuvers.

I grabbed the rucksack and tried to walk in what I thought was an efficient but unhurried stride. Peter was now leading the crew of mechanics, having proven his skills weren't hampered by his disability. I found him deftly checking to make sure all the systems were ready for takeoff. He had admirable concentration and attention to detail for one so young. There were few people at the office I would miss, but he was one.

"Do you want me to put that somewhere?" Peter asked, pointing to my rucksack as I took hold of the ladder to ascend to the cockpit. "You won't want it in the way."

"I'm taking this. Most of the pilots will have a pack with them. I want to simulate the extra weight." He didn't question the lie, but

I could see my behavior struck him as odd. If he mentioned this off-handedly to anyone in command, I could be grounded. If someone demanded to look in the bag, I'd be detained. No one carried a bag of cash, jewelry, and travel papers if they didn't plan to flee.

I was about to ascend the ladder when a half dozen SS guards marched into the hangar. Before they came fully into view, Peter took the rucksack and tossed it in a nearby bin.

"Do not enter that aircraft, *Gräfin* von Oberndorff," the one in front called.

Ansel.

I removed my foot slowly from the rung of the ladder.

"To what do I owe the honor, brother?" I said, emphasizing the familial link.

"Your husband has been accused of attempted assassination of the Führer and will be dealt with precipitously. You, *Gräfin* von Oberndorff, stand accused of conspiracy in this heinous act. I am here to take you into custody so that you can stand judgment for your crimes against the Reich, Germany, and the German people." His lips curled in a sneer as he recited the words he'd clearly rehearsed in his head on his way to apprehend me.

One of the guards clapped me in handcuffs and escorted me to the back of one of their sleek black cars. I was left only to wonder if Harald was still alive, and indeed how many hours it would be before I found myself at the gallows.

CHAPTER
THIRTY-ONE

Reentry

MAX

August 12, 1947
Los Angeles, California

"Your mother is faring better today," Dad announced as he entered the kitchen with a tray of empty dinner dishes. I sat at the table with papers spread before me as I'd done every night since Dad complained about the long hours I kept at the office. Ma was on the mend now but had fallen grievously ill right around the end of the war. A neglected cold turned into pneumonia with a dangerously high fever. While she was ill, they discovered a cancer in her breast that was weakening her and making the pneumonia almost impossible to treat. The pneumonia was gone now, but the cancer persisted. She'd suffered for two years, but the disease hadn't yet taken her.

"Hmmm," I said, looking down at the list of French and German addresses I'd copied down from my latest call to the State Department. I'd spent hours composing a letter of inquiry asking for any information on Margarethe and our child. For months, my secretary, Sarah, typed out copies when I should have had her working on patient files and the like. She'd typed the thing dozens of times by now, using onionskin paper and carbon to make triplicate copies each time. I sent them out as quickly as she could type them until the day came that she gave it up as a bad job and insisted on taking the thing to the nearest printing press. She commissioned two hundred copies, which cost me a pretty penny, but it allowed me to send the letter to a wider audience. Sometimes I included a personalized note with it if I had reason to believe the lead was a strong one. I was at it for several hours every night, papering every refugee agency I could come up with in hopes of finding some hint of Margarethe's whereabouts.

The baby would be two years old now. Did he look like me? Did she tell him about me? Was he babbling a few words and taking steps yet? Margarethe had insisted the baby was a girl, but whenever I pictured her with our baby in her arms, it was always a smiling boy with my dark hair and her bright-blue eyes.

I'd hoped to stay in Europe long enough to find them on site, but because Ma was so unwell, I was discharged almost immediately after V-E Day. Dad had written to everyone he could think of, and apparently his pleas reached the right ears. I should have been grateful for the reprieve, but I couldn't muster many feelings beyond regret. I considered staying behind, orders or no, but I couldn't leave my father to mourn for my mother alone if the worst were to happen. I was decommissioned and sent back home with only a few days' leave in Paris before returning to Los Angeles. I spent those precious few days contacting every refugee center I could manage and combed every lead I had in Paris while I could. The streets of Paris, now that the revelry was at an end, were somber. The people were gaunt with a hunger that food alone would not satiate. It was bizarre to see some of the streets completely untouched, while others were so heavily pockmarked.

The war was much like the massive wildfires that would erupt in the summer in the hills outside Los Angeles and the lush forests to the north. It might take weeks to get the blaze in hand, and there would be nothing but the charred memories of trees and wildlife left behind. Slowly, the green sprigs of life would sprout from the ruin, the birds and woodland creatures would reappear, and things would return to a state of normalcy. Not as they had been, but a new version of what once was. So would be the case in France, Germany, and everywhere else that had been trampled by this war. It would take a generation, but a new version of normal would emerge from the ashes again. Though in truth, saplings had only just begun to sprout from the horror of the previous war, so I still harbored the fear that another madman with a match would surface to ignite it all once more.

My days in Paris yielded no results, and I cursed myself for knowing almost no vital information about the woman I loved. She never even shared her surname, in service of protecting us both. I boarded the ship home and traversed the country by train. I returned to my parents having left more than a little of my soul behind. The only mercy was that my return spurred an improvement in Ma's health, though an incomplete one.

"Son, you need to put all that away and get some fresh air," Dad chided as he rinsed Ma's dishes in the sink.

"I walked home from the office," I said, not lifting my head from the envelope I addressed.

"Three blocks. A man like you needs more than that. You don't want to lose your health like your poor mother."

"Enough, Dad. You know what this means to me."

"I've seen you spend hours every night at that table for two years. What has it amounted to, son?"

"Form letters. A lot of nothing," I admitted.

"You fought in a war and lived, Max. You need to honor that gift and live your life."

"But what about the baby? Am I to leave her to fend for herself?"

"It's been two years, son. You've given your information to every organization from here to Berlin. If she wants to be found—if she *can* be found—she will be. In the meantime, seeing you brood isn't doing your mother any good."

"I'll go and read to her," I offered. She liked it when I read the Psalms to her, or occasionally an Agatha Christie.

"I think she'd prefer to see you go out, son. She'd love to know you're settled before the cancer . . ."

"Dad, the treatments seem to be working. There's no reason not to hope."

"I know what my heart tells me, son. There's no ignoring the ache that's settled in there."

I wrapped an arm around him and kissed the thinning hair atop his head and nodded. He returned to Ma in their bedroom and I sat again, tossing the pen aside. I leaned back, fingers laced behind my head, and stretched the muscles in my back that tightened into steel after hours bent over a dental chair and then the kitchen table.

I placed the letters back in the printer's carton, stacked the envelopes on top of them, and tossed in the roll of stamps. As I placed the box with the last of the letters on the bookcase in my room, I felt hollow. All that was left was the same piercing ache in my heart that Dad felt in his.

CHAPTER THIRTY-TWO

LEFT BEHIND

BETH

June 2, 2007
San Diego, California

Greg was out back scrubbing the built-in grill as he did every Saturday. Some men attended church on the weekend, others devoted themselves to watching sports. Greg tinkered in the yard each week with the same religious zeal. The half acre was Greg's refuge, and only the heaviest rain would keep him from mowing the expansive lawn. Even then, he would still tend to the grill and everything else sheltered on the covered patio. It was the sort of patio that home improvement stores used in their advertisements to lure unwitting consumers into buying three tons of flagstone and stainless-steel grills large enough to cook meals for entire football teams. It was manicured and orderly, missing the element of tropical chaos that Dad's little corner of paradise had had. Greg had allowed one plumeria—the deep-red kind that smelled of grape Kool-Aid—to reside in the far corner. It had been gifted from Dad to us after our honeymoon, and it was one of the few things I regretted having to leave behind. There might be another yard one day, though, and it could be one of my own design.

I hadn't been back to the house in over nine months, but Greg's routine hadn't changed. Everything looked basically the same but for the lack of my personal effects. I couldn't figure out if I should be sad that my absence should affect the atmosphere so little, or if it just meant I was never fully present in it.

"You didn't answer the door, so I let myself in. I hope that's OK," I said. He looked up from the grill, wire brush still in hand.

"Beth, the day you're not welcome in this house as your own is the day I've failed as a human being." Greg set the brush down and closed the heavy stainless-steel lid to the grill. He meant it too. He probably still slept on the right side of the bed, leaving the left for me. He didn't envision the day when he'd find someone else and my welcome would be rescinded. But I knew it was coming, and likely not in the distant future.

"It's not my home anymore," I reminded him, hoping I didn't sound cruel. "I want to respect your privacy."

"I suppose I deserve the frosty treatment. I'm sorry for how I behaved at the hospital. I'm glad Max is doing better."

"You've never been at your best when you're tired. I shouldn't have texted you," I said with a shrug.

Greg opened his mouth to retort, but snapped it shut. "Let's go inside," he said finally.

I followed him to the den we'd used as a communal study. My desk and books were gone, but he'd spaced his out to make the bare shelves look less spartan. He took his spot in the chair behind his desk and I sat in the guest chair on the other side. I felt like I'd been called into the dean's office for a meeting, rather than having a conversation with the man I'd once shared my life with.

He handed me a stack of my mail. Even after nine months, a fair amount still wasn't forwarded. He saved it all—every catalog and flyer.

"You could have just dropped this all in campus mail like usual," I said.

"Well, I also found this and didn't want to trust it to the mail—campus or otherwise," he said, passing me a photo album with a weathered leather cover.

"God, I'd forgotten this existed," I said, opening it to see the pictures Mom and Dad had collected from my youth. Eighteen years of birthdays, graduations, my bat mitzvah, gatherings with my grandparents before they passed. Mom had compiled it all and given it to me as a wedding gift when Dad had given us the tree. Being Mom, she'd used archival-quality paper and glue, and each page was laid out as perfectly as a spread in *Vogue*. Despite her efforts, some of the pictures had yellowed and faded, much like my memory of the events in them. I couldn't recall the flavor of my eighth birthday cake or what our neighbors had given me as a bat mitzvah present, but the memories were still there. Mom was featured prominently throughout the album, as Dad had been the family photographer since time immemorial. I had her dark, glossy hair and high cheekbones. Her attention to detail and her desire for order too. One picture in particular grabbed my attention. In it, I was looking intently at the candles on my sixth birthday cake while Mom beamed directly at the camera. At Dad. The look of love in her eyes went deeper than skin and bone. It seeped into her soul. She adored him.

Could she possibly have known about Margarethe? About the child Dad and his wartime love might have shared?

I couldn't imagine that Dad would have kept such a secret from her, but there was a part of me that hoped she'd been spared the knowledge.

"Are you still with me?" Greg asked.

"No," I replied automatically. But his question wasn't what I'd interpreted it to be. "I mean, yes. Sorry. Nostalgia lane."

"I can imagine you're prone to it these days," Greg said. "Change does that. I've caught myself looking over our wedding photos a time or two myself."

The wedding photos. He'd kept them, and it hadn't even registered with me that I hadn't asked for them. I used to take them out every year on our anniversary, and we'd look over the glossy photos of me in my flowing Vera Wang wedding dress and Greg in his tux dancing and eating cake at his parents' country club. We'd drink the same vintage champagne we'd had at our wedding and dance to "Wonderful Tonight" in the living room.

"God, our anniversary is tomorrow," I said, horrified at the realization. "Would have been," I corrected.

"You'd forgotten?" he asked.

"Not so much forgotten as haven't had time to really breathe," I said. It was true enough. Beach trips notwithstanding, between hunting for Margarethe, visiting Dad, and deliberately burying myself in work, I'd not allowed myself the free time to gather a coherent thought.

"I didn't," Greg said. He opened the drawer to his desk and produced a black velvet box and set it in front of me.

"Why on earth would you have gotten me a gift?" I asked, dreading the contents. I'd returned the engagement ring that had been in his family for three generations. He'd given me some nice pieces over the years, but I rarely wore anything beyond a simple necklace and occasionally a bracelet if I was feeling the need to be dressy. My gold wedding band sat collecting dust in my jewelry box. It was silly to keep it as I never planned to wear it again, but it seemed wrong to sell it. Keeping it tucked away in a box was easier than taking action.

"Call it nostalgia," he said. "You've had a hard year, even without the divorce. I wanted to do something nice for you. Open it, please."

I reached for the box, dread burbling up in my stomach as I cracked it open. Nestled inside was a pair of princess-cut diamond earrings. Good-sized ones to boot. They were beautiful, but something I'd take out to wear perhaps twice a year. I'd be too afraid of losing one to enjoy wearing them. But it was the sort of thing Greg did when he wanted to make a grand gesture.

"This is way too much, Greg," I said. "Very generous, but I can't accept them."

"You can," he said, standing and coming around to my side of the desk. "Please do."

He perched on the desk in front of me and pulled me to my feet, then wrapped his arms around me. He lowered his mouth to mine, kissing slowly, deliberately. I allowed myself to relax into his embrace, enjoying the nearness of another person. He still smelled of Old Spice and mint gum. Wholesome and familiar. So very Greg.

"We can try again, baby," he said as he pulled away. He rested his forehead on mine as his ragged breath grew even. "I can do better. Focus on us. We'll take vacations and make love more often. Whatever you need."

I took a step back, blinking as I considered his words. To come back. To come back *home* would be so easy. But it was a step backward.

"I'm sorry, I can't, Greg. I just can't."

"Can you at least tell me why? I think I deserve that much."

"The reason hasn't changed. You say you want to focus on us and to have more sex and travel to make me happy. I want those things to make you happy too. If they don't, there's no point."

Greg exhaled deeply and pulled me back into his arms for a hug.

"I knew it was a long shot, but I'd never have been able to live with myself if I hadn't tried."

CHAPTER THIRTY-THREE

CHARLOTTENBURG

JOHANNA

July 21, 1944
Berlin, Germany

Ansel delivered the news to me personally. Harald had been executed that morning with no trial. He'd been accused, along with two others, of conspiring to kill the Führer. They had been closer to success than many of the previous attempts, which was part of the reason for the hasty justice. Had it not been for a heavy wooden table in the meeting room where Harald had detonated the bomb, he would have succeeded in his plan.

They brought me to a small, windowless concrete room with only two chairs and a table. Ansel had been given the honor of questioning me. Whether it was out of deference to our relation or despite it, I wasn't sure. I wanted to break down and sob for my sweet man, the gentle academic who was forced into the ranks of these brainless thugs.

I wanted to wallow in tears as was my right as a widow, but I would not give this hateful man the satisfaction of seeing me broken.

"Tell us what you know about the plot your husband orchestrated," he said as he took his seat. He at least did me the courtesy of removing the handcuffs they'd placed on me for transport.

"Nothing. Why would he involve his wife in such matters?" I asked, appealing to the male-centric values the Reich espoused.

"Come now, I am not some greenhorn detective, Johanna. You two spoke of everything. You can't expect me to believe that he kept something like this from you."

"He did," I insisted. "I suspect he wanted me to be able to answer truthfully that I knew nothing in case I ended up in this very situation."

"You never noticed his behavior to be odd? Making strange phone calls in the middle of the night? Acting strained or distraught?"

"Of course his behavior was strained. There's a war on, and he was part of your highest ranks. He was working like a dog. He would leave before dawn and come home after midnight almost every day. I can't imagine any sane man wouldn't have been strained. We barely had time to speak, let alone for him to involve me in any plotting."

"But you had a plane at the ready."

It was the ace up his sleeve. I'd been caught ready to flee and looked as guilty as Harald himself. I could not afford the slightest slip in my answers.

"A standard test flight that had been in the books for two weeks."

"And this plot was not concocted overnight. You were clearly prepared to run. Answer me truly, were you to be Harald's escape pilot?"

I took a deep breath. The ice of his gaze chilled my marrow. I felt fear constrict around my voice box as Ansel's searing eyes willed me to lie. He was aching for a reason to crush me.

"Harald did tell me I might need to be prepared to leave with a plane," I admitted.

"And you didn't think to alert me or someone else in the party?"

"Ansel, he'd been a dedicated member of the SS for months. For all I knew he was enacting a plot on behalf of our Führer, not against him."

"All the same, you didn't think it wise to question him about his motives?"

"No, Ansel. I can tell you that in all my years as a married woman, I never did my husband the dishonor of questioning his motives when he made a request of me. I can take that point of pride to my grave."

Ansel cocked his head to the side, perhaps pondering how soon I might be on my way there.

"You swear you had no knowledge of your husband's plans?" he pressed.

"No, brother. I did not. Furthermore, if I had, I would have advised him against it."

"Is that so?" he said, crossing his arms over his chest and leaning back.

"It is," I said. "No matter what he believed, I would never have had him sacrifice himself for his cause. I married a man, not a martyr."

"Now he is neither," Ansel said, standing. "He is a mere traitor whose name will never be remembered. The Führer, however, will be remembered as the greatest leader in the past hundred years, if not in the history of mankind."

"That the Führer will never be forgotten is something we can agree on," I said.

He opened the door and motioned for the guards to collect me and return me to my holding cell without another word.

I could hear Harald's voice in my head telling me to be strong. To face whatever future lay before me with the strength and dignity befitting the countess von Oberndorff. But I did not feel grace or strength in that moment. I curled up on the bunk and let the grief have me. I didn't dare sob too loudly and annoy the guards, so I buried my sobs in the flat, filthy pillow that had surely seen plenty of tears prior to my own.

"Jojo." I heard a loud whisper at the door of the cell. "Jojo!"

I lifted my head to see Metta standing on the opposite side of the bars. I didn't dash over to her, but stood warily, as if my movement might betray that this vision was just a mirage.

"My God," I said feebly as I walked over to her.

"Shhh, I haven't much time, Johanna. If Ansel knew I was here, he would have my hide."

"He hasn't hurt you, has he?" I said, reaching through the bars to touch the side of her face. Indeed she looked well. Fashionable yet sturdy clothes. Well groomed and well fed. Whatever his faults, Ansel was still providing for her.

"Please worry about yourself for the moment," she hissed. "It's your life on the line here, not mine. You must get up and not act like a defeated widow. I can only imagine how much you're hurting right now, but you need to hold yourself together. Show them how useful you are. Ask to work from your cell. If they see you like a wet dishrag of a woman, they may decide the most useful thing to do with you is to make an example of you to anyone else who wants to plot against the regime."

"How do you know this?" I asked.

"I've watched these people work for years now, Johanna. If you're useful to them, you might stand a chance of survival. You're a woman and related by marriage to Ansel. These things will work in your favor . . . but you must show them how clever and necessary you are to the war effort. Do you understand me? You won't do any service to Harald's memory by dying at their hands. Honor your husband by escaping with your life."

"Yes," I said against the tears welling in my eyes.

"You won't see me again here," she said. "Ansel is furious with both you and Harald. And himself for recommending Harald to such a high post. But this is the advice he would give you himself if he wanted to save you from the gallows."

"But he doesn't, does he?"

"Thankfully for you, he doesn't get to make those decisions unilaterally. Not yet anyway."

She was right. I would have to work. But for that night, I could be alone with my tears for Harald, who was now lost to me forever.

⁓

The day after Metta's visit, I was informed with my tray of breakfast that I was being taken to the prison in Charlottenburg. Ansel hadn't found it within himself—or perhaps the scope of his authority—to release me, but neither was I being sent to the executioner. It wasn't exactly a relief, but it was something of a reprieve. It gave me the gift of time.

I had stayed up the entire night thinking about Metta's words. I couldn't act like a despondent widow if I wanted to survive. I had to show these people I was of use to them. Too valuable to kill. Too penitent to make a martyr. I had to stay alive.

I was taken in cuffs to the prison just before midday. The redbrick buildings were old-fashioned and made in a time when architectural style still kept pace with function. I wasn't given a uniform or made to change, and I wasn't sure if that was a signal that I was being treated with privilege or if they didn't plan to keep me alive long enough to make a uniform worth the effort.

"You will be staying here," the warden said with a jab of his billy club toward a private cell. "You're to be housed away from the others."

I assumed that was standard practice for traitors and other high-level criminals. It looked more like a dreary servant's bedroom than a prison cell, which was an improvement over the workings of my imagination. It even contained a small table that could serve as a desk.

"I don't suppose you might ask if I could continue my work while I'm here?" I asked. "Of course, I don't know the duration of my stay, but I'd prefer to be useful to the cause if I can be."

He turned and looked as though I'd suggested that I go scrub the mortar between the exterior bricks with my own toothbrush.

"I'm not sure such a thing will be possible, you understand, *Gräfin* von Oberndorff," he said, adding my title and a touch of deference to his tone.

"Naturally, I'll abide by whatever you and your colleagues decide is appropriate, but I'd be happy to continue my design work if at all possible."

"I'll bring the request forward. Is there anything you might need to make you more comfortable?" he asked, looking as though he was startled at the question as it rolled off his lips. For a moment, he seemed more like a kindly innkeeper welcoming me to his establishment rather than a jailer.

His lips reflexively turned up in a smile, which I returned, though I lowered my eyes in an attempt to be demure. He didn't seem the sort that cared for bold women. Speak quietly, act coyly. Shyly even, though not overly so.

He'd be easy to influence so long as he never noticed I was doing it.

Metta had been right. Industriousness was the key to this warden's heart. I would have to seduce him with hard work and charm. My stomach turned at the idea of seducing him in a literal sense, but I would do what was necessary. I couldn't honor Harald's memory if I were dead as well.

Since I didn't have my work with me, I decided to rearrange the three pieces of furniture in the cell to make a more functional workspace. I moved the table and chair closer to the cell window to take advantage of what natural light there was. The bed I moved to the darkest corner in the slim hope that it would improve my sleep. The bedding was dusty, so I removed it and beat it against the chair. It wasn't a perfect solution, but I met with some success. I hoped the warden would see these efforts as fastidiousness rather than impertinence, but I couldn't afford to take half measures with my life. I said a silent prayer of thanksgiving for the comforts of a window and a small sink. If nothing else, I would have some light and could maintain a basic level of hygiene.

Three hours later, the warden returned, Peter by his side. A bag was slung over his shoulder.

"Your request has been approved," the warden said. "This young man is to report at four in the afternoon each day to collect your work and bring your next assignments."

"How wonderful," I said, hardly able to contain my glee at having something to do to fill the void of endless hours. I had no desire to further the Nazi cause, but it would keep me alive. I couldn't do much to resist if I were dead. "Thank you for taking this matter up, *Gefängnisleiter*." I tempered my enthusiasm, but gladly accepted the bag from Peter.

"Please tell *Flugkapitän* Mueller I am grateful to remain on the project," I told Peter graciously.

"I'll relay the message, *Flugkapitän* von Oberndorff. But my duties aren't finished for the day, so I'll say goodbye until tomorrow."

"Thank you, Peter."

"You really are a flight captain?" the warden asked incredulously. "Your father permitted such a venture?"

"Indeed, he did," I said. "Goaded me on, more accurately. It was my mother who objected."

"I can see why. It's a dangerous profession for a woman," he said.

"Indeed, but even dangerous tasks must be done in times like these."

"Well put, young lady," he said, standing straighter. "And I do like what you've done with your cell. It looks very efficient."

"I think it will be," I said. "And I'm grateful to have the chance to be of use."

"I shall leave you to work, then. If you find you are missing anything that you need to complete your work, I'll do what I can to accommodate you."

I emptied the contents of the bag onto the table. It was largely filled with the schematics I'd been working on as well as an assortment of office supplies I would need to do the job. A bar of chocolate was hidden in the inner pocket along with a blank notebook. Inside the notebook was a loose scrap of paper with Peter's tidy scrawl.

> *J~*
>
> *If you need anything at all, scribble a note on the paper from this book and send it back in your bag when I come to swap it out the next day. I can't make promises, but I will try. In the interim, I thought keeping a journal would be a comfort to you, but be careful what you write. Destroy this.*
>
> *~P*

I took a pen from the collection of office supplies Peter had delivered and crossed out his words until they were illegible. I then ripped the paper into minuscule pieces and washed a pinch full of the shreds down the sink every few minutes so they wouldn't clog the drain. That would be an effective solution for today, but I would have to find other solutions for the future. Trips to the lavatory and mess hall would have to serve in this purpose as well.

I settled in with the schematics for the landing gear for the Junkers Ju 88 and sketched and redesigned until I lost myself in the work. I had to assume they'd run my work by another engineer to make sure it was up to par and that I wasn't giving them design plans that would cost the Reich time, money, and resources. They would find nothing amiss.

Only the guard summoning me to take my evening meal alerted me to how much time had passed. I wasn't permitted to dine with other prisoners but was allowed to eat in the empty dining hall when they were finished with their meals. The food was roughly equivalent to the mess at work, so at least I wouldn't be miserable on that score, though the chocolate bar now stowed in my pillow would be welcome when I returned to my cell.

I was permitted five minutes in the lavatory after my meal, and immediately escorted back to my cell by the guard, who seemed positively bored with his duties.

He locked the door, and I tried to ignore the feeling of the walls closing in on me. I lay down in my bed, almost instinctively reaching for Harald, who would never sleep by my side again. I allowed myself the indulgence of tears for a few minutes, but then forced myself to dry my face and return to work for a few more hours. It would be a solitary life, but better than none at all.

I'd cursed Harald for his recklessness in being involved in the plot to kill Hitler more times than I could count in the past few days, but he'd been the one to take a stand. I no longer cursed his folly . . . I was ashamed of my own cowardice. It was time to atone for my past wrongs and be of use to the right side of the fight.

CHAPTER THIRTY-FOUR

TAKING A STEP

MAX

August 13, 1947
Los Angeles, California

Sarah was a good-natured woman in her midforties; a war widow who was eager to find a job to fill the lonely hours and to provide for her two young boys. It seemed like the number of women in her situation were countless. I was happy to give Sarah gainful employment as I set up my practice, but there were so many others who weren't as fortunate. Her short stature, red hair, and ready smile put the patients at ease, and her efficiency in running the office was impressive.

"A full load today, Doctor," she said, plopping a neat stack of manila folders into the inbox on my desk. "Word's getting out about you."

"Glad to hear it," I said. It took time to grow the practice, but the bank didn't take that into consideration when collecting loan payments. I hadn't missed one yet, but it had been tight more than a few times, and medical bills had Dad more strapped for cash than I was.

"Any word yet?" Sarah had spent so many hours typing copies of the letter seeking Margarethe's whereabouts that she never went a day without asking after her.

"No," I said, rubbing the bridge of my nose and leaning back in my chair. "Not so much as a form letter in a month."

"That's a shame," she said.

"You think I'm insane, don't you? Spending all this time looking for her." I folded my arms over my chest to gauge her reaction.

"You're . . . loyal," she said. "There are worse things to be said about a person."

"True enough," I said, picking up the pen nearest me and tapping the cap against the polished oak. "But . . ."

"But what?" she said. "I'm not going to go out of my way to offend my boss. I like my job and want to keep it."

"Sarah, you're the only thing resembling a friend I have at the moment. I won't fire you for honesty."

She took the seat on the opposite side of my desk. "OK, the 'but' is this: it's been two years, Max," she said, adopting my given name as she was wont to do when the conversation veered into personal areas. "Don't you think you should maybe consider . . . not moving on, but maybe moving forward? You can't say you haven't tried to find this poor girl. No one could expect more."

"You have sons, Sarah. Could you just 'move forward' without them?" I tossed the pen to the far left of my desk, disturbing a pile of papers that Sarah tidied reflexively.

"I lost my husband, Max. I've had to move forward *for* them. I know it isn't exactly the same situation, but it's not so different that I can't imagine what you're going through."

"I'm sorry, Sarah. That was thoughtless of me."

"I can't say I didn't say and do some thoughtless things after I got my telegram. And you don't have the benefit of that finality. I'll let it slide this once." She cast me an imperious look.

"So, what do I do now?" I asked, feeling bile rise in my gut.

"Do something other than work and go home. Start making a life for yourself. Even if she's out there, you know she wouldn't expect you to wait forever."

"Easier said than done, Sarah. I could no sooner ask a girl out than fly to the moon. It feels wrong."

"I went out on my first date three weeks ago. My sister set me up," Sarah admitted. "Before then, I hadn't been on a date with anyone besides my Joe since I was seventeen. I survived a fried chicken dinner with a complete stranger. I was bored to tears half the time, and I'm pretty sure I won't see him again, but I survived. What's more, I have another date next week. I know my Joe wouldn't want me to be alone, and this girl of yours wouldn't want that for you either. Not if she deserves you."

"You're probably right," I said.

"I usually am, and I know it feels awful. But I trust it won't feel this way forever."

"If it does, I'll die a confirmed old bachelor," I said, rubbing my temples.

"None of that. A date. I have a niece who would be perfect for you. She's not too much younger than you, and she's a war widow like me. Too young to be alone, in my mind. You two would get along famously. She's pretty and smart as a whip." She leaned forward and rested her elbows on the table like she was a hotshot businessman in the final stages of brokering some big deal.

"I'm not sure how wise it is to date a family member of my employee," I said, sitting up straighter. "And I don't want to be set up."

"I think it's the best option you've got going for you. You couldn't run this place without me, and if you don't at least show up and act a gentleman, I'll leave you in the lurch. And spread the word among Jewish secretaries the world over. You'll never hire another."

"There are secretaries from other faiths, Sarah," I said, rolling my eyes and suppressing a laugh.

"So they claim, but are you really willing to risk it?" She cocked her head defiantly.

"Heaven forbid," I said, throwing up my hands. "Fine. Set it up if she's interested. Make a reservation someplace nice and tell me when and where to show up."

"My, my, if my duties now include matchmaker, I may have to demand a raise."

"Don't press your luck," I said, shaking my head and reaching for the top patient file. "No matches have been made yet."

CHAPTER
THIRTY-FIVE

She Touched Perfection

BETH

June 3, 2007
Encinitas, California

After so many weeks going over his war photos, I thought Dad would enjoy seeing pictures of happier times. When Mom was young and vibrant and the world was full of possibility. When Dad was growing as a pillar of the community and he still had his health.

"Your mother spent weeks putting this together, you know," he said, his face glowing as he traced the outline of my pudgy cheek that was puffed to blow out the candle on my first birthday cake. "She got copies of every photo your grandparents ever took, in addition to the ones we already had. She wanted you to always have us with you."

I felt a lump in my throat, realizing that I'd left the book behind when I'd moved out. I was grateful that Greg wasn't the vindictive sort who would have pitched such a memento out of spite. I felt a confession on the tip of my tongue. Should I tell Dad that Greg had asked me to come back—sincerely and honestly asked me to give our marriage another shot? What would his advice be? I wanted to know what he thought but was equally afraid of his answer. If he wanted me to go back, could I honestly endure another forty or fifty years of no more than pleasant companionship in a marriage that had all the warmth of a drafty museum?

"I'm glad Greg thought to return it," was all I managed to say.

"How is he doing?" Dad asked. "Always such a nice man."

"He's fine," I answered truthfully. He might have missed me, but I sensed the worst of his grief for our marriage was behind him. The scuttlebutt around the office led me to believe he was doing more than adequately at work.

"That's good," Dad said, patting my hand and flipping the page of the photo album. "Your mother looks beautiful in this one, doesn't she?" he asked, admiring the silhouette of Mom dressed in a smart emerald-green dress fashioned from raw silk. It must have been for a holiday party of some sort that she and Dad hosted when I was about two. I was perched on her hip in a dress in the same shade with an elaborate lace Peter Pan collar. I gazed up at her with childlike adoration, while her gaze and smile were focused on the client of Dad's with whom she was chatting.

"She's beautiful in all of them," I said. "She always was. See the way I was staring at her? I was spellbound."

"Most everyone who met her was," Dad said.

"Everything she touched was perfection," I said, looking at all the arrangements she'd placed at precise intervals throughout the living room and the magazine-worthy spread of appetizers just visible in the corner of the photo. At these parties, the food was kosher, so our Jewish friends could eat, but nothing was so traditionally Jewish that our Gentile friends might find it too "exotic" for their tastes. The room would have been kept warm enough to be cozy, but not sweltering. And if I were a betting woman, I'd have laid odds that Dad's vest and tie were the same shade of green as our party dresses. "It was sometimes hard being the one thing in her life that didn't measure up."

"Bethany Miriam Blumenthal. If you think you weren't the light of your mother's life, you weren't paying attention."

"Don't bust out the middle name on me, Dad. I just know that she had high expectations for me, and I didn't always meet them."

"Of course she did," Dad said, sitting up straighter in his chair, wincing at the effort. "She was a Jewish mother. It was part of her genetic code to push you. But you never once fell short of her hopes. After almost twenty years of marriage, we'd given up even dreaming of having children. You were everything she ever wanted."

"Dad, I know you defend her, but I saw the look on her face when someone else outperformed me at a piano recital. When someone else got better grades. Later, when her friends' daughters married younger to more successful men than Greg. Had babies. You saw how she and I were together."

"She wasn't the warmest mother, I admit. But she had her reasons. Before I met your mother, she went through a very dark time. As did I. We helped each other through it. But her hardships had been worse than mine. If she seemed cold, it had little to do with you and very much to do with the life she had. Trust me. I know that she wanted to do better."

"I believe you, Dad," I said. I adjusted in my seat, summoning some courage. "Did you ever tell her about Margarethe and the baby?"

"Yes," Dad said. "Though by the time I met her, I'd lost hope of finding them. She forgave me for my transgressions far more easily than I forgave myself."

"I'm glad she knew," I said. I would have hated for their marriage—and consequently my very existence—to have been built upon a lie of omission.

"You know your mother had a very unhappy marriage before she met me," he said. I did know that about Mom—it wasn't a hidden fact. But she never, ever spoke about her first husband, and somehow I knew asking her about him was off limits. "I spent my entire life after I met her trying to make up for it," Dad continued. "She repaid me by making sure you were the best-looked-after child in all Southern California. And I'll be damned if she didn't succeed in her job. I hope you see that, darling girl."

CHAPTER THIRTY-SIX

WATCHED

JOHANNA

September 2, 1944
Charlottenburg, Germany

I was summoned to the warden's office on a bright day in September six weeks after I'd been imprisoned. The guard, as was their way, was humorless and not given to conversation, so I didn't bother asking if he knew why I was being summoned. My stomach lurched as we approached the wing where the warden and his highest-ranking men kept offices.

When we turned the corner to the warden's office, the bleak concrete floors and dingy white walls gave way to handsome wood paneling and marble tile. In this corridor, full of the grace of a bygone time, one would never imagine the grime and despair that reigned only a meter away.

I tried to master my countenance as the guard knocked on the warden's door. I'd never been summoned to see the warden before, as he seemed to prefer to call on me in my cell. Mercifully, his intentions weren't untoward, and I hadn't had to submit to his baser desires.

Indeed, he'd acted more like a kindly father. In most cases. He brought me a lamp to work by and permitted me some small liberties the other prisoners did not have, such as free access to the lavatory and the occasional stroll out of doors. In turn, I did whatever I could think of to be a model inmate. The guard left, and the warden gestured to the open seat across from his desk. It was plush and covered in thick velvet.

"*Gräfin* von Oberndorff, I won't belabor you with niceties. I've been ordered to offer you release from Charlottenburg."

"How wonderful, *Gefängnisleiter*. I am thrilled."

"As I knew you would be. Though there are two conditions set before you. Neither of which I think you will find too onerous."

"Of course," I said, leaning forward.

"First, you must agree to go back to work immediately. While you have been able to do good work in our care, the government feels you will be able to work more efficiently from the DVL offices as you've done in the past."

"Naturally," I said. "I'll be able to test my own aircraft."

"Precisely," he said. "And the second condition is that you will no longer use the von Oberndorff name, nor will any of your husband's relations. You may retain the title you earned through your husband but will be known as *Gräfin* Schiller."

I paused for a moment. The von Oberndorff name had been as much a part of Harald as his brown eyes or patrician nose. It would be losing another part of him. But what choice did I have?

"I accept the terms, sir," I said. "I will be pleased to return to work and to some semblance of a normal life."

"As I knew you would be, my dear," the warden said. "I've never said this to another inmate before, but you will be missed. If all our prisoners were as diligent and responsible as you are, this job would be the easiest in the world."

"Thank you very much, *Gefängnisleiter*. I will be forever grateful for the kindness you've shown me these past weeks. You allowed me to be of use, and that is no small gift."

I was ushered back to my cell to collect my things and was given a ride back to the little lake cottage that Harald and I had shared so happily. It seemed entirely foreign without his presence there. The SS had ransacked the place, but nothing of import was broken. Harald's clothes and personal items were strewn about our bedroom as cruel reminders of the man who would never return. I began to throw all his things in boxes for donation, hoping that ridding myself of his jackets, ties, books, and bric-a-brac would make his absence less painful. It only served to make the house look empty.

Metta arrived about an hour after I did, looking relieved. She enveloped me in her arms. "Not too much the worse for wear, are you?" she said, taking a step back to inspect me.

"Indeed no," I said. "Being allowed to work was a great kindness."

"I'm so glad," she said. "It took all my persuasion to get Ansel to argue for it. In the end, they figured that you couldn't leak state secrets from a prison cell.

"The problem is now you're not locked in a prison cell. You are going to be watched. Closely. You have to keep yourself out of trouble or they will snuff out your life as easily as a cheap cigarette. I've used up every bit of familial loyalty Ansel possesses in order to keep you safe. I have nothing left to protect you now."

"Thank you for your warning. I'll watch myself and do nothing to attract undue attention."

"See that you do. Ansel would love nothing more than to have you removed. He sees you as a blight on his name by mere association."

"He sounds beastly, Metta," I said, speaking honestly. "He's not unkind to you, is he?"

"It makes no difference," she said, shaking her head. She led me to the sofa in the living room and cleared off some of the books and knickknacks that had been strewn across it, so we could sit. "Johanna, I didn't just come to warn you about Ansel. I'm afraid I have bad news. Mama got very ill after you were sent to prison. It came on suddenly. The doctors seemed to think it was some condition of the nervous system but wouldn't pinpoint it any further than that. They're far too busy with the war effort, you see. I didn't think it was right to tell you while you were in prison and could do nothing about it. We had a small funeral for her, and we mentioned you, of course. I'm so sorry you couldn't have been there."

I took Metta in my arms and let the tears flow. For Mama. For Harald. For Papa. For the life Metta should have had. For Oskar, who was all but lost to me. Metta pressed her lips to my forehead and I could feel that her eyes were as wet as mine.

"I'm so sorry you had to bear that without me," I said. "I wish I could have been there for you."

"Hush now," she said, wiping my tears with her thumbs. "None of this was your fault. You would have been there if you could."

"I would have," I agreed, nodding through fresh tears. "When was it?" I asked, forcing my shaking hands to still themselves. I'd been on the point of calling Mama to invite her back to the cottage when Metta arrived. I'd thought to have her back under my roof within a week once I'd gotten things cleaned up.

"A month ago, Jojo. I'm so sorry to have to tell you this way."

"Thank you, Metta," I said, taking her in my arms once more. "It just seems impossible that we'll never all be together again." The telltale lump formed in my throat, and I wanted to indulge in a good cry, but Metta pulled away and held me at arm's length.

"I have more news, Johanna. Ansel has been snooping through the family papers since Mama died. He's become obsessed with the records that were lost on Papa's side. He doesn't like the fact that I haven't fully proven my Aryan status. I'm worried he's going to dig until he finds something that could be dangerous for you. Or all of us."

I blanched. To tell her the truth would be to give her the information that could lead to her own death warrant. To them, she was as good as Jewish and had tricked a lieutenant colonel into marrying her to boot.

"We found Papa's birth certificate and baptismal record, but nothing for his father or any of his forebears," she continued. "Do you know anything more? Something that might appease him?"

"There's good reason you haven't found anything. All the records from *Opa* Hoffmann were lost in a fire before he moved here from Poland. There was a fire in the church where he was baptized, so far as the story goes." The lie was a practiced one and I was confident I delivered it convincingly.

"He won't like that. He'll go on yet another rant about how disorganized the Polish are."

"It was a long time ago," I reminded her. "Before many of our modern methods. It's why I had to apply for honorary Aryan status."

"You did?" she asked. "I had no idea they made you."

"It came last year," I said.

"Ansel will be fuming."

"Tell him the truth. Papa rarely spoke of *Opa*, and I didn't think it wise to make it known that I had to apply for honorary Aryan status. It might have raised unpleasant questions if the news fell on meddlesome ears."

"You're right to be discreet, Johanna, but I'm not sure this will be enough to keep him happy . . ."

"I do have a letter that Harald's attorneys drafted saying that the records were irrecoverably lost," I said. I popped up from the sofa and rummaged about Harald's desk where he'd kept copies of important papers. It didn't take long to find, even though everything had been strewn about by Ansel's henchmen.

She read it over and nodded. "This may mollify him. I can hope. He's astounded that Papa didn't tell us more about his family."

The truth was that Papa cared very little about his lineage, mentioning only that he was born into an old respected German family that had settled in Poland for a time. "Remind Ansel that you and Oskar were still schoolchildren when he passed away. One doesn't trouble schoolchildren with such matters as family paperwork, now do they?"

"Perhaps not," she conceded.

Metta squeezed my hand in solidarity, and I knew she was going back to face a furious husband.

The biggest kindness I could do for her was to ensure she never knew of our grandfather's Jewish heritage, but Ansel had tools for research beyond my imagining, and I worried that I would be unable to shield her from his wrath.

—

I went back to DVL the next day, as per my agreement. Louisa didn't even do me the courtesy of a greeting. Her obdurate gaze stared past me and over to Peter, who was tainted by his association with me, but the less repugnant option before her. She thrust a dossier into his hands.

"The gun positions on the Ju 88 still aren't right. Do them again." She stalked off without another word.

"Not exactly pleased to see you, was she?"

"She never has been," I said. "Why would that change now?"

Peter just shook his head and followed me into my office. It was in shambles, clearly having been searched multiple times during my incarceration.

"I'm sorry, *Flugkapitän* Mueller wouldn't let me tidy it up. She wanted you to see it this way."

"She's quite right, Peter. It's good for me to see the disruption I caused," I said, a penitent answer to please unsympathetic ears.

Because he was usually so reserved, I was shocked when Peter crossed the room and pulled me to his chest by the shoulders. He lowered his lips to my ear.

"You are being watched, closer than you know. If you step one foot out of line, prison will seem like a lark. Be careful, trust no one."

"Even you?" I whispered back.

"That's up to you," he said. "But I know what I've heard and seen over the past six weeks. They want to find a reason to execute you because of your connection to Harald, but there has been enough push to keep you alive that they're reluctant to do it."

"Thank you, Peter," I said, placing a chaste kiss on his cheek. If anyone saw, I hoped they construed it as a sisterly kiss to a much-loved assistant. If he was right, and I was certain he was, I couldn't afford to have any slander associated with my name or Peter's. He raised his hand to the spot I'd kissed on his cheek and lowered it just as quickly.

I buried myself in schematics until the office began to clear out. I didn't want to be the last to leave, but certainly not the first either.

I rode my bicycle home to the cottage, willing myself to ignore the headlights from the car that followed me slowly. When I got to the house, I saw two men with stern expressions eyeing me as I unlocked the front door. As soon as I was inside, they sped off into the night.

This is how I was to live. Followed to and from work. Every trip to the grocer's under scrutiny. Every excursion to the cinema or the music hall, if I summoned the heart to go. But movies and music had been among Harald's dearest pleasures. To go without him seemed utterly disloyal.

I wanted nothing more than to consult him on what was best to be done. To crawl into bed with him and curl up against him, letting the world fall away.

But that was exactly what I couldn't have, and never would again. Not with him.

I calmed my hands by preparing a meal. I wasn't hungry, but I wouldn't waste the food in my rations. Chopping carrots and browning chicken was familiar and restful. That I was cooking for only myself felt as strange as a green sky or a purple ocean. I ate my meal reluctantly but left nothing to waste.

Later, as I lay in bed, the schematics of Junkers Ju 88s swirled in my head. I loved my work. I was passionate about the job. But I'd deluded myself for more than seven years, and it was time to stop. I could not divorce the work I was doing from the politics it served. Harald had advised me to keep working, even though we loathed the regime and all it stood for. In order to remain safe, we never made a fuss when the regime stripped away some freedom or another.

All it did was make us complacent and powerless.

If only we'd anticipated how bad things would become. If only we'd taken Hitler to be the dangerous madman he was and not dismissed him as a fool.

I could have worked for the air force in Britain or America. I could have used my gifts on the right side of history. I wouldn't have had to fear for my life because of the religion of a grandfather I'd never met.

But that was the music of regret, was it not? The woodwinds played a melody of coulds. The strings played the plaintive song of woulds. The brass, a hollow symphony of shoulds.

None of that was of any importance now. No matter how clearly I saw my folly, the only thing I had control over was the here and now.

I would bide my time at the office, but I would find a way to break free from the bonds of the Reich and the madman who led it.

The question was how to escape the quicksand when I was already buried to my chest.

I lay awake thinking of a million scenarios for escape, all of which ended in my death.

The most useful thing I could do was somehow ferret away information for the other side so that they could learn from our techniques, either to adapt to their own aircraft or improve upon if they could.

But the questions remained. How would I find someone to pass on my schematics, and how could I do it without losing my life?

Peter. He had thrown my incriminating rucksack away from the watchful eyes of the SS when I was arrested. He had delivered my work to me each day while I was in prison and was able to sneak me innocent contraband and notes without attracting untoward attention from the guards. He'd learned that skill somehow. And I'd have bet Mama's favorite pearl brooch that it was through some courier work for a resistance movement. He wouldn't have stuck his neck out to warn me that I was being watched if he was truly sympathetic to the Reich's cause.

I wasn't sure how to ask if he was willing, or if he had any contacts that could make use of my design schematics, nor was I certain anyone would have use for them, but it was at least a start.

Peter was at the office early the next morning, my assignment from Louisa already in hand. She needed more changes to the navigation system, which was always fiddly work. The sort of work I enjoyed when I wanted to be lost in it for a good long while.

"Peter, would you mind going on a stroll with me around lunchtime?" I asked, examining the request from Louisa. "I have a few issues I'd like to go over with you, and I thought we might as well do so in the open air. It'll be winter before you know it."

His eyes widened a moment, but he mastered his expression quickly. "If that's what you require, *Flugkapitän*. Naturally."

He disappeared back into the outer office and I dove into the navigation system. It was notoriously unreliable, and I'd wanted a chance to scrap the entire design of the navigation system and start from scratch, but time would not allow for that. I'd have to use the basic system as it was and do what I could to improve upon it. The lunch hour would have come and gone if I hadn't kept my meeting with Peter in mind. He appeared at my door, carrying a lunch box. We usually dined at the mess, but even in times like these, there were still plenty who chose to pack a lunch and enjoy the final moments of summer heat before it faded into a dignified autumn chill. We would just have to hope the daylight would keep the Allied bombs at bay for an hour or so.

"I was surprised you wanted to talk with me over lunch, *Flugkapitän*," he said once we were outside. "You've never made such a request before."

"If anyone asks, I miss my mother and Harald terribly and just needed a friendly shoulder to cry on. No one will wonder at me not going to Louisa for clearance first."

"No, that they won't."

"Can you walk comfortably as far as the lake?" I asked.

"Not a problem at all," he assured me. "Can't imagine a nicer spot."

"I never thanked you for hiding that rucksack. You saved me from the firing squad. And for going to the trouble of bringing me my work while they had me locked up in that awful place," I said as we sat on the grass. We'd rise with damp bottoms, but it was of little matter. I chose a spot far enough from the nearest employees that there wasn't a chance of their being able to make out the conversation.

"No need to thank me. You've always been kind to me. You helped me move up the ladder at DVL to become your assistant. It seemed only a fair return."

"Well, it was a kindness in more ways than you know," I said.

"I can imagine a bright woman like you would run mad with nothing to do," he mused.

"I would have. Thank God they allowed it," I said, looking out on to the rippling water and pulling my knees to my chest rather than opening my lunch box and eating. He knew it spared my sanity but might not have been aware of how key it was in securing my freedom.

"If the reason you've asked me here is to help you escape your surveillance detail, I'm afraid anything you might suspect about any . . . abilities or influence . . . I might have is overblown." I could feel his eyes on my face, so I kept my gaze fixed on the water.

"So, you have some, do you?" I asked. "I suspected as much."

"I told them you would," Peter said. "If they have one weakness it's that they underestimate your cleverness."

"Who is *they*, if I might ask?"

"It would be wiser if you didn't."

"Well then, whose side are they on?"

"Germany's," he said. "Germany as she should be. Germany as she hasn't been in quite some time. Where good, law-abiding people don't have to live in fear of being whisked off in the night. Where those spared don't wake up to find their friends and neighbors vanished and streets full of nothing but shattered glass and broken hearts left behind."

"You speak passionately, Peter. And well. Though I'd be careful."

"Oh, I am. You needn't worry. So, now that your suspicions are confirmed, what are you going to do? Turn me in? I wouldn't blame you, with who you have for a brother-in-law. But I won't betray the others, that I promise you."

I paused. The thought hadn't occurred to me to use this kind young man, a man who had gone kilometers out of his way on a lame leg each day to bring me my work, as a pawn to gain Ansel's favor. I felt a moment of relief that my soul wasn't so far gone that I would have considered it, but saddened that we lived in a world that Peter could possibly assume it of me.

"Peter, you saved my life. I'd never betray you. What's more, I could hand them Churchill, Roosevelt, and Stalin right at Hitler's office door and they still wouldn't trust me fully after what Harald did," I said. "And I don't think these goons are much for making deals. They just take what they want anyway."

"I think that's a fair assessment, yes," he said. "So, what can I—attempt—to do for you, *Flugkapitän*?"

"I think you have the question reversed, Peter. I'd like to help *you*. I have a feeling that by helping your people, I'll be helping to end this war. That, regardless of the outcome, would be of benefit to Germany."

"Do you really think the outcome doesn't matter?" he asked.

"It would stop the killing at least," I said.

"I thought you were cleverer than that, Johanna," he said, my name sounding foreign on his lips. "The killing wouldn't stop. That madman in charge would just regroup. He'd murder off anyone with enough brains to resist him and start this bloody mess all over again. Expand territory as soon as he could rebuild his army. He would move slower next time. He wouldn't anger Stalin a second time, perhaps. But the killings would never stop. Not for a single day. In your heart, you know I'm right, don't you?"

I nodded. "This needs to end. They need to win. We just have to hope they'll be kinder to us than we deserve."

"Amen to that," he said. "I admit the reason I volunteered to be your assistant while you were in prison was partly to ferry your designs to them. They would take pictures of them and send me back along my way."

"Excellent," I said. "Well, we don't have the built-in excuse of sending you as my courier any longer, not that I can exercise any sadness on that front. Could they procure you a small camera? I could claim to be archiving the design work or some such."

"I'll ask tonight," he said.

"I won't meet with them," I said. "I can't be seen anywhere out of the ordinary." As I uttered that sentence, the horror of its truth weighed in my gut like a stone. "But if I can help in any other way, I'll do what I can."

"Any information you might have on any strategies would be the most helpful. Or anything that might give them the element of surprise. I don't know too much about their main objectives, though. I fetch, I carry, I see, I listen. Above all, I find things."

"It must be useful to them to have a DVL employee among them," I said.

"They appreciate what I can do for them," he said, trying not to sound smug, but his pride was evident. He was proud to be useful and appreciated in a way the Reich would never bring itself to do. Because of one deformed leg, the Reich had discarded him as a waste of flesh.

The benefit was that it made him invisible to them.

And invaluable to their enemies.

Louisa's plan came to mind, and I felt a smile tug at my lips. "I may have the very thing they want."

CHAPTER THIRTY-SEVEN

MILKSHAKES FOR HORSERADISH

MAX

August 16, 1947
Los Angeles, California

Sarah's niece Rebecca slid into the passenger side of my car with grace. She'd been waiting on the sidewalk by her building in South LA rather than having me go to the trouble of parking and collecting her from the seventh floor. Sarah had explained that after Rebecca got word of her husband's death in the South Pacific, she'd moved from their home in Fairfax into a small apartment to conserve funds. Even so, the time was coming, and soon, when she would have to entertain the possibility of moving back in with her parents. Sarah helped her as much as she could, but I wasn't in a position to pay Sarah well enough to be as generous as she might like to be. It was probably more information than Rebecca would have wanted her aunt to disclose, but Sarah tended to get gabby over lunch. If nothing else, I could give Rebecca a good meal and a night away from home, which I expected would be welcome.

Rebecca wore a smart-looking cocktail dress. It was modest with a delicate collar made of white lace flowers and a row of simple pearl buttons down the front. The material of red satin kept it from crossing the line over to matronly or dowdy. Her dark hair was coiffed neatly, and she seemed perfectly at ease as we drove. Only the too-tight grip on her evening bag betrayed her nerves. It was a solid half-hour drive to the fancy steakhouse in Beverly Hills where Sarah had made reservations. I'd have to remember to keep in mind Sarah's expensive tastes when spending other people's money when I wrote the check for her holiday bonus the following winter. I should keep some funds in reserve in case she had other dates in store for me.

"Aunt Sarah couldn't say enough nice things about you," Rebecca said, keeping her eyes fixed on the road.

"Of course she raved about you as well," I said. "But she'd be a disloyal aunt to do otherwise."

"She is a lamb, isn't she?"

"More of a lion when she wants to be, but she's wonderful at her job."

Rebecca's laugh was like the tinkling of crystal. "You've got the measure of her, then."

The rest of the ride passed with companionable chatter.

The restaurant was known for its prime rib, so I ordered the dinner as they suggested with horseradish, salad, potatoes, and Yorkshire pudding.

When the waiter turned to Rebecca, she replied, "I'll have the same," without having looked at the menu.

I thought to question her, but let it slide. Perhaps she'd been raised to believe it was polite to follow a man's lead in a restaurant, and I'd make her uncomfortable by asking. Though my parents and I had eaten out rarely, Dad always insisted that Ma order whatever was to her liking.

Rebecca's responses to any query I made were thoughtful and her questions insightful. Almost rehearsed, in a way. She reminded me of a girl at my high school who had been determined to marry the son of a rabbi. She wanted the status and influence the position afforded. She paid attention to people and what they wanted and used that information to get people to like her, and she was highly effective at it. Rebecca was certainly more polished and poised than a high school girl, but there was still something very measured about her mannerisms.

"Tell me something no one knows about you," I suggested. Something, anything, to help her throw off her veneer.

A shadow passed over her face, and her smile slipped for the briefest of moments.

"Doesn't that seem a little personal?"

"I'm just trying to get to know you. Isn't that the point of dating? To get to know someone?"

"I—I don't care for horseradish," she admitted.

"Then please don't eat any more of it," I said. "I don't want you to eat something you don't enjoy. Would you like to order something else?"

She bowed her head for a moment. "I shouldn't have said anything." Her air of confidence vanished.

"I'm glad you did," I said, reaching across the table to place my hand on hers. "I want you to enjoy your evening. That includes the meal."

"Does it bother you that the potatoes aren't kosher to have with the meat? They have cream and butter in them," she said, a little more boldly. "Aunt Sarah said your mother keeps a kosher kitchen."

"I spent almost three years trudging through mud in Europe eating whatever I was given. I gave up my squeamishness pretty quick. I just don't advertise my indiscretions to my mother."

"M-my . . ."

"What is it?" I pressed.

"My—late husband. He insisted I keep kosher."

"And insisted you eat the same thing that he did whenever you went out."

She nodded.

"Well, it doesn't bother me one bit what you eat, Rebecca. Especially when my mother isn't in view."

She emitted a small chuckle. "You're fond of her."

"A kinder woman was never born," I said. "But unfortunately, she won't be with us long."

"Aunt Sarah said. I'm so sorry to hear it."

"Thank you," I said.

"You'll forgive me, but she also told me about your German girl. And the baby."

"Of course she did," I said. "Bless her, but she's not the most discreet person in the world, now is she?"

"Not in the least," she said. "Which makes her a useful matchmaker."

"I see your point," I said.

"I'm sorry you never found them. It must be terribly hard for you."

I nodded and cleared my throat. I'd managed not to think of Margarethe for the course of an entire evening, and it was impossible to tell if my feelings of guilt or relief were stronger. Then I felt a fresh wave of guilt that relief had surfaced at all.

"I'm sorry, I shouldn't have said anything." She looked crestfallen, as though she'd ruined the evening with her inquiry.

"Let's get out of here," I suggested. I waved over the waiter and paid the bill for the meal. Hers was largely untouched, and I was embarrassed I hadn't noticed her aversion to the food.

We went back to my car, but I hesitated before starting the engine. "What's your favorite food? I want you to eat something you actually enjoy."

"Promise you won't laugh at me?" she said, looking down at her hands.

"Cross my heart," I said, making an X on my chest with my finger.

"Cheeseburgers. With milkshakes."

We both broke into peals of laughter despite my promise. "If he was so strict about keeping kosher, how did you have the chance to try a cheeseburger? And adding extra dairy, to boot?"

"After Saul died, maybe three days after the telegram, I'd been out running errands for the memorial service. It was probably three in the afternoon, and I hadn't even thought to eat breakfast, and I realized I was so hungry I was shaking. The only place nearby was a burger stand. The waiter got my order wrong. I'd ordered the burger without cheese and a Coke, but he brought me a burger dripping with cheese and a chocolate milkshake. I was so hungry I didn't have the heart to send it back. It was the most delicious thing I've ever tasted in my life. I've had three since then."

"If we were Catholic, I'd send you to confession. But since we aren't, I'll take you to Nick's. Best greasy spoon in all LA."

She smiled and patted my knee. "That sounds nice."

Twenty minutes later we were seated in a booth in the dingy diner, looking much better dressed than was called for. She ordered the cheeseburger, fries, and milkshake barely above a whisper, as though she were divulging a damaging secret rather than ordering a simple meal. I ordered a slice of the apple pie and a coffee so she wouldn't have to eat alone.

"I'm going to bake Aunt Sarah her favorite cake tomorrow," she said after she swallowed her first bite. "You're every bit as nice as she said you were."

"Well, I'm glad I came up to snuff," I said. "Though a burger and fries hardly seem like a very impressive first date for anyone over the age of sixteen."

"It's more impressive than you know."

CHAPTER THIRTY-EIGHT

FINAL FLIGHT

JOHANNA

March 9, 1945
Berlin, Germany

Peter ferried my designs to his resistance group, now directly from my offices at DVL. I provided them with other tidbits whenever I was able, but in the beginning, I focused chiefly on sending them all the information I could about Louisa's program. If the Allies thwarted the attacks early, the Reich might call it off altogether. It was now obvious that only a miracle would win Germany the war. For those of us who had long since given up on miracles, the choices were clear: give up and hope to minimize our already staggering losses or go down fighting. Plans like Louisa's were the ones favored by a regime that could never envision a path to an honorable defeat.

Two months into our exchange, Louisa's program was officially scrapped. Whether it was because they had reason to believe it had been compromised or simply because they felt that the sacrifice of so many good pilots wasn't worth the gains to be had, we didn't know, but I allowed myself the sensation of having won a small victory.

Louisa had been unbearable at first, but the reality of the war's imminent end sobered her out of her sullenness. There was much work to do, and even if she didn't get the accolades of leading a project, we all had to look beyond those things now.

I was tucked into my work when I heard Peter turn the doorknob.

"Some reports for you, *Flugkapitän*," he said, handing me a stack of the papers with detailed descriptions from the mechanics of repairs made to various test aircraft.

"You can go ahead and file those, Peter. I won't have time to get to them until tomorrow or Thursday."

"*Flugkapitän*, I think there are one or two that you'd be interested in reading now. Please."

I looked up from my work and saw that Peter was the color of a starched sheet fresh from the laundry.

"Very well, Peter. I'll get on this immediately if it's urgent."

He turned and exited without a word.

I leafed through the stack of papers, knowing the official reports themselves were of no import.

In block letters he'd written:

THEY KNOW EVERYTHING. HANGAR 4 NOW.
BRING HELMET. DON'T RUN.

Icy sweat popped up on my brow as I tucked the letter into my pocket. This was how it was all going to end. At any moment the SS would come marching in to collect me and I'd be taken to Plötzensee to be executed. There would be no jail sentence or kindly warden this time. There would be the gallows.

At Peter's behest, I brought my flight helmet and billfold with me and hoped I wasn't leaving behind anything I might find myself wanting.

Everything looked like a usual, if busy, day in the hangar. I spotted Peter next to one of my preferred aircraft, a Bücker Bü 181, going over the systems for takeoff. I hadn't worked on the systems in the Bü in weeks, so there was no reason for me to take it out, but I would have to trust Peter's judgment.

"All systems go, *Flugkapitän*," he said as I came into view.

"What's this?" Louisa asked from the opposite end of the hangar. "Who authorized a test flight today?"

"Gerhardt gave the order, *Flugkapitän* Mueller. I mentioned that some of the other pilots had issues with the throttle sticking, and he agreed that *Flugkapitän* Schiller should make a test run." He was smart, invoking the name of our commander. And he was out of the office now, so she'd be unable to verify that he'd issued the order.

"Next time, I'd prefer you come to me first," she said, crossing her arms over her chest, glaring at us. "You've broken the chain of command. I need you working on the bombing guidance systems."

"This won't be a long run," I promised. "I'll have them to you long before the end of the day."

"See that you do," she said, storming off.

"She still orders you around like you're her staffer," Peter said, shaking his head. "That cost us time we don't have. Get in. Head southwest. Everything you need is inside."

He looked to either side and pulled me into his arms. His large brown eyes blinked back tears. He never expected to see me again.

"One kiss?" he whispered.

I nodded.

He lowered his lips to mine, and just as quickly, he pulled back. "Thank you for treating me like I matter. I know you'd never have feelings for me, but I've loved you for seeing me as I am."

"Peter, anyone who doesn't see what a remarkable man you are is a damned fool. Come with me."

"I'd just slow you down. You can't wait any longer. Go!" he ordered.

"Stay alive," I commanded in turn. I planted a kiss on his lips with a prayer it would somehow keep him safe from the evil that was coming for us.

I scaled up the ladder and into the cockpit, fully expecting a thunder of jackboots on concrete floors to echo off the hangar walls, but none came.

I took off unencumbered. Even under the circumstances, it was thrilling to be in the cockpit again. I'd only had the chance two or three times since my release. It was clear they had me chained to a desk to keep an eye on me.

I noticed that my rucksack, the one from my first attempt to flee, sat in the space the copilot would usually occupy. Once at altitude, I locked the throttle in place and rifled through it. One of the luxuries of flying, compared to driving, was that the chance of hitting an obstacle up here was next to none.

The contents were virtually the same as when I first attempted to flee. But to my papers and cash, he'd added a few more practical items such as a change of clothes, maps, a bare-bones first-aid kit, as well as another note.

> *Johanna,*
>
> *If you're alive and reading this, then there is one small mercy left in the world. The hideout was raided this morning, and your design work was everywhere to be seen. It's enough to have you hanged. You must flee to France if you can. Do not try to find your family. It will be too late for them by the time you see this. I'm sorry I can't do more for them, but saving you will be the best thing I've done with my life. It makes the sad reality that*

it will likely be ending soon a little lighter burden to bear.
Thank you for the kindness you've shown me. It meant
more than you'll ever know.
　　With love,
　　Peter

I wiped the tears from my face and returned my attention to the business of flying. France would be just over three hours in perfect conditions, and I had to leave German airspace as soon as possible if I was going to escape with my life. I didn't dare die now after Peter had gone to such lengths. The letter itself was a huge risk, but it was the only method at his disposal to save my life.

I flew, keeping my course set toward France. I had no real plan once I landed. Nothing beyond seeking out Metta and Oskar, with the help of the Allies, if possible. I could divulge all the information on German aircraft and engineering I had stored in my brain and work for the other side. It's what I should have done from the beginning. Found a way out and given my knowledge and expertise to the side that wasn't trying to kill an entire race of people, to trim anyone deemed useless or lesser from the population for the benefit of the strong and privileged.

In that moment, I said a prayer of thanksgiving that I'd been born to a half-Jewish father. Had my ancestry not made me vulnerable to the Reich, I might not have been as sympathetic to those who hadn't been as fortunate as I was. Still, I'd been numb enough to their suffering to do nothing to stop it.

I was over two hours into the flight before I saw more than a cloud or flock of birds in the sky. It was an American aircraft, based on the paint job, though I couldn't identify the make or model. It must have been doing reconnaissance work but would be heavily armed for defense. I was in an unarmed light aircraft, and shouldn't have been a target, but by the time they took aim at me, it was too late for me to take any evasive maneuvers.

He opened fire, and two rounds were enough to take out my engine. I wrestled with the throttle to keep from dipping into a steep dive, but the effort was in vain. The best I could do was urge the plane toward an open field. I had enough control that I was able to level out some and avoid a total catastrophe, but I landed so hard I could have sworn I felt every bone in my body rattle in its socket.

I wasn't sure how long it was before the young couple wrestled me from the plane, but they were kindly and gentle as the darkness surrounded me.

⁓

I woke up in a bed in a dimly lit cabin. A woman with brown hair and a caring face sat on the edge of the bed and held my hand.

"She's waking," she said quietly in German to the rest of the room. I hadn't crossed the border.

"Keep her lying flat," a male voice called. "We don't really know if her spine has been damaged."

"I wish the American doctor were here," she said. "We could use his help."

"I've wished that more than a few times these past months," the man said.

He finally came into view. He was a tall man and probably handsome if he weren't in dire need of a good bath and a shave. I couldn't see much of the room, but it didn't seem to be equipped with any sort of modern conveniences.

"Can you speak?" he asked. "Don't tire yourself, but can you?"

"Y-yes," I said, trying the word on my tongue. My throat felt like it was coated in thick glue, but the sound emerged.

"Are you in pain?" the woman asked. "Can I get you anything?"

"Water," I said. Was I in pain? I hadn't taken stock yet, preoccupied as I was with my surroundings. My left arm suddenly erupted in flames of agony. All I could do was whimper and point.

"It's broken," the man explained. "Quite badly. The rest of you took a good beating too, but your arm and the concussion seem to be the worst of it. We're trying to get you some pain medicine now, my dear."

"Thank you," I said, both to him and to the woman who came with a large glass of clean water.

"Can you feel your toes?" she asked. I wiggled them and nodded. Satisfied, she helped me to sit, propped up by dust-laden pillows that had seen happier days.

I drank from the glass of cool water and felt the viscous coating of my throat dissipate with each sip.

"We were surprised to find a woman in the cockpit," the man said. "Not that we were expecting a plane to crash practically right on our heads."

"No one does," I said.

"Do you think it's wise to be friendly?" the woman asked with a pointed glare at the man. "She's one of them."

"One of whom?" I asked.

"We don't know that for sure. She's not wearing a uniform," he protested.

"Come now, that was a government plane. Unless she stole it, she's Luftwaffe."

"You're both right," I said, realizing that trusting these people was really my only choice. "I am Luftwaffe, and that is a government plane, but I did steal it."

"Why?" the woman asked simply.

"They learned the truth about me, and I was trying to leave. I was trying to get to France so I could surrender and work for the Allies."

They exchanged glances that carried on full conversations, the way only deeply devoted couples could do.

"Jonas, Heide! What was the smoke I saw? Are you both all right?" A voice sounded from the front door.

"We have a guest," Jonas warned.

I sat upright, my head spinning in protest, then forcing me to lie back down.

A vision of Metta's face appeared over the shoulder of the man she'd called Jonas. Clearly the trauma to the head was worse than I realized.

"Johanna!" she cried in recognition. "My God, what's happened to you?"

"She crashed in the field not far from here. I couldn't just leave her there."

"No, but I'm glad they haven't followed you here," Metta said.

Heide made the sign of the cross to ward off misfortune.

Metta turned to me. "If you had to crash your plane, you couldn't have had much better luck with it."

I fought to sit up again in case the vision was real. "You're not safe, Metta. You have to go."

"Calm down, dear," Jonas said, looking to Metta. "How do you two know each other?"

"She's my sister," Metta said. "She's safe."

"They know I've been running information to the other side for months. They're coming for me." I didn't try to sit up again but grabbed for her hand.

"Yes, they are," she agreed. "I heard Ansel fuming about it just this morning. Well done, by the way. I didn't think you gave a fig for anything other than flying. Politics was too much of this world for you."

"Not anymore," I said simply. "Though way too late to claim any honor in it."

"Well, brava, anyway. Thank heaven we're not still stationed in Berlin or Ansel would be pulling apart the cottage with his own teeth trying to find any clue to where you are. He's livid."

"I just can't believe that these words are coming out of your mouth. Sweet little Metta, involved with the resistance. How did this happen? When?"

"Earlier than you might expect. I heard things in that infernal bride school Ansel sent me to that would make you ill. I started sniffing around for a way to help, and I used my connections at *Frauen Warte* to find one. I've been running propaganda ever since."

"My God, I never would have thought it of you."

"Which is why I was the perfect choice for the job. No one ever suspected me."

"Through sheer dumb luck at times. I'd say the pair of you have it in spades," Heide said, crossing her arms over her chest. "That you managed to crash under our noses is the only reason you're not in a Nazi holding cell right now, Johanna. But will they come looking for the source of the fire?"

"Not unless someone gives them reason to, since it seems the fire's put out. They have enough fires to put out of their own," Metta said, her face somber. She clearly knew exactly how bad things were for Ansel and his lot and how vicious they were capable of being when cornered.

"He's going to find me," I said, shaking my head. "He's relentless."

"He hasn't figured out that I've been running propaganda right under his nose. Don't give him credit for being cleverer than he is," Metta scoffed. "I swear these Nazis wouldn't have gotten half so far as they did if we stopped fearing them like wrathful demigods and treated them like the schoolyard bullies they are."

"Well-armed schoolyard bullies," Jonas countered. Metta conceded the point with a nod.

"How badly are you hurt?" Metta asked, turning to me. "I might be able to get us some medical supplies."

"My arm is broken," I said, not needing a doctor's assessment. "Maybe badly. Apart from that, I think I'm going to be fine."

"If we set your arm, could you travel? You're still over one hundred kilometers from the French border. Two or three hours by jeep if we're lucky."

I nodded.

"Good. I can find the supplies to get that arm set for sure. Getting you out of here may be a bigger trick. They're looking for you, so we need to act quickly too."

"Thank you, Metta," I said, extending my good hand to take hers in mine. "I thought I'd never see you again."

"There will always be a way, sister," she said, kissing my knuckles. Despite the dark circles under her eyes and shoulders stooped from fatigue, she looked remarkably well. And filling out like a proper woman, though she'd been a mere girl just yesterday. I realized that it wasn't just transitioning from girlhood to womanhood that had altered her figure.

"You're . . . going to have a baby?"

She smiled meekly. She was able to conceal the bulge well with her clothes. She was maybe five months along, but she barely showed signs of her impending motherhood.

"How wonderful to think that amid all this horror, a flower can still bloom. I'm so pleased for you, Metta."

"As am I," she said, rubbing the expanse of her abdomen. "Four more months now."

"You have to be careful," I warned. "For the baby. Please."

"I still have work to do," she said. "What kind of mother would I be if I let her be born into a world like this?"

"You know it's a girl?"

"You sound like her father," Metta said, squeezing my hand.

"Ansel is pleased, I take it?"

A cloud crossed over her eyes. "Over the moon. Naturally. Now get some rest, I have some work to do to get you out of here."

CHAPTER THIRTY-NINE

ONWARD

MAX

June 7, 1948
Los Angeles, California

Rather than leave for our honeymoon immediately, we took two days after the wedding to settle in together and move my belongings to the house we'd bought a block south of my parents'. It wasn't large or luxurious, but it would serve the two of us well until our family grew larger. Rebecca had taken up residence as soon as we signed the papers two months back, so it was just a matter of moving the contents of my childhood bedroom to the new house. It was no more than two trips in the Studebaker to get all the boxes moved, and it took only a couple of hours, but it was important to Rebecca to have the house set up and ready for housekeeping as a married couple. She wanted to come home with things properly arranged for our life as it would be, and I could see the wisdom of her plan, though I'd rather have held with tradition and gone right after the wedding.

"I hope you like the sofa," she said as I sat with my after-breakfast coffee and the newspaper. She flitted about the room with a dust rag, wiping away particles of dust that no other person on earth would have noticed. "I worried it might be too plush for you." To stay afloat, she'd sold off many of her household goods after her first husband had been killed, so she'd been charged with the furnishing and decoration of the new house. With the help of wedding gifts, she'd created a cheerful haven within the constraints of the modest budget I'd been able to provide for her.

"It's perfectly fine," I said, wiggling a bit in place. "Very comfortable. Sturdy. Nice color. You chose well."

"I'm glad you like it," she said, though her head still drooped a bit.

"Rebecca, in the last two days we've had this conversation about the sofa, the dining room table, and the dresser. You've done a fine job picking everything out. It's all lovely."

"I just want you to be comfortable and happy."

I patted the expanse of sofa next to me and she joined me, carefully folding her dust rag before sitting.

"I am incredibly happy, darling. And it would take more than a lumpy sofa or a wobbly leg on the kitchen table to change that. What's got you worried?"

"Nothing at all. My father always says, Whatever job you have, act like it's the most important one in the world. My job is to take care of you and run this house. I don't want to do a passable job; I want to excel at it."

"You do," I assured her. "I know we're only two days in, but you're already due for a raise."

"Hardy har har," she said, kissing my nose. "If only my position were paid."

"Oh, isn't it?" I asked, batting my eyes and pulling her to my chest. I laced my fingers in her hair and pulled her mouth to mine, kissing her deeply until she pulled away.

"Oh, I suppose it's sort of a payment in kind," she said, winking.

"Rebecca, I don't just appreciate what you've done here. I admire it," I said, kissing her cheekbone. "If anything is amiss, I promise I'll let you know. Or better yet, fix it myself. I don't want you to drive yourself crazy trying to please me."

She leaned in to claim another kiss. "I believe you, Max. I really do."

"Forgive me for saying this, but I'm not Saul. I'm not going to lord over you and this house like a tyrant."

Rebecca exhaled and her shoulders sagged. She clapped her hand over her mouth but managed to fight back a sob.

"What's wrong, darling?" I asked, wrapping my arm around her.

"With Saul it wasn't just the food or the furniture. If anything wasn't as it should be, he—he would lose his temper."

"Did he hurt you?"

She nodded.

"That son of a bitch," I said, pulling her to my chest again. "I'm just sorry the enemy killed him so I didn't get the pleasure of doing it myself."

She stood and went to the case where we displayed our books. She removed her copy of her Haggadah that she would use as her guide for preparing the Passover Seder. She opened the cover and removed a photograph that had been tucked inside and handed it to me. It was maybe six years old and showed her heavily pregnant. Her hand was poised on her belly and she wore a tentative smile.

"Two days later he beat me so hard I lost the baby," she said, crossing an arm over her chest, bracing herself against the agony of the memory. "It was the only time I ever saw him contrite. He promised me we'd have another. I couldn't get pregnant and keep it after that, though. I should have told you."

"Yes, you should have," I said. "But not for the reasons you think. I want you to always feel safe, happy, and loved. Knowing what you went through in the past will help me be better at *my* job. Let's promise to not keep things from each other, OK? I want us to get started off on the right foot and stay that way for the next sixty years."

"It's a deal," she said. "Anything you need to get off your chest?"

"Not that I can think of," I said.

She crossed back to the bookcase, returned the Haggadah to its place, removed a stack of papers that hadn't yet been filed away, and handed them to me.

The letters asking for information leading to Margarethe and the baby.

"Do you think you can really move on from her?" she asked, regaining some of the confidence that had flagged. "I love you, Max, but I don't want to live in her shadow for the rest of my life."

"I haven't sent one out since I met you," I said. "I can't promise that she won't haunt me from time to time, but I won't make it your problem."

She reclaimed her seat next to me and snuggled into my side. I set the papers on the end table and circled my arms around her once more.

"You're not angry that I brought it up, are you?"

"No, I was going to thank you for trusting me enough to tell me how you feel."

We sat, with her curled up in my arms, for what seemed like hours. I felt her breathing grow even, her muscles relax as she became more comfortable in my presence. At length, she sat up and announced that it was past time for her to start preparing lunch.

She walked to the kitchen and began to hum softly over the rattle of pots and pans. I crossed the room to my den, already cleverly appointed by Rebecca so I could review patient files in the evening or unwind with a book and a glass of scotch in comfort. I tossed what remained of the letters Sarah had printed for me in the bin, hoping that wherever Margarethe and the baby were, they were loved and cared for.

We spent three weeks on the north shore of Kauai, near Hanalei Bay. For the first few days, Rebecca was still just as tightly wound as the nervous housewife in the living room of our tiny Los Angeles bungalow. Then one day, as we toured some of the lushest gardens I'd ever seen, I saw the muscles in her neck uncoil, her shoulders drop, and her breathing grow deep and even the longer we walked.

"Roses and pansies seem positively prosaic after this," she said, more to herself than to me or anyone else. One of the blooms, a yellow-and-white plumeria, hung on a low branch. She reached over to smell it and seemed consumed by the scent of lemon that emanated from the heart of the delicate flower. Her lips turned upward, her eyes closed, and she looked more at peace than I'd ever seen.

In that moment, I vowed that she would feel this tranquil at home, even if it meant bringing the islands to her.

CHAPTER FORTY

ACROSS THE WINDING RIVER

JOHANNA

March 10, 1945
Near Remagen, Germany

Metta returned the next day with a splint and some pain medication. She was dressed in a sturdy maroon suit and perfectly coiffed—the picture of a smart young German matron. There were dark rings under her eyes, and a trace of regret in their blue depths that contrasted with her smile. I wanted to know what she was thinking, to know what she'd really been up to these few years, but there wasn't time to probe her. What's more, the pain in my arm was a skilled thief of words. I could barely unclench my teeth long enough to utter more than a syllable or two.

"You need to save the rest of this painkiller for your trip unless you think you're going to faint," she warned, seeing the pain in my face. "These are your travel papers, and a tidbit from Ansel's desk to make the American refugee camp a little more welcoming. A friend told me there's always room for those willing to share information."

"I can tell them plenty," I said. "Don't make Ansel angry."

"They want proof. They'd have to take whatever information you gave them on trust. This is concrete. We can't risk them turning you back. Take it. I promise it will all be fine."

"If you think it's necessary," I said. "I wish you'd come with me."

"You need those papers more than I do. The war is ending, whether Ansel and his cronies want to acknowledge it or not. Crossing the border will be a lot easier to do soon enough. I'll do what I can to follow you in a few days."

"You'd better."

She squeezed my hand. "Let's just worry about getting you safe. I need to go back before I'm missed. Ansel has been keeping me close these past few weeks."

Of course he would. In his bones, he had to know the war was ending, and he wanted the comfort of his wife by his side.

She kissed my cheek and went out into the fledgling spring sunshine to rush back to Ansel. The sun bounced off her perfect crown of blond plaits, bathing her in golden light.

Jonas, apparently used to navigating by stealth, managed to get me from the cover of the woods to the road that would lead to the French border. I spent the next two hours in the cab of a rickety truck Jonas drove, with each bump jostling my broken arm.

Not many months before, the French border would have been guarded by German soldiers, but now, fresh-faced American boys took their place. Jonas stopped the truck a half mile from the border. I was going to have to walk the rest on foot, so that neither Jonas, nor his ancient pickup truck, would be seen.

Such a distance seemed interminable with the extent of my injuries, but I forced each ragged breath in and out of my body.

Once I crossed the border into France, I would be safe.

Safe from Ansel.

Safe from the Reich.

Safe from the specter of my own ancestry.

I thought about life in France with Metta and the baby. Would she want to stay there until the baby was born? Go somewhere else that hadn't been ravaged by war? We'd be starting over, but it would at least feel less like starting from scratch.

I held up my hands at the border and surrendered myself as a refugee. I soon found myself in the hospital tent of a camp for displaced persons. The American medical staff was attentive and kind, despite my accent and country of birth. I'd expected cool indifference, but my nationality didn't seem to matter to them so long as I had injuries to treat. When I was well enough to be questioned, I was ushered to a young American lieutenant, William Patterson, who walked with a pronounced limp. Lamed during the war, no doubt, but he hadn't accepted discharge home. He believed in his cause, that much was certain.

He rattled off a list of questions, which I answered as best as my substandard English would allow. He surprised me by slipping into more than passable German to clarify when I fumbled.

"You must think me very feeble," I said, feeling the heat prick in my cheeks. "Languages were never my strong suit."

"Given your background, I would expect mathematics and science would be more your cup of tea," Lieutenant Patterson mused in German.

"Exactly right," I agreed.

"What information do you have for us?" he asked. "The American government will be grateful for whatever you have to share."

I passed over the paper that Metta had taken from Ansel's desk. I hadn't even taken the time to read it, but it certainly piqued the lieutenant's interest.

"Who did you say this paper came from?"

"It's my brother-in-law's. My sister took it from his desk."

"Why didn't she come with you?" he asked.

"She wanted to make sure I wasn't found," I said. "Her absence on top of my being at large might have resulted in her husband organizing a proper search. She wanted me to get away."

"A kind sister," he observed.

"The very best of them," I said.

"Well, you're welcome to stay in this camp for the duration of the war," he said. "I'm sure we can arrange for it."

"I can share whatever information I have about the air force," I volunteered. "Anything at all."

"That's generous of you," he said. "We may take you up on that. God willing, this whole mess will be over soon and we won't have need for it."

"Whatever I can do to help, please let me know," I said. "I do want to be of use."

I felt as though I were echoing my early days in prison, though this time I didn't think my life was on the line.

Lieutenant Patterson offered me a smile, and I was escorted to a bunk in a crowded gymnasium.

This would be my home until the end of the war, and the foundation on which I would have to rebuild my life.

CHAPTER FORTY-ONE

ANSWERS FROM ACROSS TOWN

BETH

June 10, 2007
Encinitas, California

We trudged to the back garden to sit under the massive canopy that the staff had installed. It gave the residents a much-appreciated respite from the oppressive Encinitas summer sun. Mrs. Patterson had come for the day. Despite the constant ache in his spine, Dad had ensured Mrs. Patterson's chair was completely shaded and that she was comfortable before he took his own seat. I'd been hoping for something to keep me at home. An urgent call from my department chair. A burst water pipe at my apartment. Anything to avoid having to admit the truth.

"What were you able to find, my dear?" Mrs. Patterson asked once they were finally settled. She'd come to visit once more last week, reveling in sharing stories about Metta with Dad. Her brown eyes were bright with anticipation. She scooted toward the edge of her chair.

Kimberly came out with a tray of pink lemonade and paper cups. She patted my shoulder and retreated into the sanctuary of the air-conditioned house.

"Nothing," I said honestly, handing Mrs. Patterson one of the paper cups full of the sticky pink liquid. "James and I reran all our searches with full proper names, but nothing. No record of a baby born at the right time. No death certificates. No references in newspapers. The only thing we saw was a register that listed Ansel as missing in action and presumed dead."

"That's more than I ever found," she said. "I confess I'd hoped you'd be able to dig up more. But after all this time, I didn't suppose it was all that likely."

"I'm sorry to disappoint," I said, handing Dad some lemonade and sitting with my own. It was a lovely garden, and even Dad with his exacting standards had to admit they did a great job making the best of a small space.

"Don't apologize, Bethie. You worked hard. It may be that we're not meant to know," Dad said.

"How long did you look for them after?" I asked. I felt a weight in my heart knowing we'd likely never learn their fates.

"I looked for Metta for a full year after the war," Mrs. Patterson said, her eyes fixed on a distant part of the garden as she recalled the past. "I wrote letters just like your father did. I'd just met the man who would become my husband, an American lieutenant, and he even got leave to take me back to Berlin before the Soviets locked the place down. Their apartment looked untouched, but their neighbors hadn't seen them since Ansel was moved to the front. They assumed he was killed in the line of duty and didn't question anything. People were all too busy rebuilding their own lives to worry about missing neighbors. There were just too many for anyone to pay any real heed."

"They were terrible times," Dad agreed. "We all had to work so hard to get entire towns and cities up and running again that details—and people—sometimes got lost in the reconstruction."

"What then?" I asked Mrs. Patterson. "Did you give up?"

"Hardly, my dear. It was ten years before I stopped my search. But you see, that charming young Lieutenant Patterson begged me to come back to America with him and be his wife just as soon as he was discharged. I'd been looking for her for a solid year at that point and was no closer to finding her than I was the day I crossed over the border and threw in my lot with the Americans. I was a widow and an orphan. And in my heart, I knew I wasn't a sister anymore either. William was all I had."

"What about your brother?" I asked. I didn't think they'd have become close, given their differences, but it was one more sibling than I was able to lay claim to.

"Oskar was killed in the Battle for Berlin at the very end of the war. I continued the search from our home in Monterey as best I could, but I never found a thing. After ten years, I didn't have the heart to keep digging, though I always wondered if I'd tried hard enough."

"You couldn't have done more," Dad said, his voice stronger than I'd heard in weeks. "As much as I've tortured myself on the matter, you and I looked long and hard for them."

"Dad's right, though I'm sorry we haven't been able to trace her," I said. "I really hoped that with the advances in technology, we'd have better luck."

"You've done your best, my dear. Just as your father and I did all those years ago."

"Well, I'm sure wherever she is, she's glad you both had happy lives," I said, though it felt like a shoddy substitute for real answers.

"That I did," Mrs. Patterson said, squeezing my knee. "My marriage to William wasn't a marriage of the sort that I had with Harald, but he was a good man and a good father to our sons. I had fifty-eight wonderful years with him, and that's quite enough happiness for one lifetime."

"That's truly amazing," I said. Greg's specter hovered in my brain. If we'd married fifty-odd years ago, we would have likely stayed married. I would have had to find a way to be content with my lot in life, and after a half century of marriage, I would have felt a good deal of satisfaction in knowing we'd succeeded in spending a lifetime together. That chance was gone, and though I did feel a pang of loss, it lessened each day. Content wasn't enough, and I didn't have to be ashamed of wanting more.

"Perhaps we weren't meant to find her and the baby," Mrs. Patterson said, echoing Dad's sentiments. "Maybe her final gift to us was to find each other and know that she'd never been forgotten."

"Maybe so," Dad said, taking her hand in his. "I sent Bethie on this chase to get some answers. I never expected to find them so close to home."

"Even now, life can be surprising. Isn't that a comfort?" Mrs. Patterson said, not releasing my father's hand.

CHAPTER FORTY-TWO

THE ROAD TO STUTTGART

BETH

June 14, 2007
San Diego, California

James had texted me at exactly eight a.m. He waited to send the message until the precise moment when it would no longer be considered ridiculously early.

> I have a lead. Come to my office.

Given that he had been so cautious not to get my hopes up, I didn't take the text lightly. I threw on clothes, drove through the nearest coffee shop pickup window for two Americanos, and went straight to the library. James was in his office, his face illuminated by the soft white glow of his computer monitor. He patted a chair he'd placed next to him without tearing his eyes from the screen.

"What sort of lead?" I asked in lieu of a polite greeting.

"I stumbled upon a site for fatherless war babies looking to connect with their families. I found a man by the name of David Bauer who believes his father was an American medic named Max. His date of birth lines up with when your dad and Margarethe would have been in contact."

"That seems pretty tenuous," I said, feeling the hope subside from my gut.

"I know," he said. "I emailed him and asked for more details. His mother's name? Margarethe Ziegler, née Hoffmann."

"Really?" I asked, my hands shaking. "Do you think it could be him?"

"The names are common enough that I suppose it's possible there might be another couple under similar circumstances, but I think the likelihood of a coincidence that large is pretty remote."

"How can we know for sure?" I asked.

"I've asked him to send a picture. We can compare it with one of Max. I mean, it's not a DNA test, but it's a place to start."

There was a soft ding from the computer as if to punctuate his words. A new message from David Bauer appeared in bold in his inbox.

"Ready to get a look at your maybe-half-brother?" he asked.

I nodded but grabbed his free hand for solidarity.

James clicked on the link. The man in the picture was in his early sixties and had salt-and-pepper hair with a lopsided smile that showed even, white teeth. Aside from piercing blue eyes and a slightly more angular jaw, he was the very image of Dad from my adolescence.

The tears spilled over and I made no attempt to wipe them free. James wrapped his arms around me, and I willingly melted into them. He felt solid and safe just then, and I was glad to have that anchor for a few moments.

"It has to be him," I managed to say. "What do we do now?"

"Well, we write back and tell him what you think," he said.

"Send him one of the pictures of Dad from the scans I sent you," I said. "And tell him that if it turns out to be true, he has a father, aunt, cousins, and sister who are all very anxious to meet him."

James typed away for several minutes and the email was sent. He wrapped his arms around me again.

"How are you doing with all this?" he asked. "It's a lot to take in."

"It is. I'd resigned myself to never knowing. But I'm so glad he's real. I couldn't bear the thought of having no one after Dad passes. I don't expect we'll be best friends or anything, but it's nice to know I'm not alone."

"You're not alone, Beth," he said, his voice low. He planted a kiss on my forehead. My body screamed to reciprocate. To up the ante and kiss him on his lips. But I was in nothing like the right headspace to explore anything with James. He was tempting. He was warm and caring and so many things Greg wasn't . . . but I didn't want to start anything while my mind was so wrapped up in finding my brother.

Finding David.

The computer dinged again. Another response. If nothing else, he was a good correspondent. Dad would be proud about that.

Dear Beth,

The picture of your father looks so much like me during my days at the university that I thought I was looking at my old photos for a moment. We have much to discuss, and I hope you and your father might consider making the trip to Stuttgart so we can meet in person. I would come to San Diego myself, but I am teaching in the summer term at the University of Stuttgart in preparation for my sabbatical this fall and cannot leave until my duties are complete in August. If you can make the trip, my wife, son, daughter, and I would be honored to welcome you into our home. Please feel free to call my home at any time.

David Bauer

"It has to be him. And he's a professor like me."

"So it would seem," James said. "What are you going to do next? Are you going to go?"

"I don't see what choice I have. I need to know. Dad needs to know."

"When do you want to go?"

"God, I don't know. There's no way Dad could make the trip . . . but I hate to do this without him."

"I'll go with you," he said. "We searched for him together, let's meet him together."

"It's not about going alone, James. I just don't want Dad to miss out on the chance to meet his probably-son." I braced myself, expecting a full safety lecture about meeting strange men online alone. Greg would, even still, pitch a fit about me meeting a stranger in a foreign country.

"I get it," he said. "But I'm curious too. We put weeks in together on this, and I want to know how the story ends. And it may be a hard time for you. You may need a shoulder to cry on. A beer-drinking buddy. Whatever you need."

"I appreciate it more than you know." I turned away from the computer screen to look at him and kissed his cheek. It wasn't what he'd hoped for, but it was what I had to give. I could see he meant what he said. He wanted to support me in this. He wasn't asking for promises of anything I wasn't ready to give. "I'd like it if you came."

He cracked a smile. "I won't get in the way. I just want to make sure you have someone there on your side. Plus, I have more vacation time than I know what to do with."

"Let's call first. We may have some crossed wires and end up spending money on last-minute tickets to Europe for no good reason."

"Well, we'd get a trip to Europe out of it, but I see your point."

"What time is it in Germany?"

He looked at his watch and counted in his head. "Around six thirty p.m."

I pulled out my cell and looked at the foreign number in the signature of the email. I punched it in and went limp against James as he wrapped a supportive arm around me.

The line rang twice before a dignified baritone answered.

"*Hallo*, David Bauer."

"Um, hello, David. I just received your email. I'm Beth Blumenthal. I do believe I'm your little sister."

"How wonderful, Beth. I have been waiting for a call like this one my whole life."

CHAPTER FORTY-THREE

FOUND

BETH

June 14, 2007
Encinitas, California

I gripped Dad in a hug before I closed the red door behind me.

"Good to see you too, Bethie. Everything OK?" Dad leaned back to read my expression and narrowed his eyes at the sight of tears gleaming in mine.

Mrs. Patterson emerged from behind him. "The boys brought me over as soon as you called. I thought it was beyond hope at this point."

"I was wrong. Dad, Mrs. Patterson, I'm pretty sure we found him."

I steadied Dad as he swayed in his spot for a moment.

"You don't mean . . ."

"Your son, Dad. Your nephew," I said to Mrs. Patterson. "My half brother. His name is David. He's living in Stuttgart. He's a professor with a wife and two kids."

"A boy? I have a son? She was wrong about that, then."

"Metta thought she was having a girl?" I asked.

"So she claimed. I often imagined a boy, though. She was so rarely wrong that it never occurred to me to doubt her."

I thought back to one of the key pieces of information from my conversation with David. "You both need to know. Metta died shortly after David was born."

Mrs. Patterson was quiet for a moment. "I think I knew that all along," she said, dabbing tears from her eyes. "She would have found me otherwise. But I couldn't give up without knowing."

"You were right not to," I said, glad that her search and my father's had not been in vain. "David can't come here just now, but I'm going to go to him."

"You do that, Bethie," Dad said. "And you take this for him."

He handed me a little wooden house I recognized from the box of war memorabilia. "It was a vow I made to his mother. I had promised to build her a house just like this in California. To help make her feel at home. Like so many other promises, I was sorry not to keep this one."

~

James held my hand as the wheels touched down in Stuttgart after our short flight from Frankfurt. For most of the long haul from San Diego to Frankfurt, I had slept with my head on his chest and his arm around me, and I found that his presence soothed the worst of my jitters.

I'd been nervous about allowing him to come along, worried that he would use the trip as an excuse to make a case for himself as a suitor, but he didn't make any attempt at another romantic gesture. He followed my lead as we rented a car and navigated the highway from the airport to David's house on the outskirts of town. I offered silent thanks to my father, who had insisted I learn how to drive a stick shift.

"Try to relax," he urged. "I'm sure he's just as nervous as you are."

"How can you tell I'm nervous?" I asked. I'd deliberately kept from jabbering on, and I was too busy driving to fidget.

"If your knuckles were any whiter, they'd be glowing. And I'm guessing after San Diego traffic, this doesn't faze you," he said, gesturing to the reasonable flow of cars whizzing by. "Just breathe and be yourself."

In the space of a few ragged breaths we arrived at the address David had provided. They lived in a row house, painted an eggshell white with a red tile roof. It wasn't the most inviting-looking house I'd seen in my life, but most of the housing on the outskirts of the town tended toward the austere and functional. The garden, however, was a riot of summer flowers nearly as lush as Dad's former garden back at home. Given the difference in climate between Germany and San Diego, David's efforts were better than admirable. Though it may have been his wife's handiwork, I reminded myself. I wanted so much to see pieces of my father's personality reflected in him—to know they wouldn't be lost irretrievably once Dad died—that I was apt to seek out meaning where there might be none.

"Are you ready for this?" James asked. He took my hand in his, squeezed, then released it without lingering.

"As I'll ever be," I said. *Focus, be objective, be calm.* I repeated the mantra but struggled to keep my hands from shaking.

I stepped out of the tiny rental and the door to the house opened, David's tall, broad frame filling it. If I hadn't known that he was my father's son, I still might have stopped him in the street to ask if he had some unlikely connection to the family. I walked up to the front steps and offered a hand for him to shake. In turn, he opened his arms for a hug. I stood in his embrace and remembered all the times Dad had held me just like this. Good times, like graduations and birthdays and my wedding day. Bad times, like failed tests, breakups, and petty squabbles with friends. He had the gift of magnifying joy and minimizing grief in a simple hug. It seemed that David had inherited that gift.

"Please come inside," he said, and his voice sounded thick.

He ushered us into his living room, which was a cozy contrast to the stark exterior. Two women sat on the sofa: an attractive blond woman in her fifties, and a much older brunette woman whose eyes were still bright and keen as they assessed me. They looked as nervous as I felt, which was oddly comforting. There was a perfectly arranged platter of cookies and a pot of coffee on the table in front of the sofa, and David began pouring with a slight shake in his hands.

"This is my wife, Emilia, and my mother, Heide. We are so pleased you were able to make the trip."

"Heide?" I asked. "I thought your mother was Margarethe Ziegler, maiden name Hoffmann?"

"You must excuse me," David said. "Heide is the only mother I've ever known. She and her late husband, Jonas, raised me from an infant."

"I see . . . And your mother? Margarethe?" I asked. "My father looked for her for ages. As did her sister. You said on the phone that she died shortly after you were born. Can you tell me more?"

"We called her Metta," Heide answered in thickly accented English and shook her head. "Shortly after David's aunt was shot down, Ansel discovered that Metta had been running propaganda. He kept her on a tight leash after that, so there was no escaping to find her sister. He actually had men guard the doors at his quarters so she couldn't leave. He allowed me to sit with her at times only because he thought I was still loyal to the cause. He wanted me to read to her from their propaganda and persuade her to see his way of things again."

"My God," I whispered. "What a monster."

"Oh, that wasn't the half of it, my dear. He became obsessed with finding the truth about her father's heritage. He thought she was hiding something unsavory from him. When he found records indicating that she had a Jewish grandfather, he went into a rage."

David went pale and his wife wrapped an arm around him. Even after all this time, he was loath to hear the truth.

"What did he do?" I found myself asking. The sinking feeling in my stomach told me that I already knew.

"He couldn't bear the thought that he'd married the very thing he despised. I walked in moments after he choked the life out of her. She knew he was capable of such viciousness. Only days before, she had begged me to protect David if anything happened to her. So when I saw him stooped over her body, I grabbed David and ran. I had failed her, but I would not fail her son. The thought of what would have happened if I'd been a few moments later still haunts me."

David took Heide's hand. "You've been an amazing mother to me from that day forward. I'm sure that my birth mother would rest easy knowing how well you cared for me." The emotion was thick in his voice, but he kept tears at bay.

She patted his hand in return. The affection between mother and son was as genuine as if she'd borne him herself.

"We kept David's identity secret and passed him off as our own."

"You were afraid of Ansel?" I asked.

"He still had enough friends that he could have caused trouble for us, so we kept as quiet as possible. Once things were calmer after the war, we had no way to find Metta's sister or David's father. Not in those days. We didn't have enough information to start a real inquiry. And we never knew where Ansel got to, so there was always the worry that he would come back for some sort of revenge against us or even little David, so we were hesitant for quite some time about reaching out."

"I can understand that," I said. "Though I'm glad you decided to after all these years, David."

"I always hoped that the American soldier was my father. It was almost more important to know that the monster who murdered my mother wasn't my father than it was to actually meet the soldier himself," he said. "I thought I was likely too late for that anyway, but I had to try. To learn that he's still alive is a gift I hadn't expected."

"He felt the same way. He tried for years to find you and your mother," I said. "He never forgot about you."

"That's good to know. I was eighteen when my parents told me that I was their adopted child. I needed a birth certificate to register for the university, and there wasn't one to provide. They didn't have much choice but to tell me then so we could get everything sorted with the government. We decided to have them listed as my parents for various reasons. I considered looking for my birth father a number of times, but it felt disloyal to the parents who raised me, somehow."

"I finally convinced him that I wanted him to find the answers for himself, and I am thrilled that he did," Heide said, wiping a single tear from his cheek. "My Jonas and I weren't able to have children of our own. The war was too hard on my body to allow it. I always thought our David was a blessing I'd never done anything to deserve. But I couldn't leave this world in peace if he hadn't tried to find the truth. I only wish I'd pushed him to do it sooner."

"I'm just grateful you've done it at all," I said. "I'm afraid Dad isn't long for this world, though. And your aunt isn't in the best condition either."

"Tell me truthfully, do you think our father will be pleased to see me after all this time?"

"David, he lit up like a child who'd been given the keys to a toy store when I told him we found you."

"I hoped that would be the case . . . but I've had decades to have nightmares about the alternatives."

"I don't like to speak in absolutes, but I've never seen my father so happy. I promise he will be more than thrilled to see you."

"Then I will see what I can do about my summer courses. If he's as frail as you say he is, I don't want to miss out on the chance to spend some time with my father before he passes on. And you too, sister. We've got a lot to catch up on."

Sister.

"We do," I said, just barely able to keep my voice from cracking. James put his hand on my knee in reassurance, and in that moment, any doubts I'd had about bringing him along vanished.

"I think you're wise," Emilia said. "You can make amends with the university, but you can't reclaim this opportunity once it's lost."

"The children will come as well," David said. "They have wanted to see America for years. Certainly they can rearrange their summer plans to meet their grandfather and lie on a beach in San Diego."

"I can teach them how to surf," James offered.

"Well, that will be a yes from Johannes, I'm sure," Emilia said.

"His great-aunt Johanna will approve of your choice of name."

"It was a happy coincidence that Emilia's favorite uncle was named Johannes, but we're glad the name can pay tribute to both of them," David said.

"That boy hasn't met a sport he doesn't like," Emilia added. "And he's more of a daredevil than is good for my nerves. He'll be thrilled to talk with his aunt about her piloting."

"Like his grandfather," I said. "Where other fathers bought their daughters dolls and kitchen sets, he bought me baseball gloves and cleats."

"Good man," Emilia said. "There's time enough for babies and kitchens later."

"God forbid Johannes take up with airplanes," Heide said. "I barely survived his little experiment with ski jumping. He couldn't be content to just ski down the mountain like a sane person. After he speaks with his great-aunt, send him to me to hear how his grandfather Jonas and I pulled her out of a wreck of a plane after she crashed. She was lucky to not break her neck."

"That would only serve to encourage him," David said, rolling his eyes. "Annika is the bookish one like you and me," he added. "She'll likely follow in our footsteps and have a career in academia. She'll start her master's in chemistry in the fall."

"Poor soul," James said with a wink. "We still have time to talk her out of it."

"We'll take her to see the campus. She'll love it," I said, nudging James playfully with my elbow.

"Come with us, Mama. The California sun would be good for you," David said, taking her hand in his. "And I'm sure Max and Johanna would be pleased to see you."

"No, my son. These bones are too old to cross an ocean. And you don't need me there for this reunion. You go and remember me to them, and I'll be a happy mother."

CHAPTER FORTY-FOUR

RED DOOR

BETH

June 20, 2007
Encinitas, California

Just four days earlier, I'd flown to Germany with only James in tow. I returned home a brother, sister-in-law, niece, and nephew richer. It was just as well that James took the wheel on the ride home from the airport. My hands shook in anticipation the entire ride, and David was hardly more restrained than I was. It was nearly dark, and we were all exhausted, but there was no delaying this reunion any further.

We offered to take David and his family to their hotel first so they could clean up and rest from the long flight, but David refused, despite a slight moan of disappointment from Annika. A raised eyebrow from her mother silenced any further complaint.

Kimberly had tied a flock of colorful balloons to the fence in front of the care home, and affixed lights to the trees that made it look as though they were alight with a glorious cluster of fireflies.

Dad stood on the front porch, gripping his walker and looking taller and straighter than I'd seen him in years. Mrs. Patterson was by his side, her hand resting on Dad's in solidarity, with her sons, Nick and Stephen, behind her.

"Welcome, son," Dad said, his eyes not wavering from David's approaching form.

David crossed the yard and stepped onto the front porch, where he towered over Dad, just as Dad would have towered over David when he was a boy.

"I am so happy to finally meet you," David said, his voice husky. He wrapped his arms around Dad in a hug, tentative at first, but neither seemed ready to let go once he finally had the person he'd been searching for in his arms.

Dad's face was red and streaked with tears when he finally pulled away. "Come inside," he managed to choke out, waving all of us inside the care home. Tears gleamed in Johanna's eyes as she took David in her arms for a hug.

"Oh, my dear boy. How I hoped this day would come. I'm so happy you're well." Then she switched from English to German. Some things were too important to say in anything but a mother tongue. I wished I could parse what they said, but it was probably best that the moment remain private.

"It's so good to meet you at last, Aunt Johanna," he said in English for our benefit.

The table was laden with food. No supermarket fruit trays to be seen. There was homemade party food of every description, from little rolled chicken quesadillas to sausage bites with cheese. A blend of California and Germany, just like David himself. Kimberly hung back, a tissue indiscreetly hanging from her hand to catch the occasional errant tear.

"Kimberly, I can't believe you did all this," I said, gesturing widely.

"Honey, I haven't seen your father this excited, ever. This is probably in the top five days of his life, and Mrs. Patterson's too. Do you know how rare it is for someone in my line of work to get to share in one of the highlights of their lives? Usually I just get whatever is left at the end. And it's sad and lonely more often than not, let me tell you."

"This is still . . . beyond, Kimberly. I can't thank you enough."

"I'm just happy to be here," she said, enveloping me in a hug. She escaped to the kitchen for more guacamole and, I expected, a few private tears and a fresh tissue.

Dad took David and the rest of his family to the living room sofa. Johannes and Annika looked ready to fall on their faces but smiled affably at everyone despite their jet lag. I hung back to allow Dad and Mrs. Patterson to chat with David unencumbered. I leaned against the archway that led to the living room, feeling a bit voyeuristic but not wanting to miss any of the reunion between father and son. James came up beside me and draped an arm around my shoulders. Dad looked up and saw the gesture and smiled broadly. He was reading more into the embrace than he should have, but today I wouldn't disabuse him of any thought that gave him joy.

"I always hoped I'd find you," Dad finally said, drawing in a ragged breath.

"Beth has told me the lengths you both went through," David said, looking at Dad and Mrs. Patterson. "I'm a fortunate man to have been so loved by people that I had never met."

"That you were, son," Dad said. "I only knew your mother a short time, but she was the most amazing creature I ever met, apart from Beth's mother. I would have married her in a heartbeat and done right by you if I'd been given the chance. Of all the things I've wanted to tell you over the years, that was the most important."

"I knew," David said. "If you were as good and decent as my adoptive parents told me, I had no doubt that you would have. They met you, you know."

Dad's brow furrowed in confusion.

"Jonas and Heide," I chimed in. "You treated him during the war."

"They raised you?" Dad asked.

David nodded.

"I didn't know Jonas and Heide well, but I knew they were good people. If your mother trusted them to raise you, she knew they were equal to the task. From the way you've turned out, clearly your mother's last decision was a fine one."

"I believe so too," David said. "I had a happy childhood and a life beyond what I dreamed was possible. That's what I always wanted *you* to know."

"I couldn't be happier," Dad said. "Not for anything on this earth."

David wrapped his arms around Dad, and I could hear the telltale sniffling from both. They'd been missing each other for more than six decades, and somehow, I felt deprived of that quest. I wished I'd known David existed so I could have missed him as he deserved.

But that wasn't the case, and I had to be grateful to have a brother in my life at all. Just a couple of months before, I didn't have him to hope for.

The evening went on, and Annika and Johannes delighted in getting to know their grandfather and great-aunt, slipping effortlessly between German and English as warranted. They didn't hide in corners listening to music on their MP3 players like so many college kids would have done. Emilia stood with Kimberly at the table, asking her about her recipes and local cuisines to try.

Johanna was enraptured listening to Annika speak of her studies, and it seemed that Annika had recognized her counterpart in her great-aunt. I imagined the two studious scientists could have become great friends if they'd been born in the same generation. Stephen and Nick, clearly very devoted to their mother, were charming as they conversed with David and Emilia. It felt like a family holiday rather than a gathering of people who had been perfect strangers until very recently.

James excused himself for a moment, and David crossed the living room to where I stood.

"Are you all right, Beth?" He leaned companionably against the opposite side of the archway.

"More than all right," I said. "How could I not be to see my father so happy?"

"You just seem a little withdrawn," he said. "I've known you for less than a week, but I do sense a change."

"Perhaps the letdown that people feel after a long quest?"

"Ah, that I can understand. I can't imagine Odysseus's homecoming didn't feel like a bit of a disappointment. I just hope you don't feel pushed out at all."

"Never," I said. "It's understandable that you and Dad would want to connect. I wanted to give you some space."

"I want to connect with you too, though. You're the sister I always wanted. I hope you'll come over to visit us as often as you can. Our home may not be Neuschwanstein Castle, but you're always welcome in it," he said. Sincerity rang in his voice, and I knew this wasn't the flighty "we should do lunch" offer between two indifferent colleagues that gets bandied about so often.

"And you're always welcome in mine, though it's cramped enough you'd have to go outside to change your mind. I'm sorry I can't welcome the four of you properly."

David laughed. "A hotel with a breakfast buffet is a good idea with Johannes along for the trip. His body hasn't gotten the message that he's twenty and not a thirteen-year-old boy heading for a fifteen-centimeter growth spurt."

"They're wonderful," I said, looking over at Annika and Johannes, who were chatting with a very animated Mrs. Patterson. "You should be very proud of them."

"I am. Unspeakably so," he said. "They're excited to have you as their 'fun American auntie.' They told Emilia and me as much last night."

"That makes me so happy," I said, already calculating ways of spoiling them. Surely Annika could use a new laptop when she started her courses in the fall. And Johannes would love a guided trek up Mount Whitney. It seemed like a way to make up for two decades of missed birthdays, Hanukkahs, graduations, and other gift-giving occasions.

"Come for Christmas," he said. "Nothing would make us all happier. Truly Germany is a beautiful place to celebrate the holiday. *Christkindlmarkts* and wassail and all sorts of fun things. It will be like no other Christmas you've had."

"It will be," I said. "Since I don't celebrate it. Being Jewish, after all."

"Oh, how clumsy of me," he said. "I should have thought before I spoke."

"Please, don't think anything of it. You were raised in a different tradition, and I'm sure it's what your mother would have wanted."

"Don't be so sure of that," Mrs. Patterson chimed in. "My sister chose an Old Testament name for a reason. To honor your father's heritage. I'd bet my last dollar on it."

Dad's head bowed at the thought, but I sensed there had to be some truth in it.

"I do feel like I should learn more about my father's culture. Perhaps you could teach me?"

"I'd be happy to, David," I said. "I'm no paragon of Jewish learning, but I was dragged to Hebrew school since I was toddling."

"'Dragged' is the right word too," Dad said, his head shaking. "At times your mother and I thought you'd never have your bat mitzvah."

"Well, you gave me a taste for the outdoors, Dad. I can't help it that they were foolish enough to have class indoors."

"I guess I can't fault you there," Dad said, his shoulders shaking as he laughed.

"Teach me with Papa," Annika chimed in.

"Of course, sweetie," I said. "And you'll teach me all about your traditions when I come for Christmas."

"I'm holding you to that, sister dear," David said.

"You can count on me," I said, shaking his hand as if brokering a major business transaction.

And he could. All of them could, because now that I had a family in my life again, I wouldn't miss the opportunity to be a part of it.

EPILOGUE

BETH

"Thanks for coming out without making me threaten you with a crowbar," Gwen said as she sipped an iced mocha at our favorite café. "I was expecting more of a fight."

Dad's funeral was the week before, and this was my first venture out of my apartment since I took David, Emilia, and Johannes back to the airport. As we'd said goodbye I had renewed my promise to spend Christmas with them, and David responded by presenting me with my ticket, which aligned perfectly with my winter break.

"Dad wouldn't want me to stay holed up forever," I told Gwen. "Plus, I needed to give you back the cutting. Dad did good work with it, and I'd hate to kill it."

Gwen looked over at the Aztec Gold plumeria she'd given Dad and suppressed a tear. "That he did. I'm going to miss him."

"As will I," I said.

She reached over and squeezed my hand. "I'm proud of you, you know," she said.

"Whatever for?" I asked. "For keeping my act together long enough to meet for coffee? Man, I must have been worse off than I realized."

"No, you weren't quite that bad. I did fear for a short while after the divorce that you'd end up with fourteen cats and get evicted, but you seem to have pulled through."

"I suppose I have. And never fear on the cat front. My roommate is allergic."

Annika had fallen so much in love with the university that she decided she'd rather pursue her master's with us. David and I helped get her preliminary exams scheduled and her paperwork together to meet the deadline, which was thankfully very late in the summer for fall quarter. She'd be staying with me, at least until a more entertaining offer came her way, but she was delightful company until someone closer to her own age offered her a room.

"She's not keeping you up all hours with her crazy rock-and-roll music and raucous parties, is she?"

"I tell you, the loudest noise she makes is the turning of pages in her textbooks."

"Do we need to show that girl how to let loose?" Gwen asked. "If she doesn't come home drunk and missing a shoe before the end of the quarter, I think we need to stage an intervention."

I laughed louder than I intended and willed the swallow of iced coffee I'd just taken not to spray from my nose. "You're absolutely right. She needs to have a good time while she's here."

"And speaking of which, how are things with James?" Gwen asked, averting her eyes as she took another sip of her drink.

"Fine," I said.

"Fine? He went with you to Germany. He spent weeks tracking down your half brother. Don't tell me you're playing coy with him."

"Not at all," I said. "Things are good. I'm just not in a rush to commit to anything serious. I'm enjoying getting to know myself again."

"That seems healthy and all," she said, playing with the straw in her drink.

"But?"

"But don't take so long that he passes you by. I have a good feeling about the two of you together. And I'm not just saying that."

"He *is* wonderful," I said.

"Then tell him so," she said. "You don't need to propose, but let him know you care. That will be enough for a while."

"You're probably right," I said.

"I usually am," she said, raising her plastic cup. "And with that, I have a class to teach. Call him. Then call me and tell me everything."

"It's so great that you respect boundaries and privacy," I said, shaking my head.

"Hey, I set you two up, I deserve the entertainment factor of getting the details."

"Go teach, dork."

I pulled out a stack of quizzes, deciding to enjoy the sunlight rather than hole up in my office. I tried to concentrate on them, but it was a futile battle. I pulled out my laptop and connected to the Wi-Fi. A cursory check of email resulted in nothing interesting, and I wasn't in the mood to let the news drag down my spirits. I randomly wandered over to the website for the nearby movie theater to check the times. If I could trek six thousand miles to find my brother, I could withstand going to see a movie alone.

"You're beautiful when you're lost in thought, you know." James's baritone sounded behind me. He came around my left side and claimed the spot Gwen had abandoned. "Don't worry, I won't stay long and keep you from your work. I'm just waiting on my order."

"Happy for the distraction," I said.

"Distraction? I hope I'm more than that to you," he said. Though his tone was mostly playful, I could hear a note of serious concern in his voice as well.

"Of course you are," I said. "You're wonderful."

Promise kept. Gwen would have to be pleased.

"Wonderful enough for dinner tonight?"

My eyes flickered back to the movie theater page and my eyes lit upon a historical film that had been getting rave reviews. I could ask James to come along, though I wasn't sure it was the sort of film to capture his interest. I could go to dinner with James and take myself to the movies another time. I only had to manage my own schedule to make that work, after all.

"Maybe tomorrow?" I asked. "Or next week?"

"That sounds great," he said, flashing me a toothy smile. "Tomorrow. We'll make a night of it."

"Can't wait," I said. "It'll be fun."

James's order was called, and true to his word, he took his white paper cup and headed back in the direction of the library, leaving me to work in peace.

I turned back to my laptop and clicked to purchase a single ticket to the seven thirty showing of the film. As much as I wanted to explore what the future might hold for James and me, I'd kept myself waiting long enough.

That idea, that two people on opposite sides of such a monumental conflict would spend their twilight years together, was an intriguing one. What if their stories were connected? What if they hadn't been in as much opposition as they thought? It all played out in a rather vivid dream one night, which led to me calling my new friend and soon-to-be neighbor with a very awkward "So I had a dream about your dad last night . . ." I shelved the idea in order to write *Girls on the Line*, which was the book that insisted on being written right then, but Max stayed with me. The idea of his story intertwining with that of the elderly German woman years after the war ended wouldn't let me go.

I knew nothing about the German woman from the real Max's life, but stumbled on a book about the female pilots of the Luftwaffe (*The Women Who Flew for Hitler* by Clare Mulley). Unlike the Russian heroines from *Daughters of the Night Sky*, very few women were allowed to fly for Germany. While Stalin sought to increase his labor force by sending women to work, Hitler sought to increase his population by sending women home to marry and have babies. For those who have read my previous novel *Daughters of the Night Sky*, you'll find that Katya and Johanna are certainly defined by their love of aviation but are very different women, largely due to the environments they work in. While women were allowed to participate in aviation in large numbers in Russia, they faced more-blatant sexism when they did so. Only a handful of German women were able to fly for the Luftwaffe, but the few who managed to climb the ranks were treated somewhat more favorably by their colleagues. As Johanna says, they were the exception that proved the rule concerning women in the workplace.

The idea that somehow the woman in Max's nursing home had some connection to the two most prominent women in the Luftwaffe was intriguing. I based Johanna very, very loosely on Melitta von Stauffenberg, the talented test pilot and engineer who had to walk a tight line to keep herself out of a concentration camp owing to her Jewish ancestry. Her foil, Louisa Mueller, was based (also very loosely) on Hanna Reitsch, who was Melitta's outspoken counterpart in the Luftwaffe and a willing show pony for the cause. For me, Johanna exemplifies the myth of political neutrality. She works for a government that would be perfectly happy to see her in a death camp if she were any less useful to their cause. Regardless of her convictions, by working for them, she is complicit in their work. This is what Johanna as a character has to overcome. Like so many of us, she's focused on her own work and family. For her, the political climate in her country is something she's not happy with, but as it doesn't often radically affect her day-to-day life, she goes on as best she can. By the time she realizes neutrality isn't an option, changing the course of events for her country, her family, and herself is next to impossible.

Beth, Max's daughter, is a successful professional at a crossroads in her life after her divorce and the death of her mother. She is very much the typical modern woman who has tried to be all things to all people, and found, much to her dismay, that she is a mere mortal. The quest to help her father find the missing woman from his past serves both as a way for her to prepare herself for her father's imminent demise and as a means for her to potentially forge new familial ties that she never knew existed. The existence of a sibling, in particular, gives Beth a sense of hope that she won't be completely unmoored in the world. Beth, too, has a lot to overcome: reconciling herself with what she considers rigid expectations from her mother, helping her father transition from this life, and discovering herself after years of being defined by her relationships with others. Writing a modern-day protagonist was liberating in many ways. It was certainly a good exercise in reflecting upon the current expectations placed upon daughters and wives. And there was a lot more research involved than I expected—cell phone technology has changed a lot in the twelve years between Beth's timeline and when I began writing this book!

Max, at the end of the day, is really the lifeblood of this book. Its heart and soul. It would have been impossible for me not to fall in love with the affable young Los Angeleno dentist, consummate patriot, and son of hardworking immigrants. Above all things, Max is driven by a sense of justice. And a dash of sarcasm. When he finds love in one of the most unexpected places in the world—Hürtgen Forest as it's being decimated by the war machine—Max is as helpless to stop his feelings as he is to stem the tide of the war that keeps him and Margarethe apart. As a medic, Max sees some of the greatest horrors the war doles out. It wounds him profoundly, but it never breaks him. This is what I admire most about him. It would have been easy for him to become jaded by the atrocities he sees, but he never does, largely because he is so able to focus on the needs of others before worrying about himself.

I decided to set many of his wartime scenes in Hürtgen Forest after learning more about that particular battle at the National WWII Museum in New Orleans. It was so very tempting to show Max's valor on the D-Day beaches in Normandy. That campaign was one of the costliest to human lives that we've known, but we remember it with pride because we made terrific gains that helped turn the tide of the war. Hürtgen Forest, however, was a long battle. It was three months of strategically difficult combat in a dense wood that became known as the Death Factory. And after three months, no side could truly claim a victory. America had thought the war would be easily won after Normandy, but Hürtgen Forest deflated a lot of that optimism. I didn't want to show Max in our finest hour—I wanted to see how he would act when victory seemed not only uncertain but sometimes unlikely. That's where real heroism shines through.

These characters allowed me to weave together three unlikely stories into one. Though really, there is a fourth narrative that is woven throughout. Though we see the world through Johanna's, Beth's, and Max's eyes, this is really Metta's story. She is a specter throughout the book. She touches the lives of every major character and many of the secondary ones as well. She is the innocent victim of hate and tyranny, bullied into an inappropriate marriage and robbed of her chance to live a full life. Like so many victims, she is left without the opportunity to tell her story in her own words. I like to think that she'd be happy with the way Johanna champions her, Max adores her, and Beth seeks to know her. If nothing else, she would know that she is beloved and not forgotten.

ACKNOWLEDGMENTS

This is always the most humbling part of the process. I have so many people to whom I am indebted, including:

- My brilliant agent, Melissa Jeglinski, for having faith in me even when I didn't. You're amazing.
- Chris Werner, the most wonderful editor in the multiverse, for believing in this story and being a tremendous cheerleader for my work.
- Jenna Free, my developmental editor, for honoring me with her tough critiques. Keep 'em coming!
- Danielle Marshall, Gabe Dumpit, and the rest of the Lake Union team. Thank you for making this crazy business a little more sane for us working authors. You've made my dream a reality.
- The Tall Poppy Writers. When it comes to the book biz, you *are* the revolution. And also the best support system a writer could ask for. Thank you for all you've done for me.
- My Badasses: Jamie Raintree, Andrea Catalano, Ella Olsen, Orly Konig, Katie Moretti, Theresa Alan, and Gwen Florio . . . you're all rock stars.
- To all the amazing reader groups such as Bloom with Tall Poppy Writers; Women Writers, Women's Books; Great

Thoughts' Great Readers; A Novel Bee; Readers Coffeehouse; My Book Tribe; and so many more. Thank you for making a writer feel appreciated for her art.

- Rocky Mountain Fiction Writers and the Colorado Center for the Book—thank you for making Denver a literary hotspot. I am also humbled to be nominated for awards by these tremendous organizations this year.

- Jason Evans, thank you so much for always taking my history-nerd phone calls. You're the best!

- Carol Stratton, again, for trusting me with Max. And Sam, Kevin, and Kyle for lending their wife/mom to me for long chats about Max over cider at The Old Mine. And Melony Black, thanks for the intro and for being a lovely friend these many years.

- My amazing band of friends and neighbors: Stephanie, Todd, Danielle, Renatta, Ryan, Owen, Amanda, Mac, Emily, Maddie, and Ben; thank you for always being there for me. I'm so lucky to have you in my life.

- The Trumbly and Runyan clans for always supporting me. Thank you for lifting me up when I need it most.

- And always, my brilliant, sweet, talented children, Ciarán and Aria. Always and forever, the best thing I will do with my life.

ABOUT THE AUTHOR

Photo © 2017 Melony Nottingham Black

Aimie K. Runyan writes to celebrate history's unsung heroines. She is the author of four previous historical novels, including the internationally bestselling *Daughters of the Night Sky*, *Girls on the Line*, *Promised to the Crown*, and *Duty to the Crown*, as well as the short-story collection *Brave New Girls*. She is active as an educator and speaker in the writing community and beyond. She lives in Colorado with her two (usually) adorable children. Visit her at www.aimiekrunyan.com.